MW01681601

THE DRAKE CHRONICLES
Military Science Fiction
HRUM
A MILITARY SCIENCE FICTION THRILLER
KARA
BOOK II OF THE DRAKE CHRONICLES
JAXTON'S GAMBIT
BOOK III OF THE DRAKE CHRONICLES
AUSTIN DAVIS
Check out all of Austin Davis's books at https://thedavisverse.com

Copyright © 2023 Austin Davis All rights reserved

The characters and events portrayed in this book are fictitious. Any similarity to real persons, living or dead, is coincidental and not intended by the author.

No portion of this book may be reproduced in any form or by any electronic or mechanical means, including information storage and retrieval systems, without written permission from the publisher or author, except as permitted by US copyright law

ISBN: 979-8990178502 (Paperback)
ISBN: 979-8990178519 (Hardcover)

Sign up for Austin Davis's Readers List at: https://thedavisverse.com/

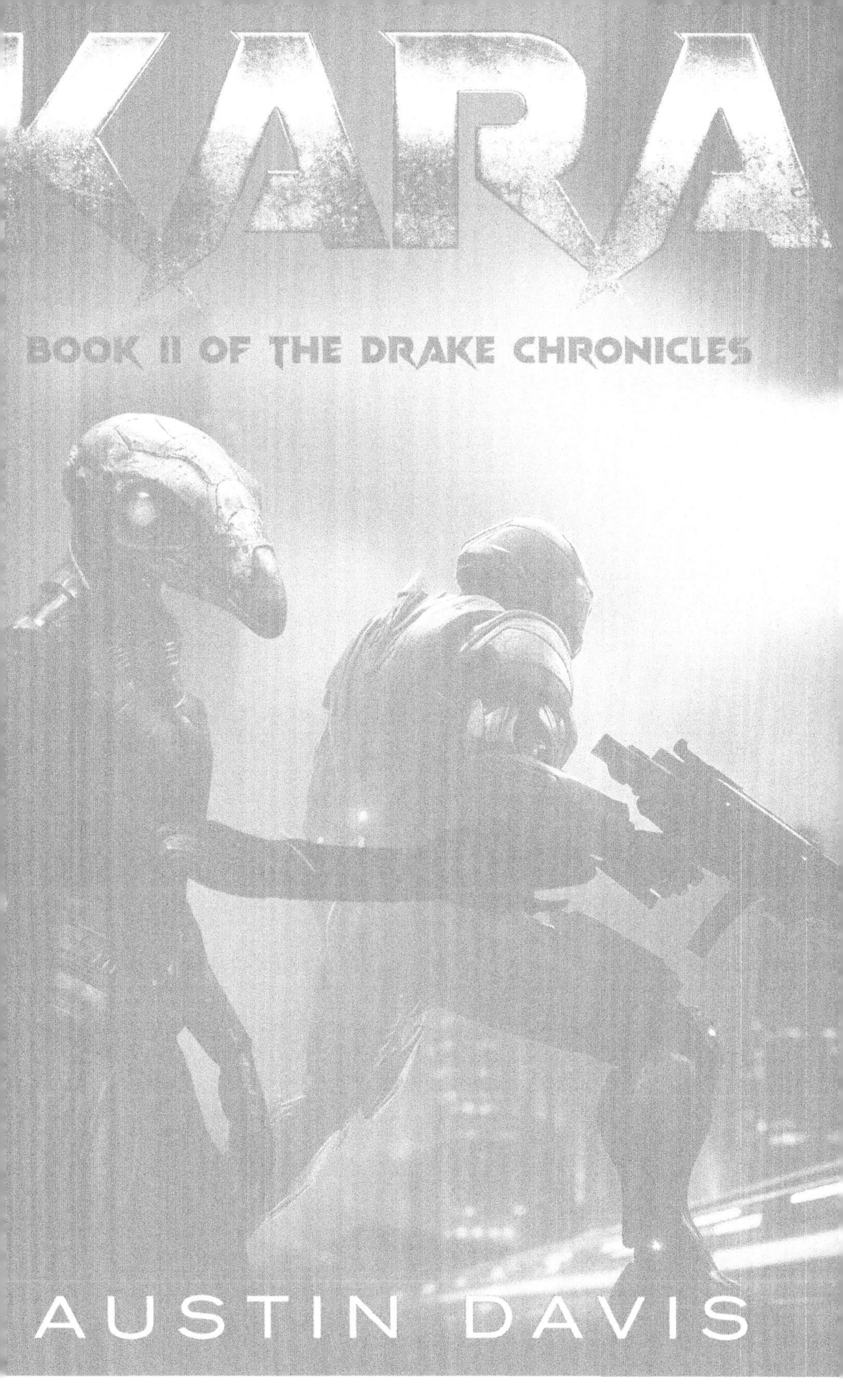
KARA
BOOK II OF THE DRAKE CHRONICLES
AUSTIN DAVIS

Thank you for picking up *Kara*.

This book marks my second step into the world of writing, and I'm truly excited to share it with you. Writing *Kara* gave me the opportunity to dive deeper into my love of storytelling and challenge myself creatively. Every chapter was written with care and with the hope of taking you on a memorable journey.

To those who supported my first book, *Hrum*, thank you from the bottom of my heart. Your encouragement and enthusiasm gave me the confidence to continue down this path. If you're new to my work, welcome—I hope *Kara* captivates you and leaves you eager for what lies ahead.

I would love to hear your thoughts and keep you updated on future projects. Please visit my website to connect and stay in touch.

Happy reading,

Austin Davis

Chapter I

In Unknown System on Battleship Arcon
Year 3326

The NIS Battleship Arcon shuddered as the Albion drives spooled down and their viewscreen began to populate. Twenty-six hours after Task Force Rogue initiated their Albion drives and transitioned out of the Jewel of Sunlight system, Admiral Jaxton Drake and his stealthy fleet entered the mysterious system into which their scout ship had disappeared. The longer than usual transition also came with a much bumpier arrival.

Once the shuddering had subsided Admiral Drake snapped out an order: “Sensor report!”

Lt. Chen barely hesitated before replying, “Nothing in our immediate vicinity, sir.” Chen looked at his commanding officer then back at his viewscreen. “I won’t have more data until we get sensor returns from our passive array, but there are no contacts, enemy or otherwise, in the immediate range of our task force. All our ships have arrived successfully. I recommend we continue on our course until we know more.”

Jaxton was about to reply when his comms officer, Lt. Stephanie Johnson, quickly interrupted. “Sir, we have a close-beam priority message from the Battlecruiser Omaha. Captain Dixon says just before he jumped to Albion he received a message from fleet command. St. George is under attack!”

“What..? Say again, Lieutenant.”

“St. George is under attack, sir!”

“Quickly, put the message up on the viewscreen. Why was his ship the only one to receive this information?”

"I am not sure, sir."

"That's not an answer, Lieutenant." Jaxton snapped back.

"Sir, if you will just give me a moment, I'm going through our incoming messages. It appears it was stuck in the buffer and before it could be fully received we jumped to Albion. Our computers automatically devote their full processing power to the calculations required, so it was not easily retrievable."

"I see."

"I am sorry, sir," Johnson managed to say, "I could've manually gone and retrieved the messages but I had no idea that it—"

After taking a breath and waving her off, Jaxton said, "Not your fault, Lieutenant. You had no way of knowing we were about to receive an emergency message." Jaxton relaxed and sighed. "I apologize for snapping at you."

"Thank you, sir." Johnson said.

"Can you please play the rest of the message over the bridge speakers?"

She did as ordered and a few seconds later, Captain Dixon's powerful voice began to play: "Admiral, I'm not sure if you received this priority message or not before we jumped. Your ship was computing the course for the rest of the fleet so they might have been tied up. We have to return to NIS space immediately. The message from fleet command indicates that not only have our ships in orbit over St. George been destroyed, these forces are likely not Hrum and potentially possess some sort of new technological edge over our ships. It is our duty to follow fleet command's orders at once. We eagerly await your orders. Captain Dixon out."

Jaxton sat back at his station and waved his XO Commander Bradley over. The computers on his ship had finally compiled the message from fleet command and he was reading through it. It didn't contain a whole lot of additional information past what Dixon had just reported, but he read it anyway. His thoughts had immediately drifted to his brother Ryan, who was on the surface of the planet.

"What do you think, Commander?"

"Sir, I think Dixon's right. The message was clearly sent to recall us back to NIS space."

"So you want to flip and go full burn back to the Albion lane?" Bradley opened his mouth as if to say something, but then stopped, a conflicted look shaded his face.

"Say what's on your mind, Chris."

"Sir, I'm not sure if we should. Doing so would light us up like a Christmas tree. Even if we flip around and slow-burn our engines, we'll still light up the area for anyone or any*thing* looking in this direction. For all we know, the same adversary that attacked St. George could be in this system, just like—"

"Spit it out, Commander, I asked for recommendations, not a sounding board. We have half a dozen anxious ship commanders awaiting orders."

"Sir, I would recommend we wait until we get more data from the passives before making a decision."

"And why's that?"

"In the grand scheme of things observing the system for a few hours won't slow us down that much, even if we change our minds and just decide to flip around and go full burn. The message had to have taken several days to get to us from the St. George system, and then we spent another day in Albion. Even if we turned around this instant, we'd still be showing up well after whatever happened happened." Bradley paused, noticing Drake's conflicted look, then continued, "On top of that, sir, we haven't fully mapped this system yet, but I would not be surprised if there's a way we can potentially use a gravity assist to flip us back around and out of here more inconspicuously. It would also give us the opportunity to see what's out here."

Drake nodded. He had been thinking along similar lines to his commander, but he'd wanted the man's opinion before he said anything. He continued to ponder what his XO said for a few additional moments before coming to a decision.

"Lieutenant Johnson..." Jaxton finally said, "Please send a tight beam message to our other ships. We are going to wait to see what our sensors tell us about this system before making a decision."

"Yes sir!"

Turning back to the commander, Drake continued. "There are no immediate threats to our ship and this way we can at least see what's out here before we return to NIS space. Work with the other captains. I want to have a conference setup with them in one hour." Jaxton took another look at the screens at his station. "Lieutenant Chen, please work with navigation to plot us alternate routes to return to the Albion lane. I want to focus on stealth. That means using whatever the planets in this system will give us in the way of gravity or concealment. I want options and I want to stay dark"

"Stay dark, aye sir," Chen said.

The next hour was busy, but passed uneventfully. Once it was determined that there were no immediate threats in their vicinity, Drake had given everyone a short break to grab a snack and some coffee. Early returns on the passive sensors indicated that there were definitely ships in this system, but without performing an active scan, it would be a while longer until they were able to get a better picture of who they were and what they were up to. Prior to their arrival in the system, Drake had ordered a communications blackout in order to keep the chances of detection down. The message from Dixon had technically broken that protocol, but he wasn't going to hold it against him because of the message's contents. Besides the one short message Jaxton sent to the rest of his fleet, nobody had spoken since they arrived. Now that they knew local space was clear, he felt comfortable that none of their signals would be easily intercepted and they could discuss the situation they found themselves in.

All the ships were in close enough proximity to one another that they could talk instantaneously without any lag. Moments after Jaxton initiated the call, the others joined and the yelling began. Before Jaxton could so much as mutter a hello, the captain of their makeshift carrier and support ship, Captain Mitchell, took over. His angry, raised voice vibrated through the speakers loud enough that Jaxton had to turn the volume down. "What the hell do you think you're doing? In all my years in the NIS I've never seen someone so blatantly disobey a direct order from the fleet command. Just because your father is a senior admiral, doesn't mean that you can ignore a direct order!"

Jax sighed, Captain Mitchell had proved himself to be a dependable and loyal officer, but not a very imaginative one. It was no wonder he had been in the fleet for close to thirty years and had not advanced past the rank of captain.

Jaxton ground his teeth while he waited for the man to finish, then forced himself to reply calmly. “Captain, I am not doing anything of the sort. As your fleet commander, I expect grievances to be voiced privately, not loudly and obnoxiously as you have just done. If you would let me speak, I will tell you exactly why we have not done anything yet.” Drake paused, almost hoping the other captain would say something that would give Jaxton a reason to have him thrown in the brig or at least written up. He could almost picture the man sitting at his desk, red-faced, steam pouring out of his ears. Nobody, especially Captain Mitchell, liked to be called out in front of his peers.

To Jaxton’s surprise and slight disappointment, Mitchell eventually mumbled, “Why, by all means, continue.”

“Thank you.” Jaxton took a quick breath before continuing. “Now as I was going to say, we have confirmed there are no threats in our immediate vicinity, and…”

“And we should be flipping around and burning for the gate at best speed for chrissakes!” Mitchell loudly interrupted again.

“*Captain*, you will not speak again out of turn or I *will* have you brought up on charges!” Jaxton said coolly while looking squarely at Mitchell in the viewscreen. “This is my meeting and I’m the one in charge, not you. Have I made myself clear?” Before Mitchell could get out a word, Jaxton added, “Actually, there’s no need to respond, a nod will suffice.” Mitchell nodded while glaring angrily. Jaxton met his gaze calmly for several more moments before continuing. “Now, we *could* flip around and burn for the Albion lane, but that could easily give away our presence in this system, which I am not sure we want to do. For all we know, the ships that we have confirmed are in the system could be the very same enemy that just attacked St. George. I think at this point it’s more important that we don’t give away our presence or more importantly, the existence of our stealth technology unless it becomes absolutely necessary. Since we arrived, I have had my crew look at alternative options that should keep us hidden from sight.

These options use a variety of small course corrections and gravity assists to flip us around and head back towards the lane without burning our engines in such a way that the ships we have already confirmed are in this system will be able to see us. I believe that discretion is more important than speed in this instance as we are able to gain some valuable insight from who is in this system while we remain hidden.

"There are three possible routes that we can take with varying levels of risk and speed as well as potential to scout the system. I will forward them to you now."

Captain Dixon was the first to reply after several moments. "Sir, I understand where you are coming from, and while I agree we don't want the ships in the system to see us, I believe it is more important to get home more quickly than it is to remain hidden."

"Why do you say that, Captain?"

"Sir, the shortest proposed route that you have here is still close to a three-day turnaround before we make it back to the Albion lane, and the longest is nearly a week. I understand the desire to finish our original mission, but I strongly advise against this course of action even if I understand why you wish to do it."

Jaxton said nothing for a moment while he digested Dixon's words. He could see the faces of the other officers casting a mix of expressions that made Jaxton feel like there was no clear consensus between them. His tenure as a leader had taught him that getting a unified decision was almost as important as getting to the right decision.

"While I am in overall command of this task force and what I decide in the end is what I expect you all to follow, I called this meeting to get all of your opinions and I will not ignore what you have said. I would like to discuss this further."

The meeting continued for over an hour before it was interrupted by Lt. Chen bursting into the conference room, nearly taking down Commander Bradley who was standing just inside the door.

"Sir! We found it."

"Found what, Lieutenant?"

"The scout ship! It's in orbit over the moon we had marked on our scans as potentially life-bearing. It appears to be attached to a space station of some sort!"

Chen quickly shared the images from his tab with Jaxton who then put them up for all the captains to see. The images were blurry, but definitely depicted an NIS scout ship. He couldn't quite tell, but it appeared that at least part of the stern of the ship had been blown off. It looked like battle damage more so than an accident.

"Work on cleaning up that image, Lieutenant. Send me updates directly to my tab in the future instead of interrupting my meetings." Jaxton sternly said as his XO slowly directed him towards the door.

Realizing what he had done, he quickly replied, "Yessir, sorry sir," and then turned and hustled back out onto the bridge.

Jaxton sighed loudly and shook his head before turning back towards the screen as his XO settled back into his seat behind him.

"Now, as I was saying… I'm going to ask each of your opinions on the matter before I make a decision. I will not be putting it up to a vote as I am making the ultimate decision, but I will let each of you voice what you have to say." Sighing internally, he continued, "Captain Mitchell, I will start with you," already bracing for what he just assumed would be a scything response.

Surprisingly, nothing of the sort came.

"Admiral, we should stay and at least observe what's going on in the system. I apologize for my outburst earlier, I lost my cool when I thought you were just going to ignore orders."

"Apology accepted. Please go on."

"I think we should perform the maneuver that will put us as close to the planet as possible in order to get a good solid look at it."

Not quite over the older captain's total change of heart, Jaxton replied, "Go on…"

"Sir, it is our duty to those crew to see if any sort of rescue is reasonable, and I believe the damage on that ship looks like battle damage rather than an asteroid strike or some other catastrophe. We should run with the assumption that the ships in orbit of that planet should be considered hostile and with that in mind, keeping our force a secret just became paramount to our success."

Thinking that maybe he had judged the officer too harshly, Jaxton slowly replied, "I find myself in agreement, Captain.... If that is all you have to say on the matter, I will move on to our next captain?"

Mitchell nodded slowly.

"Okay then..."

In the end, nearly all of the captains wanted to stay and at least observe what was going on in the system with the exception of Captain Dixon. He emphatically made it clear that he believed that they should be burning for the gate as fast as humanly possible. Even so, Jaxton was in charge and decided they should stay. He called for his marine commander, Major Stevens as well as Major Brewster to join the conference in hopes that they would have some insight or ideas on how to perform a rescue effort. He asked the other captains to do the same. If the station was hostile, and they had captured the scout ship, then it would be up to Stevens' marines to rescue them and Brewster's fighters to keep them covered in the meantime.

In the time it took them and a few other key individuals to arrive, the bridge crew had managed to put together a better look at the ships in orbit over the inhabitable planet. The ships, while not exactly like the Hrum cruisers they'd faced so far, appeared to be built along the same lines. To Jaxton's trained eye, it was incredibly unlikely that another alien race built ships in the same style that the Hrum did. After a brief discussion, they all agreed that it was unlikely that they were in the system with an entirely new alien race. It was Dixon who voiced the thought that these might be newer Hrum warships which made nobody happy, but it was something they could not rule out because there were just too many unknowns.

As the additional officers joined the conference, Jaxton again spoke. "For those of you who just joined us, please read the briefing packets being provided to you by your captains. We haven't alerted the rest of the crew yet, but just prior to us leaving the JOS system, we received an emergency message from fleet command that indicated that St. George was under attack by an unknown enemy." He paused looking at the new faces on his viewscreen for a moment to let them absorb what he was saying before continuing. "We were provided little else in the data packet other than they do not believe these new hostiles are Hrum. Now, your captains will brief you on the specifics, but we have not turned around yet because we are not alone in this system. The ships that we have detected are *similar*, but not the *same* as your typical Hrum warship. I find it very likely that these ships are at least associated with the ones who attacked St. George. In addition, we have spotted our missing scout ship and it appears to have been attacked. We called you in because we are going to make an effort to board the ship and potentially rescue any crew who may still be alive. This will also provide us with an opportunity to gather some intel on the enemy station and possibly its inhabitants."

Jaxton paused to pull up a projection of the system, but before he could continue, Captain Dixon cut in again. "Sir, I don't think that rescuing the crew from the scout ship should be the priority of the mission."

A grumbling rolled through the officers from around the room for a few moments before Jaxton replied.

"Would you care to elaborate?"

"With all due respect, sir, we have no idea if the scout ship crew is still alive, let alone aboard the station. The priority should be to secure the ship itself, make sure there is nothing to be gleaned from an intelligence standpoint by the enemy, and then either reclaim the ship and escape with it, or scuttle it so nothing else can be gleaned from it."

"You wish to condemn the brave crewmembers of the ship to whatever fate the enemy might have in store for them?" Drake replied sharply.

"Sir, I'm not saying we shouldn't rescue the crew if the situation arises, but the priority of the mission should be to the betterment of the fleet as a whole rather than a handful of crewmembers who may or may *not* still be alive. We should not risk our whole fleet for such little gain."

His cold, but calculated explanation calmed Jaxton a little bit. He saw where Dixon was coming from, even if he thought the real reason was that Dixon did not want to remain in the system any longer than they had to.

Jaxton drew a measured breath and replied, "Captain, I see your point. I don't completely agree with you, but I understand where you're coming from and will consider your thoughts in our plans." Turning back to the projection of the system, he addressed the rest of the people on the call. "Here's what we've gathered so far from deeper in the system. As you know we cannot do a high-powered scan. Our stealth would be compromised, and that's currently our greatest advantage. We have between twenty and twenty-five contacts in the system in orbit around the largest planet. From what we can tell, the planet is inhabited. Luckily, there only appears to be three ships in close proximity to the station where our scout ship is docked. We'll be going with the gravity assist in option C. This option brings us closest to this station which will assist us in performing the rescue operations. It is unlikely that we'll be able to assault the station without being detected, so keeping our speed up speed holds the utmost importance. We don't have to make our minds up yet on the details, so I expect all captains to work with their officers to provide options for when we do finally reach the station. We will keep our communication windows short in order to provide as little opportunity for detection as possible. I want options ranging from a quick hit and run where we simply scuttle the scout ship, to a full on assault on the station. Captains, I expect proposals to be provided to me in four hours. Admiral Drake out."

He closed the conference on his screen and sat back in his chair, closing his eyes for a moment before opening them and turning to his XO and the two other officers who were in the room with him. "What do you think, Major Stevens?"

"Sir, it all depends on what our goal is."

"Go on..."

"We have enough marines to take full control of the station, but even with our new weapons and the surprise of our stealth systems, fighting twenty or twenty-five enemy capital ships is a tall order for a fleet of seven ships."

"We do have a full wing of fighters," Brewster replied.

Stevens waved him off. “Okay. Fine. Even with six warships, a carrier, and a wing or two of fighters. I don’t think we would be able to take them all out even if we take them completely by surprise. I don’t see a way for us to do anything other than a quick hit and run type attack. I’m not an expert on starship travel, but I assume we can’t afford to loiter for more than a few hours before we have to flee from the enemy ships in the vicinity when they become aware of our presence and react accordingly.”

Jaxton nodded. Nothing the major said was untrue. “Okay then,” he said. “So what is your recommendation?”

“Keeping in mind that we need to be quick,” Major Stevens began, “I think we board the station in three separate locations. Near engineering, near our scout ship, and where the command center is likely to be. If the enemy uses the Hrum language and is laid out in a similar fashion to their other military installations, we can find where our people are being detained if they are still on station. If we take control of the engineering section, we can disable any defenses the station might have, and finally the scout ship can be inspected to see if we can salvage it, or if it has to be scuttled.”

“What do you think, Greg?” Drake replied, turning to his best friend.

“I think Stevens is correct, sir. We can swarm the station with fighter craft to cover the marines, but we won’t be able to linger long once the enemy in orbit over the planet is alerted to our presence. I do recommend we hit the three ships before we hit the station though.”

“Agreed, I expect the rest of our captains will come up with something similar to this,” Jaxton said. “But please write up your proposals with the commander.”

“Yessir.” both Stevens and Brewster chorused before getting to their feet.

“You’re all dismissed.”

Drake again sat back in his chair as his officers left the room. He was concerned that he was making a mistake not immediately returning to NIS space. Captain Dixon had a tendency to get under his skin, and even though Drake felt his own logic was sound, a small voice that sounded a lot like Dixon kept saying: *You’re making a mistake.*

Being in overall command had its perks, but it also had its headaches. He just had to hope this was one of those times he made the correct decision and that he wasn't going to get himself court-martialed and tossed into a windowless box on an icehouse planet somewhere. His thoughts turned to his brother who was on St. George. Jaxton wondered if Ryan was even still alive, or if his father's good friend Admiral Winters, who had been in command of the battleship that was picketed over the planet had managed to escape. He cursed silently. Just when peace seemed within reach, it all fell apart.

Chapter II

On St. George at The Grand Monarch's Estate
Year 3326

As quickly as the flashes in space began, it was all over. The partygoers at the Grand Monarch's luxurious estate were now packed out on the balcony. They'd said nothing while the sky continued to flash, but the moment it stopped, they had begun talking amongst themselves. The ones with more sense had attempted to use their communicators to contact someone to see what was going on, but they quickly discovered, as Ryan had, that their devices were not able to acquire a signal and were useless. Ryan turned as Marvin shoved his way through the crowd considerably less gracefully than he had swung the older baroness across the floor only minutes earlier.

"Sir, I tried to contact the rest of our men at headquarters, but I got nothin'."

Ryan nodded in agreement before replying. "I'm not sure if we're being jammed or they destroyed all the satellites in orbit, but jamming seems more likely."

"Ya think?" asked Marvin.

Ryan turned and squinted up at the sky. "What sort of technology has the ability to instantaneously jam an entire planet?" he asked out into space. He looked back at Marvin. "But it seems unlikely they spent time destroying every satellite while engaged with our ships in orbit."

"What should we do, sir?"

"I think we need to prepare for the worst. Let's see if we can hitch a ride and get back to headquarters. We need to get all our men armed and ready if whoever just attacked us decides to come down to fight us."

"Yessir."

"Also see if you can get ahold of a military comm set. The military comms devices may be able to punch through the jamming."

"On it, sir."

Marvin then turned and began shoving his way back through the crowds with Ryan right behind him. They were almost to the grand entrance when they were stopped by two of the

Grand Monarch's guards who had to physically block them from passing.

Before Marvin could take a swing, Ryan grabbed his arm and said, "Not a smart move blocking a ghost from getting where he wants to go."

The guard, who Ryan realized was about as fresh-faced as some of his recruits, replied,

"Captain, The Grand Monarch requests your presence in the imperial bunker. She asked that I bring you to her as soon as possible."

"I need to organize my men and prepare them for whatever is coming," Ryan replied hotly. "I've got no time to hobnob with the royalty."

"Sir, begging your pardon. I was informed it was of the utmost importance and I am to bring you in by any means necessary."

Ryan was about to snap out an angry retort when he realized the youngster was on the

verge of panic. He took a calming breath and replied, "Can you arrange a way for my man to get back to the hotel? I'll go with you, but my men need to be warned."

"Yes..um yessir, I can do that," he replied seemingly relieved. "Thank you, sir."

The guard quickly turned to his even younger-looking companion and quickly ordered him to get Marvin a ride and an escort to the hotel. After that was done and the two men were hurrying out the door, the guard continued, "Sir, if you would follow me."

Ryan only nodded and gestured for him to lead the way.

It was not a far walk, but soon Ryan found himself deep underground where the building was considerably more heavily built and much less ostentatious. Ryan approved of the defenses and realized that these monarchs may have been greedy and power hungry, but they weren't all stupid. The guard led him through a set of heavily fortified blast doors with two more soldiers blocking ingress, but they quickly moved to the side when they saw Ryan and his escort.

The command center was a hive of activity and they appeared to be coordinating with people outside the bunkers. To Ryan, that confirmed that their communications were being jammed and the civilian devices just didn't have the juice to get their signals through. They made a beeline for a massive command table with an enlarged view of their planet and the space around it. It was an impressive setup. The Grand Monarch and her permanent shadow, Commander Yellen, were deep in conversation with several military officers in planetary militia garb. She stopped as Ryan approached and graciously gestured for him to join her.

"Ah, yes, Captain, I wanted to fill you in on the situation around our planet and hoped that you might have some insight or ideas as to prudent courses of action. We received confirmation that all of our low-orbit ships were destroyed with the exception of a lone destroyer that managed to evade the ambush and flee to the outer system. The enemy was pursuing, but we believe it managed to escape to hopefully warn the rest of our fleet."

"Are the enemy ships Hrum? How did we not see them coming?"

The Monarch looked over at Yellen who replied, "We are not sure how they ambushed so effectively. The limited data we have does not indicate that they have any sort of stealth technology, but we do not know how they got into the system. We cannot speculate as to who they are, other than the fact that their ships are not of Hrum origin."

Yellen paused and pulled up a grainy picture that was transmitted to them from their ships in orbit before they were destroyed. "As you can see," he continued, "they have several classes of ships, none of which are the cruisers that the Hrum so heavily depended on."

Ryan viewed the image for several moments before a novel idea occurred to him. "What are the chances that there are two different alien civilizations that build ships along the exact same lines of a Hrum cruiser?"

"What do you mean?"

"I mean if we didn't know the Hrum only used cruisers, how would we know these are not Hrum ships?"

The Monarch's shadow looked puzzled, and it was Izabella herself who answered as she caught on to what Ryan was getting at. "You are saying that these could very well be Hrum ships, just a different class." She looked over at Yellen and noted, "Although slightly different color and size, they are almost identically shaped as the cruisers we know the Hrum use."

Smiling at her, Ryan replied, "Exactly."

Yellen, looking none too pleased at the fact that Ryan pointed out something that should have been obvious, cut in, "I see, well with the loss of our ships in space, the number one priority should be evacuating the Grand Monarch from here. We have several imperial bunkers scattered throughout the region that are known only to a small number of people. This location is too obvious if their target is to capture you. We should evacuate you immediately."

"I will not..."

"It's a good idea, your majesty," Ryan interrupted before she could reply.

She fixed Ryan with a royal death glare before replying. "I already wasn't here to help my people once when they needed me, I will not be leaving them again."

One of the other military officers whose chest was covered in medals jumped into the conversation. "Your majesty, please. I cannot protect you and organize a defense at the same time. If I know you are safe, I can focus my efforts on coordinating our defense. Please allow Commander Yellen to escort you to a safe location."

Yellen leaned in and whispered something in her ear. Ryan saw that she visibly deflated as she listened. Whatever he had said calmed her down and made her listen to her officers' suggestions.

Ryan agreed with the other generals, but kept his mouth shut as he was not sure how Commander Yellen would react to him jumping into the conversation.

Eventually, they came to a decision and separated. The commander turned towards Ryan. "I personally think this is a mistake trusting a foreigner with this information, but I will be requesting you and your men to assist me in guarding her majesty in the imperial bunker. Simply put, I don't have enough men to adequately guard her and she insisted that we bring you along."

Ryan met the man's eye for several moments before nodding and replying. "It would be my honor. I have my men gathering at the training grounds, awaiting orders. I assume that military comms are still up?"

Yellen nodded.

"My men will be monitoring the command channels and Marvin should arrive there shortly. If you can give them coordinates, they will meet us wherever you need."

Yellen turned towards one of his men and barked orders which the soldier scurried to obey. Then he turned back to Ryan. "Your men will be given the coordinates of one of the bunkers. We will only stop there briefly before moving to another one further outside the capital. We depart in ten minutes. Corporal Virgadamomo, please escort the captain to the armory. Have him take whatever he wants from there."

As soon as he finished speaking, Yellen turned towards some of his men to make last minute preparations.

Ryan made brief eye contact with Izabella who offered him a hint of a smile before the same baby-faced soldier who'd brought him down to the bunker asked Ryan to follow him.

They moved quickly down the hall to a sizable armory stocked with an impressive array of weaponry. Ryan quickly donned a set of light body armor and helmet before eyeing the rifles. A whole bunch of exotic-looking rifles gleamed in rows, none of which he recognized, but his fingers itched to try. He decided that it was not the time to try something new, and luckily they did have some standard NIS infantry rifles, so he grabbed one, checked it over, and then stuffed a bunch of magazines into his vest. He was about to walk out when he noticed some wicked-looking bladed weapons. Unlike regular knives, these were molecularly sharpened. They could cut through steel and wouldn't be any worse for wear or require a sharpening afterwards. He buckled one of them to his hip, gave it a slap to ensure it was secure, then hustled back out to the command center. Several of the Grand Monarch's attendants were strapping on a much smaller set of armor and a pistol to her thigh. Ryan couldn't help but think that she looked cute more so than fierce. It cracked a smile on his face that he quickly wiped away when Yellen hustled up to him and provided him with a comm set.

"Let's go, we have several armored imperial transports in the vehicle pool. We decided that air travel was too conspicuous and we'd be better served to stay on the ground. This part of the planet is heavily wooded and hilly, so it'll be hard to track us from space."

Ryan simply nodded and gestured for him to lead the way.

Moments later, Yellen quickly led the Grand Monarch out the doorway with half a dozen men who Ryan followed. They hustled down several hallways until they arrived in a large underground room housing a wide variety of vehicles. Everything from an imperial limo to full-on assault trucks. They beelined for an armored transport and piled into it. The vehicle's electrical motor barely made a sound as it whirled up and peeled out the garage. Several other identical trucks with roof-mounted guns followed quickly behind. Ryan thought it wasn't the most inconspicuous escort, but they would be useful for taking out any shuttles or aircraft that the enemy might send their way.

"Commander, how long until we reach the bunker?"

"It's about an hour and a half drive. If you are wondering about your men, they acknowledged the command and will meet us there. Marvin indicated that he was going to wait for the rest of them to assemble before heading out himself, but he sent the first two squads to follow us immediately."

"Thank you. Have you heard from Nord at all? I know he was overseeing an operation halfway around the planet."

"We have not. Our communications are unable to reach that far with the jamming. We were able to scramble our armed forces around the capital. Most are digging in for an assault, but at the end of the day, we don't have the air superiority to challenge more than a squadron or two of enemy fighters. We're going to have to lay low. Luckily, this's a large planet, and the enemy doesn't appear to have enough troops to attack more than a few targets."

"What's the enemy been up to? They targeting population centers like the Hrum did and how are they jamming us so effectively?"

Grimly, the commander responded, "I don't have a lot of information yet. They've only sent down a few dozen shuttles so far, but it appears they're targeting nobles estates, government centers, and a few other select targets."

The inside of the truck was deathly quiet. The Hrum, when they attacked, didn't seem to have a specific target. They just tended to land somewhere outside a population center and then march through, shooting everything that moved. This wasn't the most effective way to attack a planet, but the sheer numbers of them overwhelmed nearly all defenses, so it had an impact. Ryan knew what everyone was thinking. This meant they weren't dealing with the Hrum. It sucked, because he'd much rather have a mindless enemy that was deadly, but predictable, rather than another whose motivations they could not yet guess. This realization comforted nobody.

Izabella, who had been quiet until now finally spoke up. "I can't believe this is happening to my people again. They've already been through so much."

Yellen put a comforting arm around her shoulder. "Your *people* are survivors, we may have been through hell once, but it's prepared us for something like this. Somehow I doubt even a single civilian will surrender. They fought for their home world once, they'll do it again."

She buried her head into her hands and rocked back and forth slightly. Ryan couldn't imagine the burden she was carrying on her shoulders. It was one thing to be forced to become something she'd never expected to be, but another thing entirely to be helpless to protect those who entrusted their loyalty to her.

The only sound in the truck was the crunching of the tires on the roads, a low and steady rumble, as they flew down an abandoned road towards their destination.

Half an hour passed without a word spoken when suddenly an explosion rocked the driver side of the vehicle. The truck rocked onto its right side wheels and seemed like it was about to tip over before slamming back on all six with a loud boom as the driver managed to regain control.

From the front, the soldier in the passenger seat yelled, "Incomingggg!" Then he said in a calmer voice, "Enemy aircraft."

There was a booming report when their truck as well as the three other escort trucks opened return fire on the shuttles. The driver, seemingly unfazed from the near miss, put his foot to the floor and the truck lunged ahead. An open section of road left them terribly exposed. The driver made a break for the heavily wooded road only a few kilometers away. The escort trucks followed, cannons hammering away at the sky. One of the shuttles began belching a thick black smoke as it was struck repeatedly by gunfire. The pilot lost control and it spiraled away before crashing into the ground with a boom that shook the truck, the Grand Monarch grabbing for a brace and finding only Ryan's arm. The other aircraft hadn't been idle, however, and one of their escort trucks took the full brunt of the shuttle's autocannon. The vehicle was shredded and swerved off the road before tumbling into the ditch, aflame. Together, their truck and their remaining two escorts continued firing and their shared rounds stitched up the side of the hostile shuttle, causing it to bank away. It maintained altitude for a few moments before it appeared to dive towards a field to make an emergency landing. The entire attack hadn't lasted more than a few minutes, but everyone in the truck sat quietly as if in shock.

Ryan was the first to speak up. "What're the odds that was a coincidental attack?"

Nodding in agreement, Yellen replied, "We have no transponders or anything in these vehicles. We swept them before we left, but I agree, it's likely they recognized the trucks."

"It's clear whoever *they* were knew where *we* were," Ryan continued. "It's only a matter of time until they send more of them after us."

"I would think that they would have sent more than two aircraft if they knew exactly where we would be, however."

"You think we got lucky?" asked Ryan.

"No, I'm saying it's more likely someone with inside knowledge of evacuation procedures, but not someone who knew exactly what our destination was, gave us away."

"How's that possible?"

"Well, the Hrum have never shown any inclination to speak with us, which makes me think these aren't Hrum," stated Yellin, his gaze as sober as a brick wall. "I think it's possible someone just got sloppy. We haven't fought what I would consider a smart enemy in a long time. I think due to that we've been lazy with security measures, cutting corners we'd never cut with a smarter enemy."

"I don't know, Commander. I feel like we're missing something here."

"Well we're in agreement on that," Yellen replied. "We'll stop briefly to recharge and wait for the rest of our troops at the safe house before moving on. I think that all the imperial bunker locations are likely compromised and it's no longer safe. Even if they didn't know exactly where we were heading, they likely do now." Yellin's brick wall face began to crack with worry.

Ryan thought aloud, "We can't go anywhere in the standard evacuation procedures, we have to assume they're no longer secure."

Again Yellen said nothing. Clearly Ryan wasn't telling him anything he didn't already know.

Izabella, who had again been silent, suddenly spoke up, "What about that summer camp on the old Ryder estates?

"Summer camp?" Yellin asked. "Ryder estates?"

"Their family didn't survive the first invasion," Monarch Izabella noted. "It should be abandoned, and the whole camp was self-sustaining and equipped with their own power generation equipment and other necessary survival goods. Maybe we can get one or more of the generators running, and the lake water should have plenty of fish and the water's clean."

The knot of worry that Commander Yellen had been wearing suddenly came free and a small smile creased his face. "Your majesty, that's an excellent idea!" He pulled up a map of the surrounding region on his tab. "Unfortunately we need a new power cell for the truck, we will not make it there on this charge.

"We still need to stop by the bunker?" Ryan asked.

"Yes. But if we make it quick, we should be able to get away before the enemy can find us."

At that moment, the driver yelled back, "Sir, you've got to hear this."

The driver turned up the communications set and a robotic voice began to growl over the speaker: "Humans of St. George. We are your conquerors. All nobles and military are to lay down their arms and surrender immediately. You will await our troops to take you into custody without harm. Failure to do so will result in your immediate extermination from this savage planet."

The message ended abruptly before repeating in a loop over the speakers. "Humans of St. George...." The other soldier in the passenger seat turned it off.

"Sir, it's on every civilian channel, and I cannot get any messages out even with our handhelds, every comms channel is just playing that message on repeat."

"Can they track us with it?" asked Yellen.

"I don't believe so sir, but I don't know for sure."

Ryan jumped into the conversation. "Two things. I still don't get how they are jamming us like this? It would take something with much more juice to so effectively blanket our signal than a dozen warships in orbit. Also, I don't know if you noticed, but they sent the message in perfect English. That means they've at minimum been observing us, at worst, they've infiltrated our population somehow.

The private in the driver seat nodded.

Commander Yellen cut in before Ryan could continue. "Private, how far out are we?"

"Sir, about fifteen minutes."

"Did you hear from the militia prior to the looping message taking over?"

"Yes sir, they should arrive less than ten minutes after us."

"I want to be back on the road within five minutes after that. I wouldn't wait for them if we could afford it, but we need more people to guard the Monarch." Yellen ordered, pointedly ignoring the glare that Izabella fixed him with.

"Aye sir."

The rest of the journey was uneventful and they turned off the main road onto a dirt strip that looked like little more than a deer trail. Ryan wasn't sure they'd be able to turn their vehicles around quickly if they needed. Commander Yellen, seemingly mirroring Ryan's thoughts, gave him a knowing nod.

"There's two alternate escape routes and the bunker itself is equipped with plenty of weapons and supplies if we need to hole up there for a while. I want to try the communications gear and see if any of our other forces made it to the other bunkers, but judging by the complete comms blackout I don't think we'll have any luck."

Ryan nodded, but didn't respond as he kept an eye on the surroundings.

When they finally rolled up to the inconspicuous-looking mound, Ryan grew apprehensive, feeling uneasy.

Commander Yellen ordered him to keep a lookout while he and his other men quickly accessed the bunker and began hurriedly ferrying supplies into the trucks. Ryan's senses were on high alert and the private who had been driving the truck looked just as uneasy.

"Private, I am going to do a quick walk of the perimeter. Something doesn't feel right."

"Aye sir, I'll let the commander know."

Ryan nodded and walked off.

As he reached the treeline, the dark threshold to the forest edge, a slightly distorted voice rattled over his headset. "Local comms are working. The commander said to let you know that the power cells have been loaded and the militia should arrive in the next five minutes. When you finish your sweep we must get back to the trucks so we can head out as soon as they arrive."

"Will do, I—" Ryan suddenly stopped as a shadow slithered among the trees.

He raised his rifle and froze. The shadow continued to slowly but assuredly move through the trees towards the bunker. The shape slowly materialized into a familiar shape that dropped a rock into the pit of Ryan's stomach. A Hrum soldier!

As quietly as he could, he tried to open a comms channel with Commander Yellen. Before he could say anything, the Hrum pivoted 180 degrees towards him, spinning on a dime, then opened fire.

Without hesitation, Ryan quickly returned fire and nailed the Hrum soldier in the faceplate.

Ryan dropped into cover and quickly reported, "Commander, the Hrum have found us. The Hrum have found us. We're under attack!"

The commander didn't reply, but Ryan began hearing gunfire in the cold shadowed distance back towards the bunker. He charged through the woods but slowed before he reached the forest edge. He paused and took a look at the situation that was unfolding. One of their trucks was on fire, but he could see Izabella and the commander taking cover in the doorway of the bunker. Ryan clicked his comms to get the commander's attention, knowing that he would know where the signal came from.

Yellen instantly noticed and while looking in Ryan's direction, signaled where the attackers were coming from and performed a chopping motion indicating that Ryan should hit them from the side.

Ryan didn't respond, but he quickly made his way through the forest's edge until he was coming at the Hrum soldiers from the side. It appeared to be half a dozen Hrum with one who was a bit smaller near the back wearing a purple version of the regular Hrum armor and acting like he was in charge. That was another unfortunate surprise. The Hrum were very obviously advancing in a tactical manner and were using suppressing fire to cover each other as they advanced from cover to cover. It was very un-Hrum like, but Ryan didn't dwell on it and opened fire into the advancing soldiers, dropping two of them before they realized the new threat from their flank. In an uncomfortably quick and organized fashion, they spun and fired in his direction. Ryan cursed as he ducked into cover. He spot-checked his gear, wishing he had some grenades or a heavier weapon than an assault rifle, but he would have to make due. He popped up quickly and fired off a few bursts and actually nailed one more of the Hrum before ducking back into his cover, which was getting smaller by the second as the Hrum focused on his location. He was gauging his chances of moving to a new cover without getting shot when the fire suddenly faded away and he heard the deep humming noise of the turret mounted on the trucks singing its death song. He took a quick peek and saw that all the Hrum were down before leaving his cover and sprinting back towards the bunker. He clicked his comms shortly before breaching the treeline to let friendlies know he was coming and hopefully not get shot. He paused and slowed to a walk as he came out to several rifles pointed in his direction, but they quickly lowered as they saw who it was.

Commander Yellen quickly advanced and said, "Great job, Captain. The distraction was exactly what we needed to eliminate the Hrum."

Ryan nodded and replied, "We need to get out of here, sir. There are bound to be more of them."

"I couldn't agree more, we are loading the last of the supplies now, and your men should be here any moment."

A frenzy of movement from the bunker followed and the bodyguards and even Izabella were quickly throwing ammunition, food, and other supplies into the truck. They were all hopping aboard the trucks when the welcomed sight of two APCs with the Monarch's logo came rolling into the clearing.

They wasted little time with pleasantries as Ryan exchanged a firm handshake with Corporal Kim who indicated that Marvin and the rest of their men were on their way, but decided that they should gather as many supplies as possible, so they were an hour or two behind. Ryan nodded and told him to keep everyone in the trucks and that they were moving out. Less than two minutes later the now enlarged convoy was moving out one of the alternative routes from the bunker and headed back towards the road. Ryan felt the beginnings of hope as they reached the main road when the turret suddenly began spitting rounds again.

"Commander, two Hrum dropships just unloaded on the highway." There was a distant explosion and a short cheer before Ryan continued. "Make that one Hrum dropship. I don't know if they managed to unload before I took them out though."

The vehicle was suddenly rocked with gunfire and the turret replied in turn.

"I think that answers that question," Ryan muttered to himself, before checking the magazine in his rifle.

There wasn't much he could do at the moment as he was near the front of the truck across from Izabella, but it didn't hurt to be ready. He watched silently as Commander Yellen barked out orders to the men. The truck jumped suddenly as they hit a larger than usual bump and bounced twice before settling back onto all of its wheels. The fire from the turret suddenly slackened and Ryan peered up the port. The young soldier at the station had a gaping hole through the front of his visor, clearly dead. Ryan quickly and gently as he could removed the young man from the turret and climbed up into it himself. It only took him a moment or two to familiarize himself with the controls, and he rotated it towards the rear of the truck where the remaining shuttle was making passes on the convoy. Luckily, it didn't appear to have any sort of missiles, but it was firing its autocannon in controlled bursts. Ryan felt a sudden sense of anger at the attacker and depressed both of the plungers on the large cannon. His first shots were high and due to the shuttle armor, many of the rounds pinged off or missed entirely, but as he walked the aim forward towards the cockpit window he saw that some rounds were beginning to puncture. The shuttle began to turn away and Ryan thought it may be retreating, but it suddenly performed a twisting maneuver and spun back in their direction, its attention now focused on Ryan's truck. Ryan had paused when the shuttle turned, but now he squeezed the plungers and focused his fire on the engines of the Hrum shuttle. Bullets began rocking the truck as the shuttles' own cannons spit out their rounds.

"Die, die, die… you bastard!" Ryan heard himself yell out.

In what felt like ages, but was likely only seconds, one of the engines on the shuttle began belching smoke and the shuttle veered off sharply, out of control. It slammed into the ground before erupting into a massive fireball. Ryan cheered loudly, pumping both of his fists into the air.

"How do you like me now!"

He recomposed himself and continued to scan the area for any more threats. Finally, the convoy reached the roadway and accelerated to their top speed. It appeared for now that they had escaped. He started to call out to the people in the truck below to celebrate when he heard a loud wailing coming from the bay. He ducked down from the turret to see what was going on. Izabella was crying hysterically, holding Commander Yellin's head in her lap while the medic worked on him. Yellin's body shifted to reveal a large hole in the side of his chest, likely a result of the fire the truck took during the duel Ryan just had with the shuttle. The Commander was still conscious, but judging by the severity of the wound, his grip on life waned without immediate access to a hospital. Ryan sat there numbly, watching the medic do his best to save Yellen's life with what little medical supplies he had. Ryan was fully trained as a field medic, but he would just be in the way if he tried to help.

Suddenly, Commander Yellen raised his hand in Ryan's direction and gestured for him to come closer.

Ryan leaned in and ducked his ear towards the commander's mouth so that he could hear him.

"Captain, protect her…"

"Commander…I…"

"I need you to protect Izabella," Yellen groaned, his voice but a hoarse whisper. "Without me, she will need someone to lean on. You aren't so bad… for a foreigner." He stopped and coughed painfully before continuing. "She can be a great leader, just needs to trust her instincts. Promise me you'll keep her safe." He raised his hand as if to grab Ryan's arm, but Ryan clasped Yellen's hand into his own.

"Yes… of course, sir, I promise," Ryan said, unable to look at the Grand Monarch directly. "No harm will come to her. I'll die before I let anything happen to her."

Yellen didn't reply and with a shuddering breath closed his eyes and all strength left his grip on Ryan's hand.

It appeared he was gone before his eyes suddenly opened with a surprising clarity and focused on Izabella. "I love you my dear," he creaked. "The daughter I never had. I wish I could've seen you grow into the leader I know you'll become."

Tears flowed freely down Izabella's cheeks, but she couldn't seem to find any words. She sat there quietly holding Yellen's other hand for several moments until finally he faded away. The medic was frantically trying to save him, but the commander was gone. A few minutes later, the medic finally gave up on his attempts to save him and sat back defeated. It was at that moment when Izabella appeared to break out of her trance and began screaming and pounding on the commander's chest.

"No, no, no, you can't leave me! I have nobody. I can't do it without you." She sobbed into his chest plate before Ryan gently reached over and extracted her, taking her into his arms where she wailed.

The medics gave him a grateful nod and began to secure the commander's body. No words were exchanged, but Ryan held her for the duration of the ride while she sobbed silently. Luckily it appeared that they had escaped and there were no more surprises in store for them.

They made one more stop to gather their bearings and check on all the others. Luckily none of Ryan's militia sustained serious casualties outside of a few minor shrapnel wounds and one concussion. Everyone appeared to be milling around sort of aimlessly when Ryan realized that the most senior soldier remaining from the Grand Monarch's entourage was the young corporal in the other truck who'd initially escorted Ryan around the Monarch's estate. Ryan took him aside and asked what his orders were.

The young soldier's eyes projected traces of panic and he quickly stuttered out, "I... umm... we need..." He began hyperventilating.

The corporal was barely out of his teens and on the verge of a full-blown panic attack. Ryan recognized the signs and grabbed him by the shoulders and gave him a thorough shake.

"Soldier, get it together. We can't have you lose your head now. The Monarch is depending on you."

The panic lingered in his eyes, but the corporal managed to stop hyperventilating, "Tha—thank you, sir," he stammered.

"I understand what you're feeling, Corporal," Ryan said. "Now breathe, and tell me… what are your orders?"

"Sir, umm could you perhaps umm take charge? I think it's what the commander would have wanted."

Ryan looked down and away, about to say no, then looked back to see just how scared the young soldier was. He sighed before nodding.

"Go check on the men, Corporal. Make sure everyone is accounted for and there aren't any casualties. I want the convoy ready to go in five."

The corporal nodded and sharply saluted Ryan. "Thank you, sir. Right away, sir." He spun on his heel and nearly fell over before Ryan grabbed his shoulder.

"One more thing," Ryan said.

"Sir…?"

"What's your name, son?"

"Corporal Virgadamomo. Zacharius Virgadamomo, sir."

Ryan paused, wondering who would name their kid such a thing, then said, "Well it's a pleasure to meet you Zach. I know you won't let me down. Let me know when everyone is ready."

Without another word, but one more salute, Corporal Virgadamomo sprinted off.

Ryan shook his head and muttered under his breath, "This day just keeps getting better and better."

Chapter III

In Unknown System on Battleship Arcon
Year 3326

As with most well-thought-out plans, everything fell apart rather quickly. Shortly after Jaxton and his captains had agreed to perform a quick hit and run attack on the enemy space station, the enemy did something unexpected. The three ships that they planned to attack remained in orbit over the planet where that space station and their scout ship resided, but the other ships, twenty-seven in total, began to move. They quickly assembled into two groups. One of fifteen and another of twelve. The fifteen ships took off in a direction opposite to Jaxton and his ships. They quickly transitioned out of the system. The other twelve were headed directly towards the Albion point that Jaxton's fleet had used to enter the system.

"Sir, those ships are headed for the Jewel of Sunlight system," reported Lt. Chen.

"Thank you, Lieutenant. I see that. The question is what do we do about it?"

The bridge was silent. Jaxton thought he heard something from the gunnery station, so he turned and looked at Lt. Lewis, who appeared to be silently scolding the roving bridge marine who was passing by his station. Jaxton looked over at the unfortunate corporal who had apparently said something to incur Lewis' wrath.

"Suggestions from gunnery?" Jaxton inquired.

"No, sir. Corporal Truly just coughed."

"Didn't sound like a cough to me," Jaxton replied before turning and looking at the corporal. "What did you say, son?"

"Sir, forgive me. It's not my position to say."

"For chrissakes, Lewis, what did he say? Don't make me order you to tell me..."

"Sir, I apologize for the language... he said 'Let's fuck 'em up.'"

A chuckle spread through the bridge as everyone listened in.

Jaxton, who had been unable to stop himself from also laughing, replied, "Well, Corporal. I find myself in agreement with you."

"Here's what we're gonna do...."

Jaxton sat back in his chair as the fleet broke into two groups. He'd quickly assembled his captains for yet another strategy meeting, but this time he simply told them what he wanted done. That didn't stop Dixon from disagreeing with him, but eventually even he did as he was ordered. Dixon had wanted the entire fleet to stay together and attack the incoming ships before turning and leaving the system. Jaxton thought it was still important to rescue the scout crew, so he rejected Dixon's suggestions and ordered the fleet to split into two.

Even though Dixon had disagreed on nearly everything Jaxton proposed, he did agree to lead the ships tasked with assaulting the space station. Drake knew that outside of himself, Dixon was the most capable of their ship captains to lead such an assault. He may not have agreed with many of Jaxton's tactics, or the importance of their mission in this system, but Dixon got things done.

It was not long before Dixon and the two destroyers tasked with assisting him were invisible on the sensors. The screen showed their projected locations based on the plan that Jaxton had put together.

At the same time, the remaining four ships of his group burned their engines gently to change the angle of the gravity assist in order to flip around and head back towards the Albion point. Originally, the entire fleet was supposed to continue along the path that Dixon continued along. A brief discussion on whether or not the ships in the system could be considered hostile ensued, but at the end of the day, these ships were in possession of a NIS ship that had clearly been attacked and they were heading towards the Albion point where the scout ship had come from and more NIS ships were at risk of being attacked. Jaxton couldn't be 100% positive that these ships were his enemy, but he felt that the risks of allowing them to pass were too dangerous to the remaining ships in JOS. In his mind, you didn't send a fleet of warships to make contact with a potentially new alien race.

Checking the plot, he knew that he had about twelve hours before he had to engage the enemy. They'd fight them just short of the Albion point, using their stealth and the incredible power of his battleship to surprise. The plan was simple, but relied heavily on the stealth systems being as good as the scientists thought they were. What made him feel better about the plan was that the ship in the most danger was his own. The other three ships would have an opportunity to escape should the plan go to hell. At a designated time, his other ships would break off to get into position, hiding along the path that Drake was going to lure the enemy ships into. He was going to get as close as he felt comfortable getting to the enemy fleet with his own ship before firing all weapons and launching a flight of missiles before turning and running as fast as his ship could take him. He'd be coming at them from an angle and would have a pretty significant initial velocity advantage due to the fact that the enemy ships weren't moving with any real urgency. Assuming that these ships were as fast as Hrum ships he'd fought in the past, his speed advantage would not last, but he was confident it would last long enough to lure the enemy into his trap. If he was wrong, he would be outnumbered at least seven- or eight-to-one, assuming he took out some ships with his initial volley. His ship was about to be put to its first real big test.

As he walked onto the bridge from his ready room, he acknowledged his crew,. "Everyone get your replacements up here," he told them. "I don't want anyone to sleep, but let the second shift crew monitor the systems until we are ready to engage. I expect you to be as fresh as daisies when we spring our trap." The last part he said with a wolfish smile. Even though the simulations were realistic, there was something considerably more thrilling about the real thing.

Taking his own advice, he motioned to his XO to take his seat, then got up to go get a snack from the officers' galley. The rest of the officers took his departure as a sign to get up from their stations and do the same. Drake was the first to the galley, so he sat down at an empty table, but the room soon filled with the rest of his bridge crew. He had made it a point to get to know all of them on a personal level, and quickly erased the notion he'd enjoy a meal alone. When they had initially resisted interaction, he started sitting at random tables and talking to the crew until they just accepted that this was the way it was going to be. The crew was always deferential and respectful, but they had grown more comfortable around him the longer they worked together. Today, he was joined by Major Stevens, the young marine Corporal Truly, his nav officer and sensor operator. From conversations he'd had with the young man, he knew that Truly's wife was due any day to have their first child and was surprised that he had not requested a transfer off the ship.

"Corporal Truly, any news on your wife from our last dispatch before we transitioned to this system?"

"Yes sir! She was headed to the hospital with her parents. I might be the father of a little girl by now."

"Congratulations, Corporal. Have you picked out a name yet?"

"Yessir, we are naming her after my mother, Alanna."

"Well I'm sure she's honored."

"She was in the Sapporo system when the Hrum attacked and fell victim to their ships when her transport was destroyed." Truly said. "I think she would have appreciated the gesture."

"Well I am sorry about your mother, but I know for certain that she would be happy to know she has such a loving son."

The rest of the meal went by uneventfully, the atmosphere was tense, but Jaxton felt that there was also an edge of excitement. It seemed he wasn't the only one who was excited to see what their ship could do.

The ship was at battle stations and the crew awaited Jaxton's orders. They were minutes away from engaging the enemy fleet. So far, there had been no evidence the enemy was aware of their ship's presence. Major Brewster and his fighters were sitting in the bays, ready to launch. The moment that Jaxton engaged the enemy, his fighters would launch a lightning-quick strike against the enemy ships. The reason they were still in the hangars was that it would break their stealth to allow them to disembark. They did not know for sure if the enemy would have detected the fighters being launched, but Brewster's pilots had trained relentlessly for a quick deployment and they were raring to go. The resulting fighter strike wouldn't be as effective, hanging back as they were, but it would still add to the surprise and firepower of the ambush.

Taking a breath, Jaxton ordered, "It's time."

All stations bustled to life with actions and mumbling of seniors to subordinates into comms.

"All weapons fire, shields to full power, give the flight deck commander the green light to launch all fighters," Jaxton added.

The bridge erupted into a flurry of activity and the lights dimmed briefly as the powerplants struggled for a moment to keep up with the massive load they were being asked to provide. To Jaxton's glee, the enemy fleet was caught completely flat-footed with their shields down. The first shots from his Evo cannon began blasting into the enemy formation, ripping enormous holes in the ships it struck. He had chosen to fire at the maximum firing rate, targeting engineering sections on the ships in an attempt to disable them before they could get their shields up and weapons armed, which would even the playing field for his fighters hanging back. His gunners targeted each ship with no more than a few bursts before switching over to the next one. There were also loud thunks as the missile silos opened and his ship launched a flight of fusion-tipped missiles. He checked his screen and saw that all twenty-four fighters had successfully launched and were also in the process of burning towards their intended targets. These fighters, like his ship, were also equipped with stealth systems. If the enemy hadn't noticed them launching, it was quite likely they never saw them at all, especially with massive bulk of his ship as a backdrop to them. It would be interesting to see how close they managed to get before the Hrum ships were aware they were there and took actions to fight them off.

The crew watched as the first shots they fired in anger intersected the enemy ships. It didn't take long for some explosive results. Of the dozen ships in the enemy formation, three were destroyed outright. The Evo cannons bolts barely pausing at the unshielded hulls before striking deep in the engineering sections. Those ships were little more than expanding clouds of gas as their reactors went critical. In addition, Drake's ship managed to damage at least four others with his Evo cannon alone. Just a couple of seconds behind that came the missiles both he and his fighters had fired. They weren't quite as effective, but they did take out two of the damaged ships and damaged a third. Not all the enemy captains were asleep at the wheel and had managed to get some of their shields up before the missiles got to them. If he'd been just a few seconds quicker, Drake was convinced he could have taken the entire formation apart with his ship alone. He continued to fire, but as the shields stabilized, his shots were not as effective anymore.

"Focus fire on one ship," Drake called out. "Let's see how many shots these bastards can take before their shields fail."

His gunners quickly adjusted fire and the shots were now focused on the lead ship. He pulled up an array of viewscreens at his station and watched eagerly. One of the screens was feeding sensor data, and it suddenly began flashing.

"Sir, we're being hit with targeting sensors," Chen said. "They've begun tagging us."

"Emergency power to the engines," Jaxton ordered, deciding it was time to make his escape. "Pull back out of estimated range and maximum bias on shields facing the enemy."

"Banking out of range, aye sir," said his helmsman, Lt. Booker, neatly pivoting the ship about forty-five degrees away from the enemy ships. Arcon began to vibrate as the engines poured millions of tons of thrust out of the nozzles to try and stay out of range of the enemy guns. The first shots from the enemy ships began to strike his shields. The weapons appeared to be very similar to Hrum cruiser munitions. They also launched a flight of missiles, but Jaxton was prepared for that and his point defense gunners as well as the fighters who had returned after launching their missiles worked in unison to destroy anything that posed a threat to the battleship. Not a single missile came close, and it wasn't long before they were rapidly gaining distance on the enemy fleet.

Then, in an unexpected twist, the enemy ships began launching smaller craft of their own.

"What's that, Lieutenant?" Drake, squinting at the center viewscreen, asked Chen.

"Seems to be enemy fighter formations, sir."

"Well, well..." Jaxton muttered to Commander Bradley. "That's new."

"I already miss the old Hrum," Bradley replied.

Jaxton nodded.

The enemy having and using fighters was a new development that indicated that NIS wasn't going to be able to use their own fighters as purely bombers and point defense. They would likely have to revert back to a mixed role of dogfighting, bombing, and point defense. which was something he was unhappy about. The utter destruction that a full wing of fighters launching missiles could have on a fleet of ships was a tactical blind spot in Hrum doctrine that Jaxton had exploited time and time again. It was what had allowed him to wipe out forces that were significantly more powerful than his own multiple times.

"Sir, Major Brewster says that he is ordering his pilots to engage enemy fighters," Lt. Johnson said.

"Override that order," said Drake. "Order him to wait until they are in range of our own point-defenses. Have him cover our blind spots."

Jax knew his friend would not like that order, but it was the right move. Fighter doctrine had not focused on dogfighting in recent years and the training reflected that. On top of that, with their new stealth systems, fighters were mostly being used as stealth ambushers rather than dogfighters, so they didn't have the correct loadout for fighter-to-fighter engagements. Jaxton was willing to bet money that Brewster would be integrating it back into their training simulations in short order. The shaking of enemy fire had subsided as Jaxton's ship gained distance on the enemy fleet. The enemy fighters also seemed to realize that they would be exposed if they charged after the battleship without their support ship and they slowed to allow the rest of their ships to catch up. The bridge suddenly fell silent except for the deep rumble of their engines. As a group, they watched over the next thirty minutes the Hrum ships slowly gain momentum and eventually begin to close the distance between them. It was no surprise to anyone aboard. While Jaxton's ship was incredibly powerful, it was relatively slow and a Hrum cruiser would have no trouble catching up. He took a quick look at their position on his screen and smiled, the smile of someone with another surprise in-store.

Ten additional minutes later, Lt. Booker at the helm announced. "Flipping the ship and killing the engines. We are approaching waypoint Surprise."

Drake acknowledged the statement with a distracted nod, but his focus was on the enemy ships. Unlike the blindly charging Hrum of old, *this* enemy was advancing in a layered formation that indicated they were aware of the benefits of overlapping shields and a combined weight of fire. This was yet another headache that Jaxton now had to deal with. He much preferred the berserker-like aggression that Hrum had shown in the past. His headache disappeared and a wolfish grin split his face when the enemy continued to advance. Either it had not occurred to them that he was not alone, or they didn't care, but just three-thousand kilometers off the Jaxton's and the Hrum's own path, waited the rest of his ships.

"Helm, full stop! Lewis, fire as soon as they enter effective weapons range."

The enemy was seemingly confused by this sudden change in direction, but still continued to advance. The formation tightened and slowed slightly, and it appeared that they were biasing their own shields towards the front, obviously wary of the power of Jaxton's Evo cannons. Jaxton laughed suddenly, causing a few of his officers to look over at him in concern. Had something happened? Had their captain suddenly lost his mind? Before they got too concerned, Jaxton managed to regain his composure.

"Care to let us in on what's so funny?" a confused Commander Bradley asked.

"The enemy is biasing their shields towards the front," a still-snickering Jaxton replied.

"And that's funny how?"

"Us facing a 'smart' enemy has actually weakened their ability to counter what we have planned. Normal Hrum would just leave their shields equally covering their ship and wouldn't so much as slow down to fight us. Them slowing and fighting us directionally is making our lives easier."

Jaxton started laughing again, and by then a couple others on the bridge had caught on to what he was getting at and had also began to laugh. Luckily Jaxton's ship didn't play a large role in this next engagement and by the time the enemy realized the predicament they were in, it was too late, and the trap had been sprung. The remaining ships of Task Force Rogue along with a massive volley of missiles from their carrier's fighter wing launched all their weapons from behind the enemy formation. The shields, which Jaxton had accurately pointed out were biased towards the front in order to fight him, barely slowed any of the shots, and the remaining enemy ships were torn apart. The viewscreen automatically dimmed, and by the time it cleared and the fusion explosions settled, there were only a handful of drifting hulks and other debris where an enemy formation had been only moments earlier. Looking over his screens, Drake confirmed that all of his ships were still intact, and only one of his destroyers was showing any damage. In addition, he had only lost two fighters. It had been a slaughter.

Now back in control of his emotions, Drake looked over at his sensor operator and asked, "Any escape pods or other emergency signals, Lieutenant?"

"Sir, none in the immediate vicinity," the officer replied. "There may however be some from the first ships that we destroyed. They weren't destroyed so completely, so there's a chance we may find some survivors, or at least corpses of crew."

"Organize search and rescue operations. Tell them to use extreme caution and take no chances if any surviving enemy is not cooperating."

"Yessir."

"In addition, send a message to Captain Dixon that we were successful in intersecting the enemy and that we will be available for support if he requests it."

"Aye, sir."

With nothing else to say, Jaxton unbuckled his harness and stood up from his seat to stretch his legs. It never ceased to amaze him how even a short engagement like the one they just had could feel like hours. In all, the shooting itself only took about ten minutes combined, baiting the trap and luring the enemy took the rest of it. He was especially happy with how his new weapons had performed during the engagement. There was no overheating even though they fired it at full power and as fast as the cannons would allow. The hard work over the past few months paid off.

As he was walking to his ready room, he decided to go check in with the engineering team as well as his scientists. He was sure they were poring over the weapons data and he could probably have just waited for a report, but he decided that it would be good for crew morale if he stopped by the various departments to congratulate them. It marked their first engagement as a crew, and they had performed flawlessly. He wasn't sure if the stealth coatings would allow for it, but it had been tradition that his ships painted on a mark for each of their confirmed capital ship kills in the past.

It took him nearly an hour, but he finally reached the engineering section of the ship where the science bays were located and he spotted Dr. Casey and her team talking animatedly. As he walked in, he realized the real reason he didn't want to wait for the weapons data report was that he wanted to see her.

"Still a sucker for a pretty face," he muttered to himself.

Chapter IV

In Unknown System on Captain Dixon's Battlecruiser
Year 3326

"Sir, the assault forces have just detached from our ship and are slowly making their way to the station," Commander Taylor reported to Captain Dixon. "They'll go full speed once we engage the three ships in orbit. The admiral's fleet should engage the other enemy fleet just short of the Albion lane. They should be engaging at any moment."

"Thank you, Commander," Dixon replied. "I'm sure Admiral Drake will handle them. Let's focus on our piece of the pie."

"Aye aye, Captain."

"Which shuttles are boarding the scout ship with our officers?"

"The last shuttle I've labeled shuttle four has Lt. Drake and her team as well as a squad of marines. The engineers with Nat should be able to either get the ship up and running or scuttle it to prevent any further analysis of it by the enemy."

"Very good, Commander. Keep me updated." Looking over to his sensor officer he continued, "Lieutenant, any additional enemy ships in range or weapon signatures detected on the station?"

"No sir, just a couple robotic drones of some sort that appear to be maintenance bots. There are several what appear to be cargo ships in lower orbit, but they aren't showing any signs of detecting our presence and the station appears unarmed."

"No planetary defenses of any sort?"

"Sir, I cannot confirm for certain, but there does not appear to be anything. Maybe the fleet was acting as the defense network?"

Dixon sat back in his chair, digesting what she was saying. Even their most remote colony planets had a basic satellite defense system or stations with a fighter garrison.

"Once we engage the enemy ships, warn the marines on the station to not get caught up in a prolonged firefight. First sign of real resistance, get out of there. I would hate to be wrong about this place not having any sort of real defenses. Number one priority is capturing or scuttling that scout ship."

Commander Taylor glanced at him out of the corner of her eye. She felt he was ignoring the fact that the Admiral wanted to make an attempt to rescue the scout crew if they were still alive. She knew Dixon wouldn't directly disobey orders, but he didn't agree with the mission to board the station in the first place. He would have been more than happy to simply blast the ship from afar and call it a day. She wondered if Dixon had an ulterior motive for sending Lt. Drake rather than herself to secure the ship. She'd logged in her situation report Dixon's claim that it was because the ship needed its XO more than its main helm officer, but she felt like he was being a little bit petty and was sticking it to Nat's brother.

"Sir, three minutes to range on the three enemy ships. No sign of detection yet."

Nat was on the shuttle in an armored vacuum suit that was far too large for her. The marine commander insisted that all crew he was being saddled with wear fully armored suits and as a result, Nat and her team of five were adjusting to the bulkier armored suits. Her team's job was to see what they could do once they got aboard the scout ship and see if they could get it operational. In addition, there was a team of five xenobiologists tagging along. She still wasn't sure why they were bringing them, but NISI Agent Hadley, who for some reason was still on Captain Dixon's ship, had insisted they were mission critical to attempt to establish relations with the aliens they assumed they were going to encounter. Five seemed like overkill and they also appeared far too calm for untrained civilian scientists, but Nat had not been able to dig into them or talk to her brother about how they didn't look or behave like any scientists she had ever known. She hadn't forgotten the weird reaction Lt. Carn had upon seeing them in the galley a few days prior. She actually still had his bottle of hot sauce in her quarters.

The shuttles were slowly drifting towards the station, waiting for Captain Dixon to engage the three enemy ships in orbit. Suddenly, the shuttle fired its engine and over the intercom the pilot said they were thirty seconds to boarding and to brace for impact. Nat wasn't able to see what was going on, but she assumed that meant that Dixon had engaged the enemy ships.

She'd never been aboard a shuttle when they breached something before, and she was quite curious to see how it worked. These shuttles were equipped with a custom breaching ring that would magnetically mount to the station before burning a hole through the walls and creating a makeshift vacuum seal that would allow the marines to board the ship quickly and through a spot of their choosing that would hopefully confuse any enemy. Airlocks were predictable, and could easily turn into chokepoints, so unpredictability was the name of the game.

Her team's target was the scout ship, but the ship's only full-size airlock was attached to the station. On the off chance the ship was flyable, they didn't want to destroy the hull of the ship with the breaching ring, so they had picked a location on the station nearby to breach instead. With a jarring suddenness, the shuttles slammed into the station and the maglocks initiated with a loud thunk. Moments later, the breaching lasers fired and the cabin filled with smoke that was quickly sucked away by the ventilation system. The only sounds was a steady buzz as it cut a large hole in the wall of the station. In less than thirty seconds, the lasers finished their work and a large panel fell inwards, signifying the existence of artificial gravity.

Without hesitation, the marines charged through the hole, smoothly transitioning from microgravity to what felt like about three-quarters normal gravity, covering all directions and establishing a protective circle for the rest of the shuttle occupants to filter into the station. Nat noticed with curiosity that all of the xenoscientists smoothly slipped between no gravity and artificial without so much as a stumble. She would eat her lieutenant bars if they were truly scientists. Even seasoned spacers stumbled quite often.

The marine sergeant signaled the all clear, and the team began to move out. So far they had not run into any resistance, but it was just a matter of time. They hustled down a corridor unmolested towards the scout ship and less than five minutes after they'd breached the station, Nat and her team found themselves just outside the ship's airlock. Nat, being the senior ship officer, approached the airlock. She had not expected the ship to be buttoned up, but it was. She plugged her tab into the access port and quickly entered the command codes that Commander Taylor had given her. It only took a moment for the airlock doors to unlock and begin to slide open with a swish of compressed air.

She moved forward to enter the airlock and prepared to enter the codes on the second door, but was taken aback when the sergeant grabbed her arm and said, "Ma'am, step back, we're not sure what to expect and I'd rather not have our Admiral's little sister get shot because she charged in ahead of her escort."

Nat was about to argue when she realized that his marines would be far more equipped to deal with any hostilities that might arise when first entering the ship.

She nodded and stepped to the side and replied, "Sorry Sergeant, just give me the signal and I'll enter the rest of the code for your men."

He simply nodded and gestured for his men to get into positions before turning back to her and replying, "Engage your mag-locks, the ship won't have gravity."

His men quietly acknowledged and he turned back towards Nat. "Do it."

Nat quickly typed in the code again and the second airlock door slid open smoothly, clearly still powered. This didn't mean the powerplants were active, but it did mean that the ship still had some juice left in its batteries. They had expected this, which was why three of the members of her team were part of the engineering crew who had experience on these ships.

The marines didn't hesitate and charged through the ship, barely wavering when they had to switch back to the lack of gravity.

The ship wasn't very large so it was only a few minutes later when the marine sergeant reported over the comms, "Ship's clear, no souls on board, only one deceased human male in one of the berthing sections."

"Thank you, Sergeant."

Nat and her team starting moving forward while listening to the marine continue over comms. "It appears he was killed when the ship was hit with some sort of weapon that depressurized the section and a piece of shrapnel pierced his suit."

"Which means that at least five of the crew were missing and potentially alive," Nat muttered, half to herself.

"Potentially, ma'am..."

"Message the ship," Nat said as she turned to the marine sergeant. "We have one crewmember deceased, but accounted for. Five are still MIA."

"Yes, ma'am."

Nat listened in as he reported what they had found. Feeling foolish, she realized that she could have done the same thing, but instead had asked the marine to do it. She tuned her own communicator into the command chat and listened as Captain Dixon indicated that he had successfully eliminated the three enemy ships, and was going to head their way shortly after SAR operations. She turned the channel down, and using her mag-boots, she quickly clomped to the small bridge of the ship and took stock, as the tech team continued on to the rear of the ship that contained the engineering section. She tried to fire up the main display but unsurprisingly found that it was dead. The bridge showed some signs of weapons fire which indicated that the crew had attempted to hole up in here when their ship was captured. She also saw a large pool of blood near the navigation console which didn't bode well for at least one of the other members of the crew. That was when a realization hit her. There was a good chance that the remaining crew was captured rather than killed. *Why would the enemy leave one body and take the rest*? Nat wondered. If all they had wanted was the ship. If they wanted to study them, she would bet money that they were more useful alive than they would be dead?

"They must've captured at least one if not all of the rest of the crew alive!" she said aloud to herself.

Nat quickly toggled her comms back to the command chat. "Sir, we're on the bridge. The consoles have no power and there was clearly a firefight here. I see evidence of at least one additional wounded crewmember, but no additional bodies."

"What do you think happened, Lieutenant Drake?"

"Sir, I believe the enemy has captured the rest of the scout crew alive!"

The channel was quiet for a pregnant moment before Captain Dixon finally replied, "Lieutenant, will the ship fly out of there under its own power?"

Nat glanced over to one of the engineers who had walked back onto the bridge and was listening to the chat. He shook his head: *No*.

"Sir, the ship is disabled, we could potentially dock it with our ship if you bring it close enough to grapple, but this ship is not going anywhere under its own power."

"You have your orders then, scuttle the ship. Make sure all the computers and other sensitive data are magnetically wiped. Hopefully the scout crew had the presence of mind to do that themselves, but I want you to make sure."

"Sir, are we going after the crew?"

"That's not your responsibility, Lieutenant. Scuttle the ship and get out of there. The marines will cover you until you have returned to the shuttle."

"But sir… they might very well be alive. If they are wearing their vac suits, we may be able to track their beacons."

"Lieutenant, you will follow your orders or I will have you brought up on charges. Have I made myself clear?"

Nat paused for a moment, grinding her teeth to keep herself from replying with a rude retort. "Yes sir." Nat sighed defeatedly.

The captain was in charge, but she disagreed with leaving NIS personnel behind, especially if they might be alive.

The computers had no power, but she hurriedly wiped the computer systems using a scrambler that the engineering team brought with them just to be safe. The engineers also went to work setting up charges on the central computer and all other potentially sensitive areas to ensure that no part of it would survive when they scuttled the ship. This all took about thirty minutes.

When they had all gathered back on the bridge, Nat realized that there was the sound of weapons fire coming from the main airlock to the ship. Making sure her entire team was present and ready to go, she hustled to the main airlock but had to quickly duck back down as enemy gunfire splattered the wall over her head.

The sergeant who had noticed her yelled. "Get down, Lieutenant!"

"Give me a status report, Sergeant," Nat said while ducking for cover.

"The enemy has apparently noticed our presence and has brought up security forces to repel us," the sergeant replied. "We have one of the other squads of marines making their way to us, but for now we are essentially trapped here. Our shuttle had to detach from the station when the enemy showed up. They are hovering nearby, waiting for us to find another way out."

The weapons the enemy were using were some sort of laser rifle. She couldn't be sure, but they did not appear to be the normal Hrum assault rifles that she'd seen footage of. They did bear a resemblance to them in shape, however, so she supposed they'd want to use different less damaging weapons aboard a thin-walled space station where an unexpected decompression could be deadly. She flinched as another shot splattered against the wall behind her. There were only four marines in the entryway returning fire using what meager cover they could find. She had no idea where the rest had gone.

"Sergeant, I suggest we retreat into the scout ship. We can use the airlock as a chokepoint. They won't be able to advance more than one or two at a time." Nat had to shout in order to be heard over the constant patter of gunfire.

The Sergeant quickly analyzed the situation before nodding his head and replying. “Mendez, Dillon, toss HEs into the passageway. We’re going to fall back into the ship. If the passage loses pressure, so be it, we have our internal tanks.”

With a quick thumbs up acknowledging, the two marines hurled grenades up the corridor toward the enemy fire and waited for a few seconds before the grenades exploded and decompressed the entire passageway of the station. In the smoky confusion that followed, the entire group retreated into the scout ship dragging one of their wounded comrades who had his gun pointed back towards where the enemy was as he was towed along.

“Good thinking, Lieutenant.”

“Bought us some time at least,” replied Nat.

“It won’t be long before they regroup and maybe use some high explosives of their own to make our lives miserable,” said the marine.

“I hope reinforcements get here in time,” Nat said with a grimace.

Commander Taylor listened in as Captain Dixon argued with Lt. Drake. While she understood his point of view, she thought that they should at least make an attempt to rescue the crew of the scout ship. Dixon had pushed back on the admiral’s assertion that it was their duty to try and rescue the crew, but Taylor found herself at odds with her captain on that issue. As long as the crew followed protocol, there wasn’t a whole lot of information the aliens could glean from the wiped computers, but the crew themselves could be a treasure trove of useful information for the enemy. You couldn’t just forget command codes or fleet positioning or even when and where your rendezvous were supposed to be with the fleet. That information could be forced out of them and that put the whole fleet at risk.

Taking a breath and coming to a decision, she finally said, “Sir, a word in private?”

Dixon turned quickly and looked like he was about to snap an angry retort her way, but he got ahold of himself and the quick retort he had on the tip of his tongue never materialized.

"Of course, Commander," Dixon said. "Let's go to my ready room. Helm, you have the conn." He quickly walked through the door to his room with Taylor in tow.

"Sir, I think we need to reconsider leaving the crew to their fate."

"Why's that, Commander?"

"Lt. Drake was right, I managed to get a signal from their suits shortly after she said they were missing from the ship."

"A signal from where?"

"They're on the station and while I can't get a solid enough lock to read their bios, they indicate that the suits are still being worn. They only activate after they are put on and an emergency is declared."

"Commander, I already told you. The risk versus reward just isn't there. I cannot in good faith risk the lives of our marines to rescue a handful of crew who may or may not be alive. Believe me, I don't want to leave them at the mercy of a hostile alien, but I don't see how we can reach them without suffering more casualties than people we would save. We put ourselves in harm's way every second we sit here in orbit. We have no idea what sorts of defenses exist on the planet. We have already given away our position by fighting those ships. It wouldn't take a whole lot for a planetary defense center to fire at us and do some serious damage."

"But, sir. We've not detected any. They have been pretty easy to spot on the surface of the other planets we've been to in the past..."

"Just cause we can't see 'em doesn't mean they aren't there, Commander. Now, if that's all, Commander. We will be ordering the team to evacuate in the next fifteen minutes so they can intercept us as we come back around."

Taylor was about to reply when the marine at the door pinged the intercom. "Captain, I have a NISI agent, Hadley, for you at the door. He's ordering me to open the door and allow him entry to your room. I don't—"

"Send him in, Corporal," Dixon said, cutting him off. "Thank you for alerting me."

The door swooshed open and the NISI agent came strolling in with a smug look on his face.

"Captain..."

"Agent Hadley..."

"It is my duty to inform you that we will make every attempt to rescue that scout ship crew."

"And why might that be?" replied Dixon sarcastically. "In fact, I should have you thrown into the brig for interrupting my meeting with the commander. Your role here is purely advisory. I had Admiral Drake show me your orders."

Still wearing that smug look, Hadley replied, "Well, in fact things have changed a little bit."

In his hand, Hadley held a small data chip. He reached towards Dixon to hand it to him. Dixon made no move to take the proffered chip. He just continued to stare at the smug, sleezy agent. Commander Taylor reached over and grabbed the chip from him before plugging it into her tab. It only took her a few moments to pull up the information on it.

"Sir—"

"Yes, Commander?"

"I'm not sure how this is possible. These orders appear to be authentic."

"What do they say, Commander?"

"Sir, he's in charge," Taylor replied, puzzled.

"Convenient you didn't share that little tidbit of information until we are unable to reach out to the NIS fleet to confirm," Dixon replied.

The captain didn't think it was possible, but the smug look Hadley wore seemed to get even more smug

"Captain, we can play word games all day, but you know a legit order when you see one. Yours truly holds overall operational command of this fleet."

Dixon looked back over at Commander Taylor, who shrugged.

"As far as I can see, they're legitimate, sir. I can have our intelligence officer review them, but I believe he'll say the same thing." She ground her teeth together as if forcing herself to continue. "Agent Hadley is in charge."

Dixon sat back in his desk digesting what Taylor said. He didn't trust NISI any more than the next guy, but orders were orders. Nothing came to mind when he tried to think of a way around doing what the agent ordered.

"Commander, order the crew to initiate a deceleration burn," Hadley ordered *his* XO.. "There's no point in pussyfooting around the planet now. Have our remaining shuttles loaded with the rest of our marine forces and signal the destroyer to send their marines as well. We are taking control of that station."

Hadley paused for a moment to let Taylor get up and hurry out of the room onto the bridge. She gave Dixon a questioning look but didn't linger.

Dixon continued to eye the NISI agent who appeared to have no intention to move before continuing. "I am not sure how you managed this, or who you have leverage over in the council, but the captain is the ultimate authority on his ship. The second I find out that these are not legitimate or that these weren't given in good faith, you are being thrown in the brig, and if you resist, I will space you no questions asked."

"No need for the melodramatic threats, Captain. I'm just doing my job. I'll be going now."

Hadley spun on his heel and walked out of the room, only pausing for a moment in the doorway. "Be careful who you threaten, Captain," he said over his shoulder to the defeated Dixon. "You'd be surprised what can happen, even in the safety of your own ship."

Dixon made a note to make some inquiries about Hadley. The admiral had to know about this. Maybe it would be worth requesting a meeting with Jaxton. Knowing him, Jax would not be any happier than he was about having this slimy agent in charge of his fleet. Dixon was a stickler for the rules, but he wouldn't bat an eye if Jaxton chose to ignore the agent's orders, and he was sure the rest of the captains would not either. He stood up from his desk and strolled back out onto the bridge, ignoring the questioning look Taylor was giving him.

"Status report. How long until our assault force arrives?"

"Sir, the last shuttle has just launched. The marines were waiting in the hangar before I gave the order, so they're already on their way. ETA of fifteen minutes."

"Very good, Commander. Keep me apprised of any updates and alert the marines already on station. Sensors, weapons, if anything out there so much as twitches, I want you to vaporize it. No point in risking our ride out of here."

Chapter V

On St. George at Summer Camp
Year 3326

The summer camp—if you could even call it that—was nothing like Ryan had ever gone to as a child. The camps he and his brother had gone to usually had small minimalist log cabins, no power, and the only water supply was the nearby lake. Not that he was complaining, some of his favorite memories with his dad and brother occurred during those trips. They explored, went canoeing around the lake, and fished. Then at night, they cooked hot dogs over a campfire because none of them were any good at fishing, and their catches usually came in the form of seaweed or lily pads. Those were good memories that he cherished.

The cabins at this camp—if you could even call them cabins—were similar only in the fact they were made out of wood. Even with the three squads of militia, and one squad of imperial guardsmen, every single one of Ryan's men could have taken their own room. Hell, most could have their own floor. Luckily for him, several of his men were engineers or tradesmen in their actual jobs and it didn't take long for them to get the generator up and running. They had also found some old, and probably expired canned foods that seemed like they would still be edible and two of his other soldiers were making food for them.

Izabella had been quiet since the death of her bodyguard, oldest friend and father figure. He had died protecting her, throwing his own body in the way of bullets meant for her. They had set her up in the largest room in the building, and one of the women in his unit, a psychologist, remained in there, talking with her.

Ryan had briefly tried to listen through the heavy wooden door, but quickly stopped when he realized it was an invasion of privacy. Now, he was pacing back and forth like a caged tiger, thinking. The situation was grim and none of the Imperial safe houses could be considered safe. They had almost no contact with anyone outside of their own small group, but what they did know was that there was fighting all over the planet. It seemed that the people of St. George weren't taking the conquest of their planet laying down for the second time. He knew it was only a matter of time until the Hrum started to simply bombard the hot spots, but he could relate to the local populace's anger and would have done the same thing in their shoes.

He hoped most of them would realize that an organized static defense was pointless and would resort to a more underground style of resistance, but he couldn't communicate with them. He was thinking about what he should do next when the door opened and his soldier came out. Her name was Fiona O'Leary. Prior to the first invasion, she had been a married mother of two working with her husband at starting up their own counseling practice. When the Hrum arrived, she had been at the office while her husband was at home with the children. In the chaos that followed, she never saw them again. Ryan had no idea what sort of pain she had gone through and she adamantly refused to talk about it, but was one of his most enthusiastic recruits. Ryan had her pegged as a future squad leader when their ranks expanded. She was smart, motivated, and fought with a passion that would inspire the men and women in her charge. She walked up to Ryan with a sigh and a slightly dejected shrug.

"She didn't say very much. It's clear that she saw Commander Yellen as a father figure. I'm sure he was in her life far more than her actual dad. I can relate to loss and we can talk through it, but there is little I can do to make it better other than say it will take time."

"Thank you, I am sure that she appreciates what you are doing for her." Ryan was never comfortable with emotional talks like this, so he felt awkward and wooden as he said it, but she simply nodded.

"Oh, and by the way, she is asking to see you."

"Ummm... what?"

"She asked to talk to you."

"Me? I can't help her through this."

"You'll do great. Just don't press. Listen to her. Let her speak more than you. There's no exact science to this, but she just needs someone she trusts there to support her."

"I think I need a drink."

With a chuckle Fiona replied, "That's the *last* thing you need. A clear mind is critical to being aware of what's going on."

Ryan grumbled to himself, but took a deep breath and nodded. "Thank you, Fiona. You can take a break. The food should be almost ready by now."

"Thank you, sir. I'll do that."

She turned and quietly walked away.

Ryan turned towards the door and approached. He reached for the handle but stopped. It felt wrong to just barge in, so he raised his fist and knocked timidly. The door opened almost instantly as if she were waiting for him. Before he could say or do anything, she threw herself into his arms sobbing wetly. Not knowing what else to do, he stood there holding her while her tears soaked into his shirt. He awkwardly patted her back doing his best to support her while looking around for someone to help him. It was a couple of minutes before she regained her composure enough to realize she was doing her best to drench his shirt. She seemed to realize how uncomfortable he was, which startled a small laugh out of her, which only confused him more. It was only a few seconds before she was laughing hysterically and he blushed beet red with embarrassment. She pulled him through the doorway and closed the door behind him. Now he was in the private quarters alone with the most powerful person on the planet, and she was laughing at him. If it was possible to die from embarrassment, he thought, this would be the time for it to happen.

"Your majesty, I um...."

"Thank you, Ryan," she gushed, managing to regain some composure and reaching forward to grab his hands. "I am sorry for soaking your shirt."

"Oh, it's um no problem your maje…" He stopped as she fixed him with a glare. "Izabella. I am sorry about Commander Yellen. He was a good man. I respected him."

He was about to say more when she suddenly threw her arms around him and kissed him. The softness of her lips shouldn't have surprised him, but it did. He felt his arms go back around her and pulled her body close to him in a tight embrace. At that moment, he felt like nothing else mattered and he was completely caught up in the moment. The next couple of minutes were a frenzy of desperate kisses that seemed destined for something more, but there was another knock on the door which broke them out of their trance and they jumped apart like scared rabbits.

Shakily, Ryan called out, "Who is it?"

"Sir, we have food for both you and the Grand Monarch."

"Come in, set it on the table please."

There was only a moment's pause before the door opened and another one of his recruits came in and hurriedly set the food on the counter and set the table to the best of his ability with the limited supplies they had before scampering out of the room, clearly uncomfortable with being in close proximity to the monarch in such an intimate setting.

Izabella and Ryan eyed each other for a moment before a chuckle escaped her lips. It was only a second longer when Ryan too couldn't help a smile from cracking his own lips and he too broke out into a full-bellied laugh. Together, laughing at the absurdity of the past couple of minutes, they laughed so hard that Izabella had hiccups, which made them laugh even more. This continued for several moments before they regained their composure and he gestured over to the table with a flourish.

"Your majesty, dinner is served."

Still smiling, she walked over to the table eyeing him mischievously before taking the seat that Ryan was offering to her. He pushed her chair in, and she awarded him with a sidelong glance that set his pulse pounding in his ears. He wasn't sure what they had been about to do, but he was not convinced that it would have stopped with desperate kissing. He stood off to the side as she settled into her seat.

"Thank you, Ryan. Please don't make me order you to sit with me. It would be awkward for both of us."

Ryan realized he was being silly, but still made sure that she was settled in before taking the seat opposite of her at the table. They sat quietly for several minutes as they ate the food that his men had prepared. Ryan was doing his best to eat like a civilized human being, which was the exact opposite of what his years in the marines had taught him. His method of eating usually involved shoveling as much food as humanly possible down his throat as quickly as he could swallow. For the second time in the short time he'd been in the room with Izabella, he felt wooden and out of place.

Izabella broke the silence with a question. "So tell me about your family. I know you have a brother and a sister, both in the service, but please tell me about them."

Ryan welcomed the distraction and replied, "Well my brother Jaxton as you probably know is an admiral."

"How much older is he than you?"

"He's almost exactly two years older."

"So he's fifty two then?" she said with a mischievous smile.

Smiling at her joke, he played along. "Indeed. We are both just short of retirement."

"I see," Izabella said with a nod, smirking.

"Nat, our younger sister just turned twenty-three or twenty-four and she's a lieutenant on a battlecruiser." He didn't mention that she was also a part of Jaxton's new fleet. He'd been pretty mum on the details, so Ryan had to assume there was something secretive about it.

"I'm sure you've heard or read about all of Jaxton's exploits."

"A big war hero," she said, as a smile crept over her face. "Youngest admiral in the fleet, I hear. Hero to humanity and all that."

"Yes, so they say."

"Though that's not what I meant. I have heard all those things, but how was growing up with him? What's he really like? Are you two close?"

"We are close. He is two years older than myself. He always followed the straight and narrow a little better than I did."

"The young maverick of the two, I see…"

"Well, not all that dramatic, but I couldn't have asked for a better big brother and role model."

"Well your sentiments honor him, for sure."

"I remember one time when I was just entering grade six, I got into a fight with a boy from his class. He brought his friends and whooped my ass—" Ryan paused and blushed. "Begging your pardon, your highness."

Izabella nodded it off.

"I was big for my age, and could have probably taken him in a fair fight, but his two friends held me down as he wailed on me. I told my mom that I had fallen on my bike, which I don't think she believed."

"Mothers always know the truth."

"Indeed, but when Jax came home while she was still tending to me and he saw what had happened, he didn't say a word. He strode out of the room, saying he had something to do after school, so he showed up at home right when we started dinner the next evening. My mom freaked out when she saw him because Jax's hands were scraped, one of his fingers was broken and he'd obviously been in a fight. He plead ignorance to his injuries, while my mom fussed. The next morning, when I saw the boy who had beat on me, he could barely walk, but fled as soon as he saw me. His two friends had both called in sick. Jaxton had broken his nose and beat on him until he promised to never touch me again. The boy claimed that he had gotten kicked during a soccer game, but both him and everyone else knew the truth and never messed with me again. To this day, we have never talked about that, but I knew he always had my back."

"That's sweet to have someone you are so close with."

Ryan nodded. "From that point on actually, I always promised myself that if it ever came down to it, I needed to have his back as well," he confessed to the monarch, pride and valor painted across his face "That's actually what inspired me to take on mixed martial arts and join the wrestling team."

Replying in her teasing manner, she said, "I am sure that was an adorable picture, little Ryan in a wrestling leotard."

"Well, I—"

"Can you tell me why that outfit hasn't changed over the hundreds of years of the sport existing? Nothing quite like tight spandex on a skinny twelve-year-old boy."

"Oh, I looked fantastic. I was quite the stud. You wouldn't believe how many ladies I had to fend off. I mean look at these muscles." Ryan replied while flexing his biceps.

He was pleased to see Izabella was laughing at him making an idiot of himself, and she even reached over the table and gave his bicep a test squeeze.

"Oh man, how did you get any schoolwork done?" she said, her facetious smile hard to hide. "You must have been surrounded by the ladies twenty-four seven."

"Or as they say on Sapporo: *thirty-two twelve*."

They both chuckled and eventually fell into a full-blown fit of laughter.

The conversation continued as Ryan told her about how Jax had joined the academy, following their father's footsteps, and how he had his own slot and had nearly joined as well, but was much more conflicted about it. He was miserable and felt trapped until Jaxton convinced him to follow his own path. The day after he committed to it, he called the academy, backed out and joined the marines instead, much to his father's chagrin. He actually wasn't sure if their father knew that it had been Jax who had convinced him he didn't have to do what their father wanted if it wasn't what he wanted out of his life. He was the master of his own destiny, Jaxton had said, and he had to own it. At some point someone had come and taken away their dishes as Izabella and himself talked more about their families. She seemed to take comfort in Ryan talking about his family. She clearly loved her own, but they weren't close like Ryan's was. He felt himself falling in love with her while she laughed at Ryan's depiction of what happened on their last leave together before they were deployed and how Nat had basically caught Jax red-handed sleeping with a random woman he had just met the night before. He had changed the story slightly when it came to how he got his black eye, implying that he was defending his brother's honor rather than hitting on a woman with a boyfriend, but Izabella didn't notice. By the time he realized what time it was, they were sitting together on a comfortable couch with their legs together and Izabella's head on his shoulder.

Ryan was thinking about what it would be like to kiss her again, when in a moment of panic, he suddenly bolted up from the couch, nearly knocking Izabella to the floor before saying,

"Your majesty, I am sorry, this is inappropriate. Yellen asked me to protect you, and I don't think he had this in mind when he said it."

"Had *what* in mind?" she asked with a coy smile.

"I am your de facto bodyguard now, and I cannot besmirch your honor by consorting with you. I mean— Well— What would the people say if they knew a simple marine was in your private chambers alone with you? Especially with me being a foreigner. They'll say I seduced you and I am—"

Izabella suddenly cut him off by standing up, and putting her hand over his mouth. In a serious tone that was at odds with the amused look on her face, Izabella replied, "I am no child, Captain Drake. I can *consort* with whomever I wish, and the people who you speak of who would eh… *talk*, well that's none of their business. You have been there for me, Ryan, through some of the hardest moments of my life, and you are an incredible man. Calling yourself a simple ground-pounder is an insult towards yourself that I will not have, and it doesn't even begin to show what kind of caring, generous, and intelligent person you are. You inspire people with your actions, you are the kind of leader that all people wish to serve under, and don't presume to think what Commander Yellen thought of you."

"He hated me. Let's face it. Every time I talked to him, he was glaring daggers at me."

"Oh, he did not *hate* you, Ryan, he was just very protective of me. He had known of you for a long time and was actually the one who suggested that I hire you as a military advisor and train my people."

"Knew me how?"

"Do you remember the soldier you had on your squad, also with the last name Yellen?"

Ryan thought for a few moments, before an aha. "Oh, yes, of course. Hank Yellen. He was killed at JOS."

"Yes... *Henry*, he hated being called that, so he went by Hank. Commander Yellen's nephew, his brother's kid."

Ryan had just thought it was a coincidence that the two had shared the same name. It happened more than you'd think.

"That doesn't really explain why he knew who I was."

"Henry's father never really gave him the time of day, so he often confided in his uncle. He wrote to him many times about how much he respected and looked up to his heroic sergeant. Staff Sergeant Drake. How you had taught him to be a better man."

"I had no idea."

"Of course you didn't. The commander may not have outwardly gone and said it, but you are the first man who he let me dance with who was not some noble's son or noble trying to move up in status. If he was able to, I don't think he would have allowed those either."

This was all news to Ryan. What she was saying made sense. Ryan always just thought that Yellen was so blunt to him because he was a foreigner, but it was really that he was just incredibly protective of Izabella. He nodded as he absorbed what she was saying, reaching out and lightly taking hold of her hand.

"Now, seeing as you are so worried about my ahem... *virtue,* you may see yourself out," she said as she steered him towards the door. "I need my rest."

Ryan was doing some mental gymnastics trying to figure out a way to stay, but he was pretty sure he ruined his chances with her by reacting so sporadically.

He turned as she edged him out the door and somewhat formally said, "Thank you, your majesty. I'm sorry I presumed anything. I had a wonderful time tonight."

That brought a faint smile to her face, and she leaned in and gave him a quick peck on the cheek. "Your welcome, Captain. Thank you for opening up to me. I look forward to doing it again some time."

She winked at him and slowly closed the door.

Ryan cursed to himself and mockingly muttered, "*I had a wonderful time,* come on man. That's about the stupidest thing I could have said to a beautiful woman."

It's a good thing Jaxton wasn't around to make fun of him. He'd have never heard the end of it. He wondered where his brother and sister were. He knew that they were headed towards Jewel of Sunlight, and hoped that they too hadn't been attacked. Although knowing his brother, if they had been, he'd have probably single-handedly done something heroic and neatly destroyed whoever it was who got in his way. He shook his head and continued muttering to himself as he walked off to check in on the rest of his men. "*Wonderful time*..." he muttered again. The couple of hours he'd spent with the monarch had been a wonderful vacation though from the chaos of the past day. He didn't know how long they could stay here, but he made a mental note to start some patrols of the area and set a watch schedule.

This new awareness the enemy was showing was an uncomfortable reality that required him to pivot his thinking. They'd already proven as much in the attack earlier in the day. Tomorrow was another day, but it was time to start thinking of what to do. First things first, he needed to reestablish communications with planetary forces and provide more security for the monarch. He trusted his men with his life, but a few squads of militia was not enough to guarantee her safety. He blissfully thought back to his time as a sergeant where he didn't have to worry about anyone except the handful of men under his command. He chuckled inwardly at what his father would say. It would probably even bring a small smile to the old man's face, knowing that his son who tried so hard to avoid responsibility ended up with a heap of it anyways.

Chapter VI

In Unknown System on re-captured Scout Ship
Year 3326

Lieutenant Natalie Drake sat quietly in the captain's chair of the scout ship. The enemy combatants had made several attempts to breach the door, but were met with a fierce wall of fire that forced them to retreat each time. The sergeant continued to anxiously check the passageway for any sign that they were coming back, but since their last attempt had been repelled, it was all quiet. He was sure they were planning something, but was unable to ascertain what it was. Nat maintained constant communication with the ships, and had been alerted that Dixon apparently had a change of heart and decided that rescuing the scout ship crew was important. She suspected Commander Taylor had convinced him, but she couldn't really be sure. They were still maintaining stealth protocol as much as possible, so the reinforcements were coming, but she wasn't sure of their ETA. The burst message she had received was kept short for op-sec reasons. She expected they were less than fifteen minutes out, but they couldn't rely on that.

There was a sudden explosion in the direction of the hatchway, quickly followed by a spatter of gunfire from the marines. It appeared their unwelcoming hosts had returned with bigger guns. Before she could do anything, the sergeant came running onto the bridge.

"Ma'am, any way we can decouple this ship from the station?" the marine asked. "They returned with some sort of portable shield and heavier weapons. We aren't going to be able to hold the hatchway for long."

"The computer's down, there's no way to do it from here," she replied.

Looking around the room, she waved one of her engineers over and repeated the sergeant's question.

The engineer paused for a moment to think before replying, "There is no way to do it from here. We could decouple it manually from the actual hatchway, but if what the sergeant is saying is true, the person doing it would be exposed to enemy gunfire. We should have closed the hatch and decoupled when we retreated onto the ship."

Nat noticed the sergeant cursing himself for the oversight. They'd wanted to keep the hatch open for when they destroyed the ship on evac, but now it was looking like they were trapped on a dead ship rigged to blow. She racked her brain for ideas, but was coming up blank.

One of the other engineers joined the conversation. "What about the manual release?"

"Manual release?" Nat said.

"Yeah. On the hull of the ship."

"This ship has a way to externally access the airlocks?" Nat replied incredulously.

"Yes ma'am, this isn't a warship, and as such, the normal securities that most NIS ships have that restrict access to the ship are not in place. We can blow the hatchway from the ship manually on the hull. The panel should have its own power source, and operate even without the ship's computer."

"I can't afford to send one of my men to do it—they're all busy holding the entry," the sergeant replied. "One of you will have to go out there and blow it," he added, pointing at the two engineers.

Nat simply nodded. She had been about to volunteer herself, but she was positive that at least one if not all three of the spacers standing in front of her would stop that from happening.

Both of the engineers nodded.

"We'll both go," one engineer said.

"I can provide cover to Ensign Mateo in case the enemy sees what we're doing," the other said.

The sergeant nodded and handed his rifle to them. "Know how to use this?"

"Aye sir! Admiral Jaxton required all enlisted to recertify their firearms certificates prior to us arriving in this system."

The sergeant simply nodded and hustled off towards the hatchway, drawing his sidearm in the process. The fire from that direction had picked up and it appeared to be getting closer.

The three sat there for a moment watching until Nat snapped back to reality. "Let's go, let's go," she said. "I assume you're going out the forward maintenance hatch?"

"Yes ma'am. It would be helpful if you could close it behind us."

"If we need to," Nat said.

"The ship's depressurized, so we don't need to go one at a time through the airlock."

"You got it, Ensign. Let's move!"

They scrambled to the front of the ship where all the sensors and sensitive science equipment was stored. It was designed this way to keep it all as far away from the engines as possible. The main hatchway was amidships, and they'd have to backtrack once they exited and were on the hull of the ship. Ensign Mateo knew exactly where to go, and he led them quickly to a small hatch and airlock that clearly could only hold one person. It was a good thing the ship was not pressurized, as the safety systems would have had to be overridden in order to manually force the airlock to stay open.

In less than fifteen seconds, there was a solid clunk and the maintenance hatch popped open. Mateo and his companion wasted no time, quickly exiting the ship. Mateo moved much more readily than the other spacer who was holding the rifle. Nat was about to close the hatch when an explosion rocked the ship. Both ensign Mateo and his companion were thrown about, but due to the rifle, the other engineer was unable to grasp anything and his mag boots failed to maintain a connection with the hull of the ship. Nat watched in horror as the unlucky spacer tried in vain to change his direction and reattach himself with the ship. The spacer was flailing and clearly panicking.

"Fire the rifle to stop your velocity," Nat attempted to yell into the comms. "It's your only chance."

She wasn't sure if the comms were down due to the explosion or being blocked, but the poor ensign continued to flail and Nat watched in horror as he released the rifle from his grasp. There was nothing she could do for the man. He had a two-hour supply of oxygen in his suit, but she was not sure if anyone would be able to save him in time.

Taking a moment to assess the situation, she turned back towards Mateo, who appeared to come to the realization that he also could not help at the same time and continued his trek to the main hatchway. Without thinking, Nat pulled out her sidearm that she had been ordered to bring and followed Mateo onto the hull of the ship. She would do her best to provide cover for him while he detached the ship from the station.

Making sure to stay low in case there were any more explosions, she made her way amidships where Mateo had already opened up a panel and had plugged in his tab. She kept an eye on the station from behind the cover of a sensor nacelle, where she could see flashes of gunfire as they ripped holes in the arm of the station that kept them in place. Through the thick windowed walls, she could see the enemy moving toward their position, steadily advancing behind some sort of powered shield that reminded her a bit of the mules that the marines often used.

So far nobody had noticed them out on the hull, and she hoped it remained that way. There was little she could do against an armored opponent with the small pistol she was using to cover Mateo.

Suddenly, there was a loud thunk and she turned and saw Mateo hurriedly unplugging his tab and retreating from the panel. It appeared he had figured out how to blow the airlock which disconnected them. As fast as one could in zero gravity, he was now retreating away from the exposed position he was in. From her vantage point, Nat saw the enemy falter as they realized what was happening. It was at that moment when they saw what was happening on the hull of the scout ship. The alien who appeared to be in charge seemed to bark orders, and several of his men appeared to dive towards the gaping hole where the airlock had been, while a handful of others peeled off and jumped towards the now exposed hull of the ship. They were coming for Nat and Mateo. She fired a few rounds from her pistol, hoping to deter them. Even if her bullets struck, they were unlikely to puncture the armored suits. Several shots peppered the area around the nacelle, but none struck her, and she spared a quick glance towards Mateo who was almost halfway back to the hatch and so far unharmed. She peeked her head up again and fired off a few more rounds from her pistol, but wasn't sure if she was even coming close. To her horror, she saw several of the aliens who'd jumped towards her land on the hull of the ship with a thud that she felt through the hull. The distance was growing from their ship to the station, so no more enemies would be coming, but even a single enemy would likely be able to take both her and Mateo out. She fired until her magazine ran dry and tried to weigh her options. She looked around, but did not see Mateo. She was well and truly screwed as she frantically looked for somewhere to retreat to. She just hoped that Ensign Mateo had made it back to the relative safety of the ship.

Suddenly, the thunking from the hull stopped. She risked a look around the nacelle and saw that the alien marines appeared to be firing at something coming towards them, something not on the ship. A NIS marine shuttle appeared from around the far edge of the station and opened fire on the aliens, wiping them from existence, and in the process saving Nat's life. The rear bay opened and a full squad of marines, equipped with their jump-jet armor popped out and began deploying around the ship while firing on the remaining aliens on the space station. Nat rested her helmet against the nacelle that had been her cover and closed her eyes.

Her comms crackled back to life and she heard a worried voice of Ensign Mateo checking in on her.

She opened a channel and replied, "I'm alright, thank you Ensign. I'll join you shortly."

She picked herself up and retreated to the maintenance hatch where an excited Mateo waited for her. When she finally closed the hatch behind her, she was swept up into a hug, and they excitedly embraced each other for a job well done. She took a moment to look at Mateo, his armored suit bore several scorch marks, but appeared to be in one piece. It was apparently a good idea that the sergeant ordered her and her team to wear the armored suits. It definitely saved Mateo's life.

They returned to the bridge where the sergeant was standing, coordinating with someone over his headset. Several wounded marines sat along a step, tended to as best as they could without atmosphere, but it appeared the team was mostly preparing to depart.

The sergeant noticed Nat approach and called out, "Ma'am, we're preparing to evacuate the wounded. Marines are scouring the station looking for the scout team. Their emergency beacons are active, and it appears they're alive."

"Excellent, Sergeant. Any word from command?"

"Captain Dixon ordered you and your team to evacuate on the shuttle with the wounded. My marines will take care of the rest."

Nat simply nodded. She had enough of playing the hero for one day. She and her remaining engineering team helped with the wounded and brought them to the hatchway which a shuttle was now magnetically clamped to and loaded everyone up.

With the wounded loaded up, Nat looked around the bridge and sighed. She was headed home.

"Marines, report in," Captain Dixon ordered over the channel.

"Sir, we are advancing steadily. I ask again, why did we retrieve the xenobiologist team from the scout ship? I don't see—"

"That's enough, sergeant. Do your duty and rescue those sailors. The xenoscientists will stay out of your way and be collecting samples from the downed enemy."

Dixon had to bite his tongue to not say anything else. He didn't want those scientists getting in the way of his marines any more than he wanted Hadley smugly sitting on his bridge. The first thing he was going to do when the fleet reconnected was have a sit-down with Admiral Drake. He glanced over at Hadley who was openly ogling Commander Taylor, who was in turn pointedly ignoring him. The NISI agent was a sleazeball, and he would be relieved to get rid of him.

Captain Dixon's crew watched as the marines advanced through the station. All appeared to be going well. The enemy was still fighting, but there didn't appear to be an organized defense against them. Watching the Marine body-cams, he saw that they had entered what appeared to be a science bay of sorts. There were big tanks filled with a bluish liquid with some traces of black swirling around inside. The xeno people appeared to be combing over the consoles and investigating the tanks more than they were looking at alien corpses, but who was he to say what they were looking for.

"Sir, we found the holding cells," the marine sergeant advised. "It appears we have three of our scout crew alive and mostly unharmed. We're going to have to put them into vac suits. A fourth is badly wounded and needs to be stretchered out. He apparently was taken away and just thrown back in here the day before and hasn't regained consciousness."

Dixon didn't reply while he waited for more information. He could see the marines breaking open the cage doors and communicating with the newly freed crew.

"Sir, they are saying that the captain of the ship is MIA. The spacers said that the aliens took him away two days ago and they have not seen him since. Permission to continue the search?"

Dixon paused for a moment and looked over at Commander Taylor who nodded to him. He didn't want to dwell any longer than he had to, but there currently didn't appear to be any threats to his ships.

"Permission granted," Dixon finally said. "Keep me apprised of the situation."

The channel closed and Dixon sat back in his seat. He spared another glance over at Hadley who was standing there with his eyes closed, appearing to be muttering to himself. That was odd behavior, but at least the man was being quiet and not harassing any of his crew. The search continued for another thirty minutes, when the marine team appeared to break into a surgical suite of some sort. Laying there, on a bench strapped down, was the captain of the scout ship. The marines hustled over to him and quickly took his vitals. The man was alive, but his pulse was faint, and it appeared that the aliens had been performing some sort of surgery on him. The comms channel pinged and Dixon opened it.

"Sir, we found the captain, we're not sure what happened to him, he's alive, but not responsive, and he appears to have been experimented on. Permission to return to the ship with him?"

"Granted. I will have medical personnel on standby awaiting your return."

"Aye, sir."

"Good work soldier, let's bring them all home, Serg—"

Before the captain could finish or the marine could reply, a loud explosion erupted and a fireball filled the screen. Dixon saw that something had detonated in the lab and flames lit up everywhere. Looking back at the marines' cameras, Dixon saw that nobody appeared to be hurt, and that they were still working to extract the captain from the surgical suite. The sergeant, who Dixon had been talking with, was barking orders to his men who appeared to be attempting to find something to put out the flames. Dixon didn't demand answers, he didn't want to interrupt the man and distract him. He saw that they had successfully extracted the captain and were ferrying him out of the science bay while the other marines had given up fighting the fire and were shooting their rifles at something off camera. They were all retreating in an organized fashion towards the waiting shuttles. Dixon was just starting to get antsy when the comms channel opened back up and the sergeant's voice came over the comm.

"Sir, the xenoscientists were in one of the lab rooms when something exploded. The fireball forced us out of the lab, and I'm not sure where xenos went. I believe they may have perished in the fireball, and now it appears the enemy has organized a defense and is pushing us back. We're going to have to retreat to the shuttles. There's nothing we could do."

"Get out of there, Sergeant. We have lingered here for too long. Something doesn't feel right and I want to get away from this planet ASAP."

"Aye, sir."

Dixon closed the channel. He looked back over at Hadley who wore a slightly smug look on his face, but was still standing there with his eyes closed. Dixon made eye contact with Taylor who also saw what Hadley was doing. She gave the captain a WTF shrug, indicating she had no idea either. Dixon had just about enough of the agent's antics and made a mental note to have him observed at all times. The rest of the retreat went smoothly enough, and all of his marines made it back to their shuttles and jetted away from the station. All of his ship's sensors were on high alert, but at the moment there didn't appear to be anything that could threaten his ship.

"Commander, as soon as the shuttles dock, please take us away from this station."

"Aye aye, Captain."

"Jaxton should be just about done wiping out the enemy ships that were headed his way. Send him a message that we successfully rescued the scout crew and are headed back in his direction."

"Aye sir."

"Also, initiate quarantine protocols for the scout team. Make sure the medical staff tending to them is also suited up. No idea what sorts of things they were exposed to while on the station."

"Already done, sir."

"Excellent, thank you," Dixon replied before sitting back in his chair.

He said nothing else, but snuck yet another glance in Hadley's direction. The man still hadn't so much as moved, and he barely reacted at all when the news of the xeno team he had ordered to the station had perished. Something was going on and Dixon had to get to the bottom of it.

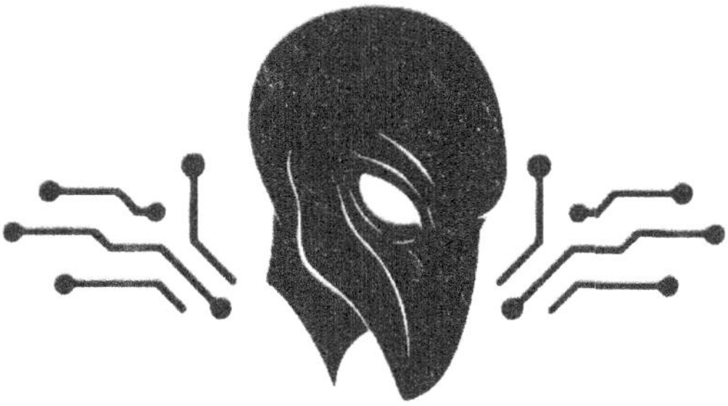

Chapter VII

In Unknown System in hidden Asteroid Base
Year 3326

Unbeknownst to the NIS fleet, the movement of the Karathian ships in the system were being monitored by more than just their ships. Several months ago, when the scout ship had arrived in system, protocols long in place but never used had awakened several of the occupants of the asteroid base hidden deep in an asteroid field. It had been over twenty-five years since any living, breathing being had been awake and monitoring these particular viewscreens showing an overlay of the Twilight of Moon system. There were four beings known to the humans as "Hrum" now occupying the command center. The most senior of these went by the name of Revalius Je and was frowning in concentration. They had witnessed the Karathian ships disable and board the alien ship before towing it into orbit over the Hrum planet they were currently occupying. This system had fallen to them almost 30 solar cycles ago to the day and the Hrum had gone into cryo-sleep once they felt that there was no chance their people would re-liberate the system in the near future. They were there to monitor and prepare any friendly ships for what to expect when they did come to free the system from the Karathians. They had not received a signal since the fateful day the planet had fallen, and due to that, Revalius ordered that they put the command center on a passive monitoring for any ships not of Karathian origin. When he had first awoken, he felt a rush of excitement, but looking at the screen, he saw that it had been twenty-five years and the unknown ship was of alien origin.

Deep in his heart, he realized that the Karathians must have won the war and conquered his people.

The war with their foes had begun unexpectedly nearly 100 solar cycles ago. The Karathians—their once-longtime trade partners—attacked without cause. While not particularly strong physically, the Karathian mind was incredibly clever. They had developed an invasive microrobot race known to his people as buggavites. These robots, when they entered the host, would multiply rapidly and slowly take over the host without them being aware of it. Buggavites were the ultimate weapon that his people had not seen coming until it was too late. Microrobots such as these buggavites weren't unheard of, and many times were used in medical and other fields, but never as weapons. The Hrum did not realize until it was far too late that these new buggavites that the Karathians created were able to jump between hosts like an airborne virus and the Karathians had already infiltrated many of the Hrum senior leaders and generals. A buggavite infestation became a cascading effect until even members of one's own family and fellow soldiers in one's unit could not be trusted. By the time it was possible to detect these buggavites and implement protections against them, the Hrum were fighting a losing battle against their own people.

Once a planet fell to the Karathian forces, massive buggavite swarms were released all over the planet and it was just a matter of time before the entire population was infected and turned into Karathian drones. Revalius realized that he and the four others sitting in his command center were likely the only five remaining Hrum who were free-thinking/living beings in the entire system.

Revalius waved a bony hand at the alarm sensor to silence it, then he narrowed his Hrum brow at the monitors. The ship of unknown origin that had been captured was the only thing of interest that had occurred since they had woken several weeks ago, and Revalius was weighing what would happen if he gave his men the order or return to their cryo pods. Morale was incredibly low, and while suicide was nearly unheard of in Hrum culture, mutiny was much more common. He half-expected his men to reject the order and put one of themselves in charge. The funny thing is that if any of them had any ideas to share that would get them out of this mess, Revalius was all ears, no mutiny needed. Of course he would not step down, his honor would not permit it, but in a very un-Hrum-like manner, he would take recommendations from his subordinates.

He glanced over to the chrono on the wall and saw that they had been sitting in the command center for much longer than their normal shift, but it wasn't like there was anything to do other than personal entertainment that the crew had brought with them when they were stationed there. The networks and all their data had long been shut down and they couldn't risk sending signals back to the planet to attempt to reconnect it. He stood up and stretched for a moment and was about to order the one other crewmember in the room to stand down when suddenly the sensor console started blinking rapidly! They had detected a blip passing near to their base. He thought that his sensors must have been malfunctioning, but after he ran a diagnostic, he realized that the blip was real. He wasn't sure how the system missed something quite so large, and he feared it was a Karathian ship lurking in the asteroids that had managed to sneak up on them. After reviewing the data for another few minutes, he ruled it out because why would the Karathians hide in their own system from their other ships? In fact, the blip that had appeared was so short and faint that he would not have been able to detect whatever it was had the sensors not been within a couple thousand kilometers of where he was stationed.

"Wake the rest of the crew," he ordered without looking away from the screen. "Something's happening here. See if we can get that blip back on the sensors. I don't believe it was a false alarm."

His subordinate rushed to obey while Revalius began running deeper diagnostics on the sensors. It wouldn't amuse anyone if the blip had just been a false signal due to something malfunctioning.

Just over a day later, Revalius was beginning to think he'd made a mistake. None of his men had managed to figure out what the sensor ghost was, and there were no other blips indicating that their sensors had detected anything. He was beginning to think it may have just been a sensor glitch, even though all the diagnostics checked out fine. The only thing of note was that the Karathian fleet was moving. This in itself wasn't that unusual, as their station had tracked and logged many instances of the Karathian movement throughout the past quarter century. The only thing unusual was that nearly all of their ships were moving at once. There were three ships remaining in orbit around the Hrum planet Twilight of Moon, a dozen heading towards the Jewel of Sunlight system, and the remaining headed out deeper into space. Revalius was born on Jewel of Sunlight, and watching the Karathian ships move casually towards it saddened him deeply. Judging by their unhurried and casual pace, he depressingly realized his planet had likely been conquered too. Two of his other crewmembers were also from that planet, and their faces bore similar deflated expressions to Revalius' own.

Several hours later, the first group of the ships had warped out, and the second group heading to Jewel of Sunlight approached the warp lane when his dark mood suddenly evaporated.

A massive contact, more than three times the size of a standard Hrum warship, suddenly appeared on the screen and had begun firing its weapons at the unsuspecting Karathian ships. In addition it appeared to be launching some sort of fighters. Oddly enough, these fighters quickly disappeared off the screen shortly after launching. This ship and its fighters had some sort of stealth technology! Thinking back to the sensor blip earlier, he wondered if it had been this same ship. The Karathian ships, caught completely flat-footed with their shields down and weapons cold, were being ripped apart. The advantage did not last, however, as it was only one ship, but it quickly turned away from the Karathian ships and blasted away as fast as its ultraheavy engines could take it. The Karathian ships gave chase, and nearly thirty minutes later, he saw that the massive ship would not be able to escape. The captain of that ship must have also realized this since Revalius saw the ship flip around and face its pursuers. Revalius approved of this. He had commanded many ships in his long career, and retreating was considered a stain on one's honor. The weapons on that phantom ship were impressive, but it was severely outnumbered and had seven enemy cruisers now bearing down on it. Without the element of surprise, he found it unlikely that this incredible alien ship would survive another engagement.

It was at that exact moment when the Karathian fleet rippled with a volley of shots from incredibly close range, blasting the formation apart. The large ship was just acting as bait! An additional three ships that had snuck in close to the fleet and were now blasting away from near point-blank range. Even while they were firing, the ambush ships appeared to blink in and out of existence and it was only a few minutes later when the last Karathian ship was reduced to scattered molecules. Revalius and his crew watched in awe at the power that these ships had shown, and were now chattering excitedly among themselves. The Karathians had another enemy, a quite capable one.

Three hours later, Revalius sat in his station as his crew looked on. These ships were clearly not Hrum ships and the limited communications signals that his men had managed to intercept were not in a recognized language. In a moment of weakness, he asked his second-in-command what he should do. After a moment of confusion where she was caught off guard by the question, she managed to say that she was also conflicted. These new aliens could very well be hostile, but they had no way of knowing if they could even speak with them. At that point Revalius felt like he had no other choice but to take the risk and hope that they wouldn't be simply blasted out of space.

"Prepare my shuttle and broadcast our first contact package," he ordered. "I want to move slowly out of the asteroid field, leave all but our navigation shields down and weapons unpowered. I don't want to give them any ideas that we may be Karathian."

He heard his second-in-command Arama Wa mutter to himself, "Well one way or another, I don't think we'll be going back into cryo."

Revalius nodded to himself absently. That was a good point. He had already decided to himself that after his crew went back into cryo, he was going to take the shuttle to the planet and try to see if any Hrum on the surface were even still alive and well, but this changed things, hopefully for the better.

Chapter VIII

In Twilight of Moon System on Battleship Arcon
Year 3326

Jaxton was sitting at his desk, reading messages. Captain Dixon's task force was headed back to where Jaxton had destroyed the alien fleet. Dixon had been slightly muted in his report, but it appeared that they had lost several marines as well as an entire xeno team who had apparently gone haring off on their own. Jaxton lacked time to fully debrief his subordinate, but that's what the initial report suggested. Another note in there indicated that Dixon wanted to meet face-to-face to discuss *personnel issues*. Jaxton squinted and scratched his head when he read this, but he agreed to meet with him. Reading through the report, Jaxton saw that they had managed to rescue four of the scout ship's crew. The others had either been killed when their ship was attacked or experimented on for reasons that Jaxton couldn't fathom. He was told that marine body cameras recorded much of what they saw in the alien station and that it wasn't for the faint of heart. His SAR shuttles and marines were currently combing through the wreckage of the ships he had destroyed. His stealth systems and the total surprise of his ambush meant that it proved a brutally one-sided affair and they had not yet found any enemy survivors. He didn't feel any remorse for what he did, especially with the video and photographic evidence of what the aliens did to the scout crew. What their motives were, he did not know, but it was obvious that they viewed it as some sort of sick science experiment.

His XO walked up to him and handed him a full coffee bulb. "Sir, we've sifted through nearly seventy-five percent of the easily accessible wreckage."

"Any survivors?"

"No, sir, not yet, but we did manage to access the bridge of one of the enemy cruisers that wasn't totally destroyed. They found bodies, all of which were Hrum. They are currently attempting to break into what appears to be the captain's quarters."

"*Attempting*? What's the hold up?"

"They're taking their time because it appears to be heavily armored to act as a sort of holdout or emergency bunker and it also appears to still be pressurized."

This information came as a surprise to Drake. The NIS had plenty of wreckage from Hrum ships that they had destroyed, but none of them had any sort of armored captain's quarters. In fact, he couldn't recall if he had ever seen a captain from one of the ships retreat to his quarters before the ship had been destroyed. In the ships they had captured relatively intact, the captain was always dead on the bridge with the rest of his crew.

"Keep me apprised, Commander,"

"Aye, sir."

"If the captain of the ship is alive, he might be of use to us."

"Sir, we have captured Hrum captains alive before, what makes you think this time will be different?"

"Well… let's see…" Drake replied, mock-rubbing his chin. "Have any Hrum you've ever fought used fighters, or advanced in formation?" Drake saw the realization dawn on his XO's face before he continued. "Ever see them operate with much strategy at all? I mean, it could all be for nothing, but maybe at minimum we can have a conversation with a real live Hrum who won't simply berserk-attack us on sight."

His XO nodded thoughtfully to himself but didn't reply.

Jaxton went to take a sip from his coffee and realized it was already empty. *Did I really drink that entire thing already? I need to cut back.* He got up from his chair, nodding to his XO as he moved. "I need another refill.. Keep me apprised on the armored captain's room."

"Aye, sir."

Jaxton used the time it took to refill his coffee bulb for the fourth or fifth time to think. The development that these new ships were Hrum-owned and operated worried him more than he let on. He had made it clear multiple times that he believed if the Hrum had tactical awareness that any space-faring species should have, that the NIS would not have managed to win the war he thought they had just won. In addition, if he did not have the advantage of these new stealth systems which they had stolen from the Hrum, he would have almost certainly suffered casualties or even lost this battle. He was worried that the most recent attack on St. George was not instigated by the normal run-of-the-mill Hrum that they were used to fighting. A lot of captains would be in for a big surprise when they ran into them. He returned to his ready room and sat down at his desk before pulling back up the report from Dixon. It appeared that his subordinate was originally simply going to make a quick pass of the station, only stopping to destroy the scout ship, but something changed his mind. As he continued to read, it became clear that meddlesome NISI Agent Hadley had somehow pulled rank on Dixon and exerted his influence to force him into a different course of action. Jaxton hadn't even known that Hadley was on Dixon's ship. At some point he had moved over there without Jaxton knowing. That worried him because he had asked his XO to keep an eye on him. He couldn't entirely blame Bradley though because without using actual ship resources, even the commanders of a ship could not blatantly violate a man's privacy. He typed a quick note to Major Stevens to work with his XO to keep an eye on Hadley. He decided that Stevens was trustworthy enough to be in the loop and would keep it discreet.

He pulled up some of the video feed from the fighting on the station. The marines' body-cam footage held way too many shots of his sister to make him comfortable. He was quite unhappy that Dixon had put her in harm's way, but did understand the logic of having an officer who could pilot the ship board with the engineering team on the off chance it was salvageable. They recovered limited footage of the xeno team disappearing, but for all intents and purposes, it seemed like they accidentally set off an explosion in a lab that they were combing through. He wasn't sure when they had transferred over to Dixon's ship either. Taking a look at the crew logs, he saw that they were a last-minute addition to the battlecruiser which Hadley had signed off on. He made another note for Stevens to monitor the remaining members of the teams that were scattered throughout the fleet. Stevens would do what Jaxton asked without question, but the admiral felt like he should bring the marine commander into the loop more fully. Something was not adding up, and it reeked of either governmental or other agency meddling. He wondered if this was what his father was so worried about. It took him nearly two hours to review the rest of the footage. He was preparing an order to have the scout ship survivors be brought aboard his ship once they were stabilized. His ship had a much more advanced medical suite than a battlecruiser's. He was just about to send off the request when an alert came over the intercom to report to battle stations.

Jaxton rushed to the bridge and ordered, "Report!"

"Sir, we have a contact rising from the surface of one of the asteroids in the field roughly three-hundred thousand kilometers from us," Lt. Chen replied. "It's a single corvette-sized ship, just slightly larger than our scout ships."

"Is it armed?" asked Drake.

"Doesn't appear to be, sir."

"Got any images of it yet?"

"Forwarding them to your terminal now, Admir—."

"Don't bother, put them up on the main screen."

Jaxton settled into his seat as his XO vacated it and retreated to his station. A moment later, the small ship appeared on the screen. It was clearly of Hrum design, just appearing to be a much smaller version of the same cruiser ships that he had destroyed so many of.

"Is the ship making any hostile moves or attempting to flee?"

"No sir, it just appears to be holding station…"

"Sir, communications!" Lt. Johnson said, cutting into the conversation.

"Whatcha got, comms…"

"Incoming communications request, sir."

"Play it."

The message began playing. It was in the Hrum language! This was the first time Jaxton had heard a Hrum voice from anything other than a translation. All of their ships were equipped with advanced translation software and the Hrum language had been integrated into all NIS warships, so the voice was overlaid with the English translation.

"Greetings conquerors. I am Revalius Je. My crew and I thank you for destroying the horrible Karathian menaces. As twists of fate would have it, we are now at *your* mercy. However, we humbly request an audience with your leadership."

Looking around the bridge, Jaxton saw all eyes were on him. "Was this message targeted to us or did every ship receive the broadcast?" he asked.

"Every ship, sir. It's an unencrypted communications signal."

"Very well, reply with this message. Send it in English, and then translate it as well: Greetings Revalius Je. It is an honor to meet you. No thanks necessary, we eliminated a threat to my people. I am Admiral Jaxton Drake of the NIS fleet. We are not conquerors and have no desire to take over this system. May I ask why you were hiding in the asteroid field spying on the previous occupants of this system?"

The bridge was quiet for a few moments while the message was translated back into the Hrum language and sent off to them. The reply message came as Jaxton grabbed yet another coffee bulb and he could sense a level of surprise.

"It seems these aliens did not expect to receive a reply in their own language," Jaxton said to his XO as he piped the message over the bridge speakers.

"Conqueror Admiral Jaxton Drake," the reply began, "I believe that all questions can be answered. I would like to formally invite you to our ship. We surrender control to your authority and I will order that we power down all systems. None of my crew carry weapons and we shall not resist you. Please do not harm us, we stand at your mercy."

There was no further message and Jax noticed that his crew was still staring at him intently.

The admiral turned to his XO who shrugged and said, “Sir, we have no idea what’s over there. This could be a trap. Send the marines and someone less important to the fleet.”

Jaxton nodded thoughtfully, consideration scrunching his brow. “I will attend!” he said.

“Sir…?”

“I will be leading a delegation onto the ship.”

“But, sir—”

“This is not up for discussion, Commander,” Jaxton said, holding up his hand for silence. “I am leading the delegation to the alien ship because I already talked with Revalius and I believe he would react better to me being there. Order Stevens to detach some marines to come with me and ask our science team to send one of their ranking members.”

“Sir, if I may… it’s not a good idea—”

“That’s enough, Chris. I appreciate your concern, but this is an order. I also want detailed scans of the area and a fighter escort to clear the area.”

His XO looked like he was going to argue more, but he turned and gave the orders.

It wasn’t even thirty seconds later when Jaxton received a communications request from Stevens, which he ignored. The man would listen to orders even if he didn’t agree with them.

Jax was already in his vacuum suit, but he clipped his helmet to his waist and drew a sidearm from the armory before heading towards the hangar. Unsurprisingly, Stevens intercepted him about halfway there and blocked his path.

“Sir, you can’t be serious.”

“Ah Major Stevens… please step aside, as I have a pressing engagement.”

“We have people trained in first contact situations,” Stevens continued, the persistence tightening his jaw. “You are the commander of this fleet, too valuable to risk on this harebrained mission.”

Jaxton apparently guessed wrong. It seemed that Stevens would not simply take his orders without making his opinion known.

“You forget your place, Major,” Jaxton said, trying to maintain authority without appearing ungrateful for his officer’s concern.

Jaxton stepped around Stevens and kept walking. Stevens, fueled by heated protest, hastening to keep up.

"Sir, you told me I could speak freely to you, and I'm freely telling you this is a bad idea. We have no idea what's over there, and you are the commander of this task force."

Jaxton stopped, looked at the floor then up into the eyes of his brave officer. "That is exactly why I have to be the one to speak with them," he told Stevens. "For all we know, it's an insult in their society to have their highest-ranking member speak with someone who isn't our highest-ranking member. Also, I have already spoken with them, and I believe he will be offended if it is not me who continues the conversation."

The marine commander didn't appear convinced, and Jaxton could sense his hesitation. He turned to begin walking again, but then stopped and added, "If it makes you feel better, Major, I will allow you and your men to sweep the alien ship before I board. Revalius Je seemed to expect us to show up in force when we arrived. He repeatedly called us *conquerors*. He emphasized that his crew would be unarmed and are at our mercy."

"It still could be a trap."

"Well then, I expect your marines to keep their vigilance. I appreciate the concern for my safety, but this has to be done."

Stevens finally relented, and allowed Jaxton to continue walking ahead of him. It seemed that he couldn't come up with another argument that would hold water with his commander.

Jaxton continued to the shuttle bay with Major Stevens in tow. Even though he relented to let Jax go, he wasn't going to let him go unescorted, and he had been talking furiously on his communicator since they finished speaking. Jax didn't interrupt him and when he got to the shuttle bay, he let the man run the show. He saw Greg Brewster standing in the bay talking to one of his fighter pilots. He gave him a smile and a wave, which Jaxton acknowledged, but they didn't speak. He was sure Greg knew exactly why he was doing what he was doing. They could often finish each other's sentences. Major Stevens agreed that they did not want the alien ship docking directly with his own ship just in case it was a trap, so they agreed to send two shuttles over instead. The first would have an entire heavily armed marine squad, and the second would have Jaxton and the selected officers who he decided to bring with.

Jaxton's crew remained in constant contact with the first shuttle. When they boarded, it all appeared to be going smoothly. Revalius Je appeared to be true to his word, and his entire crew was waiting, unarmed, in the bay of their ship for his marines. Jaxton's shuttle stayed on station waiting for the green light for nearly thirty minutes before Stevens' marines finished their search. It appeared they wanted to be as thorough as possible. The marines stayed onboard, but the shuttle detached, allowing Jaxton's shuttle to dock. He was interested to see that his engineers had fitted the Hrum airlock conversions to the shuttles in the short heads-up that they were given before Jaxton boarded. He made a mental note to applaud his deck boss and reward the crew for attending to such a critical detail.

A solid thunk brought him back to the matter at hand, and the airlock began equalizing the pressure between the two ships.

Stevens, who had chosen to ride with Jaxton, leaned over to him and said, "Sir, the air appears to be breathable, but I would recommend leaving your helmet on."

Jaxton nodded, but didn't say anything.

"Apparently the ship smells quite… ripe," Stevens added.

The Hrum ships they'd been on had been mostly sterilized prior to his boarding, and the planets they visited hadn't had any foul stenches that he could recall. Alien yes, but not foul, not that Jaxton could remember.

As the pressure equalized, and the hatch opened, Jaxton got to his feet and stepped out of the shuttle and down the ramp. Standing there, flanked on both sides by his marines was a male Hrum, dressed in ornate clothing. Mentally preparing himself, he released the latches on his helmet and removed it. Just like the major had said, the stench was quite overpowering, but Jaxton forced himself not to react before speaking.

"Greetings, my name is Admiral Jaxton Drake of the NIS space navy. I am the commander of this task force. May I board your ship?"

The alien paused for a moment, listening to the translator device that was clipped to Jaxton's chest before replying.

"Greetings, I am Revalius Je. My lowly self is at your mercy, please come aboard. We have a room for discussion and there is much discussion to be had."

The ornately dressed Hrum bowed deeply, causing his marines to stir slightly, but they didn't move to stop him. Apparently they were still on edge. Jaxton only paused for a moment before stepping off the ramp. He was not sure if the aliens had the same significance of asking permission to board that NIS captains had, but he wanted to do everything in his power to avoid antagonizing him. He also realized the significance that he was likely the first NIS officer to speak with a real live Hrum. As he walked forward, he spared a glance over to Dr. Casey who unsurprisingly was one of the scientists who had come with him to this meeting. She and two other scientists were a part of the ambassador party who had come along. He nodded in approval as he saw one of them was recording everything.

Revalius led the party to what appeared to be a conference room. There were two other Hrum seated in the room along with another half a dozen of Stevens' marines. There was little conversation as they took their seats in surprisingly soft, yet alien, chairs.

Once everyone was settled, Revalius continued, "Thank you for not harming me or my men." He nodded to Jaxton, who nodded back. "It has been a long time since we have interacted with a friendly alien race."

Jaxton wasn't entirely sure how to respond, being called an alien was mildly amusing. Although he supposed that it could have been just how the translation device understood what Revalius said.

"I promise that as long as you are no threat to my crew or my fleet, that no harm will come to you," Jaxton began. "I have a lot of questions, but I want to start with the elephant in the room. What were you doing spying on a planet filled with your own people? Why are you talking to us? None of your kind has ever seemed interested in talking to us before. And finally, why did you attack our people?"

Revalius seemed bemused at the analogy that Jaxton had made, but as the translation continued, seemed to understand. "I am not sure I understand why you are talking about a large, gray, tusked creature, but I can do my best to answer the rest of your questions. Before I begin, and with your permission, I do want to inform you of one thing and warn you of another."

Jax nodded for him to continue.

"The people on the planet are not *my* people anymore. The inhabitants were infected by the Karathians."

Jax looked around the room and saw a lot of confusion, but nobody interrupted.

"It is hard to explain, and I hope that my language translates, but we have been at war with another alien race that we call the Karathians for nearly one hundred of my home planet's solar cycles. The beings on the planet were once my people, but the Karathians have taken them over with tiny microrobots that we call buggavites, which—"

Before he could continue, Dr. Casey cut in. "Do you have any—" she paused and cleared her throat. "Begging your pardon, Mr. Je, do you have drawings or images of these buggavites?"

Revalius looked at Jaxton, but said nothing, apparently waiting for him to say something.

"Please go ahead and answer her question."

Revalius nodded and replied, pointedly looking at Jaxton and not Dr. Casey, "We do." He gestured to one of his subordinates to hand over the tablet that the marines had returned to them and tapped the screen a few times. The wall of the room lit up and images of tiny bug-looking critters filled the wall. "These are buggavites. I do not know what your species uses for measurements, so I hope the translation works, but in a single drop of blood, you can embed nearly a hundred of these."

The room was quiet as he scrolled through several images of these buggavites. Jaxton looked over to Dr. Casey who looked astounded.

"Sir, I believe the closest translation to these would be nanites," Dr. Casey informed Jaxton. "Although if what the gentleman is saying is accurate, these are much smaller and more advanced than our own."

Jaxton nodded thoughtfully before turning back towards Revalius. "Thank you, Revalius, can you please explain how they work?"

"Of course, Admiral," the Hrum leader continued. "Buggavites are biological parasites, first genetically modified for medical purposes, but now weaponized for warfare. They enter the target and with the ability to take over their live host. They too are more advanced than what you called nanites that my species had access to."

"You said they take over the *live* host? How do they do that?" Dr. Casey asked.

Before replying, Revalius again looked towards Jaxton who nodded. "Once the host has been infected with these, they self-replicate using the body's materials as a resource until eventually they are able to control the neural pathways in the brain, nerves, muscles, and more. They can even shut down the body, killing the host."

"They can control the thoughts and actions of the being they infected?" Jaxton asked.

"I do not know if the host is still *alive* in anything but the barest sense of the word," Revalius replied. "We never managed to figure out a way to remove the nanites from the host without killing him or her."

Jaxton tapped on the table and squinted, then sighed. "What do you think Doc?" he said, looking over at Dr. Casey.

"Our nanites have limited medical uses and some other specialized things, but they're expensive, and just don't work that well. We've never been able to create self-replicating organisms, nanite or otherwise. They always have a limited usefulness before they die or shut down." Casey looked down at the table, then straight at Jaxton. "This is beyond anything that I can imagine, sir," she added, trying not to grimace.

"Revalius, you said earlier Karathians released clouds of them on the population. Are you saying they can jump between hosts?"

"Yes."

"Yes?"

"Yes, that's what I am saying, Admiral Drake."

"How does that work?"

"I am not an expert in this technology, but in similar ways that a disease or virus spreads, they can too. You only need a few dozen nanites to make it into your system for them to replicate into clouds, fog the air, and eventually take over."

"Did they infect other creatures? Cattle, wild life, pets?" Dr. Casey inquired.

For the third time, Revalius didn't respond, but looked towards Jaxton.

"Revalius, with respect, I'm not sure if there's a cultural or societal barrier here, but please answer any questions that Dr. Casey asks," Jaxton insisted.

"Of course, I apologize for being rude. In my culture, I am not permitted to answer questions from anyone except the leader until given explicit permission." Revalius turned and looked at Dr. Casey for the first time and proceeded to answer. "To answer your question, Dr. Casey, yes they can jump between hosts of my species, but no they did not jump between our food animals or pets. The Karathian so deeply infiltrated our society that when we finally figured out what was going on, it was too late, and many of our planets had been lost to them, and we were stuck fighting our own people, brother against brother, sons fighting fathers. We did develop detection methods, but they weren't perfect, and as far as I am aware, we have not determined a method of cleansing a host once they are deeply infected."

The room went silent as he said this while everyone digested the information and nothing was said for several awkwardly quiet moments.

It was Dr. Casey who then again broke the silence. "Would you be willing to show us what planets were lost to these Karathians?"

Revalius hesitated, and Jaxton quickly picked up on why.

"How about this? We show you which planets we're visited that have your people. Would you be able to tell us if the Karathians have invaded them?"

Drake realized that Revalius, out of territorial protection, may hesitate to reveal where his race's planets were. Telling Jaxton might even equate to treason in their culture. They were still basically strangers at this point. Jaxton's guess was accurate, and Revalius' look, which had been troubled, lightened considerably.

"Yes, Admiral," Revalius agreed. "I would be able to do that." Revalius picked up on the olive branch that Jaxton had extended.

The room was quiet for several more minutes while Dr. Casey had one of her team pull up a star map of the known Hrum space and pulled up the planets that the NIS had invaded. She brought the tablet over to Revalius and showed it to him. The alien's face took on a pale gray tone as he looked at the map. Jax realized that he was likely unaware that at least some of these planets had fallen to the Karathians.

A few moments passed before Revalius regained his composure and spoke. "Admiral, I apologize." He paused and cleared his throat. "It is a hard thing to realize that one's own people are all but exterminated. When my team went into cryo, only two of those planets had fallen to the Karathians. I had hoped that we'd have managed to stop them, but it appears that their victory was total."

For a moment Jax said nothing, but nodded. He understood how the alien seated in front of him felt. The entire room seemed to be reliving the emotions of when their own planets had been attacked.

"Revalius, I need you to work with our science teams. We need to understand this buggavite threat."

Turning towards Dr. Casey, he continued, "Dr. Casey, am I safe to assume that these nanites are not transferable to humans? We have had lots of contact with the Hrum over the years and I have seen no evidence that we have been compromised."

"Admiral, I cannot say with any certainty, but now that we are aware of it, I ask that we work with Revalius Je's team to determine how they detect the presence of these nanites, and begin taking precautionary measures on our ships."

Jaxton nodded. "Make it happen. Start with our ships that were involved in the attack on the space station. Let's not take any risks. I want to have quarantine measures in place. Yesterday.."

Jaxton watched as Dr. Casey coordinated with one of the other scientists at the table. She turned and looked at Revalius then spoke into a communicator. “Sir, would Revalius Je please have his most knowledgeable subordinate work with Dr. Bert here. We want to understand what we are dealing with as soon as possible.”

Jaxton looked towards Revalius who nodded in return to the Hrum female sitting next to him. She got up and followed Dr. Bert out of the room, flanked by two NIS marines.

“Next order of business is to explain to you the situation as best as we can explain it,” Jaxton said. “To put it simply, we’re not sticking around in this system. We only came here to investigate what happened to our scout ship. I cannot give you the details, but we have secured the ship and the crew and are regrouping with our fleet as we speak. I’d like any and all tactical information you can give me on the Karathian. Do they have ships of their own? Or do they only use your ships? What do they look like and so on. After we figure out a way to guarantee you are not carrying any nanites in your systems, and you go through quarantine procedures, I ask that you come aboard our flagship so that we can communicate further. I’m not authorized to extend any sort of cease-fires or truces with your people, if they even are your people, but we’re definitely willing to look into the existence of these nanites and we will go from there.”

“That is all I can ask, Admiral. I said it before, but I am at your mercy. I will share all the information that I can.”

Jaxton leaned back in his chair. This was going to be a very long day. Especially now that technically he wouldn’t be able to return to his ship until he was cleared.

Turning to Stevens he asked, “Major, please figure out a way to get coffee and snacks brought over here. Work with the scientists to make sure we don’t risk infecting anyone else. Also, go into my ready room and access the third drawer on the left. There is a bottle of genuine Kentucky bourbon in it. I think we’ll need that as well.”

Major Stevens nodded and ordered one of the marines to get on the task. A realization seemed to hit him as he spoke. “Sir, what about the captain’s room on the damaged Hrum cruiser?” Stevens asked.

Revalius’ nearly nonexistent ears seemed to perk up at the Major’s comment, but he again said nothing.

Jaxton, noticing this, spoke, “Revalius, please don’t hesitate to speak if any of my crew say something of interest. It’s in our best interests that you convey any and all pertinent information to us.”

“Apologies Admiral. Major... *Stevens* was it?” Revalius said, clearly struggling with the pronunciation. Stevens just nodded. “Is this *captain’s* quarters you speak of an armored room just off the bridge of the starship? Far more ornately decorated than any you have seen previously?”

Again Stevens just nodded, which Revalius seemed to understand.

“What’s the significance of that?” Jaxton cut in.

“Admiral, you may have captured a Karathian puppeteer.”

Jaxton frowned at the odd translation that came from his unit. “Meaning what exactly?” he asked.

“Meaning, if the occupant of the capsule is still alive, you very well may have captured a Karathian who is capable of commanding the buggavite drones infecting my people. We didn’t get to this yet, but imagine a stringed creature, being commanded by another.”

“A marionette, or a puppet.” Jaxton replied.

“Exactly. Think of these Karathians as puppet masters and the buggavites or nanites and the host they control the puppet.”

Jaxton’s eye’s widened as he pondered the implication and turning to Dr. Casey. “They behave almost like a hive mind.” He turned back towards Revalius. “What would happen if there was no *puppeteer* there to pull the strings?”

“They operate with whatever simplified orders they were given prior to the puppeteer departing. They are capable of little more than basic commands and behave more like animals than anything else. Bare instincts if you will.”

The entire room seemed to come to the same conclusion that Jaxton had previously arrived at. The reason for the Hrum behaving like they had behaved was that they were essentially on auto-pilot! Without Karathians controlling them, they behaved as little more than animals. The room burst into an excited chatter. The years that they were at war with the Hrum, they were actually at war with these Karathian drones who had infected the Hrum. There were many more questions to be answered, but this one conversation with Revalius supplied them with more information than they had acquired from the years of war and study.

The discussions continued as more questions were asked. Eventually the requested supplies were provided, including Jaxton's bottle of whiskey, which he shared with everyone in the room. When he offered it to Revalius, the alien looked concerned, but took the small glass in his hands and gave it a curious sniff. His eyes lit up with the realization of what it was.

"Your species has created fermented liquid as well," he bellowed, which caused the others in the room to chuckle.

"Yes, we call this *whiskey.* It was made on the planet of my species origin."

"Then this is a great honor. Do you mind if I scan it? I wish to taste it, but want to make sure it is safe to consume for my species." This brought another laugh around the room.

Jaxton hadn't considered that it would be unsafe for the alien to consume, and felt slightly foolish that he hadn't thought about it. "I insist you do. We have much to discuss."

"Well let's see what Arama says…"

"What's what?"

Revalius appeared excited, and quickly handed the glass off to his second-in-command who pulled out a device from the large satchel that the marines had given back to her. She dipped it gently into the liquid, where it made a whirring noise before beeping several times. She nodded at her commander who retrieved the glass from her.

"Arama says that it is safe to drink. On my planet, it's customary to send thanks to the provider of a beverage before it is shared."

Jaxton nodded. "We do something similar, we have many different languages, but in my language, we simply say 'Cheers' and clink the glasses together."

"Well then I insist we do the same. *Cheers*, Admiral. Thank you again for exterminating this system of Karathians."

"Cheers." Everyone around the room said, before taking a sip of their own glass of whiskey.

Jaxton smiled to himself. It seemed that some things were universal among species, and sharing an alcoholic beverage was one of them.

Chapter IX

In Twilight of Moon System on Captain Dixon's Battlecruiser
Year 3326

Captain Dixon was just returning to the bridge from what he considered a well-deserved nap when his Comms officer flagged him down.

"Sir, we have new orders from the Admiral. They are waiting at your station."

Dixon thanked the officer before settling into his chair and pulling up the screen.

"What the hell," he muttered to himself.

They were receiving orders to not resupply with the fleet, and to enact strict quarantine protocols among the ships. This meant no transferring personnel between the ships, and no transferring the wounded to the more advanced medical suite aboard the battleship. The message indicated more information would follow, but the preliminary report was a potential alien bug with the ability to take control of a living host. It didn't really make sense to Dixon, and the report seemed like a bunch of garbage, but he took it seriously. He waved Commander Taylor over to his station as she also returned to the command deck and shared the message with her.

She took a few minutes to read through it. "Sir, is this a real message?" Taylor eventually asked.

"It appears so, it bears the admiral's watermark and signature, and it passed all the security checks."

"Well, we can quarantine the marines in grunt country, but by now, those who have visited the med bay and those who have returned to their bunks have already come into contact with others aboard the ship."

"Agreed, Commander. Nobody was directly exposed to the alien atmosphere either—other than the scout crews who are already being quarantined. But coordinate with medical to ensure anyone who may have been exposed on their staff quarantines as well."

"Aye sir."

"The marines were using their stored air the entire time as far as I am aware, but keep them all restricted to grunt country to be safe," Capton Dixon added. "I find it incredibly unlikely a biological component survived in vacuum and even if they somehow got into the bottled air, the filters in those suits are incredibly advanced, and should've filtered out any biological contaminant before it got to them."

"I'll also forward the report on to our two destroyers."

"Thank you, Commander. I'm going to return to my office to compose a message to Admiral Drake. He mentioned a follow-up report, but they wanted to make sure that we quarantined as soon as possible."

With that, they parted ways.

Dixon walked quickly to his office, deep in thought. It wasn't until he had sat down at his desk, that he realized someone else had followed him in. With a nonchalant motion, he spun his chair, pulled a sidearm from under his desk and pointed it at the unwelcome intruder.

"Agent Hadley, funny seeing you here," Dixon said, half-relaxing his gunsight-squinting eyes. "To what do I owe the pleasure?"

The NISI agent slowly walked forward with his hands raised to show that he was unarmed.

Behind another of his smirks that Dixon wanted to smack off his face, Hadley replied, "Now captain, that's no way to greet your commanding officer. I would expect more respect from a *subordinate*."

The pistol in Dixon's hand barely wavered. "Commanding officer or not," Dixon said, "this is still my ship and I'd be well within my right to shoot you dead where you stand for entering another officer's quarters without his permission."

"Is that so?"

"We *are* on war footing after all," Dixon added, with a smirk of his own.

"Oh no need for the dramatics, Captain," in a semi-affable tone that surely masked mischief.

"One man's dramatics is another man's due diligence," Dixon replied.

"Besides, I emptied that pistol long before you came in here. I have to say, I was surprised that a by-the-book officer such as yourself kept an illegal firearm in his ready room."

Dixon slowly lowered the pistol. A quick glance at the side of the gun showed that what Hadley was saying was true.

"You still haven't said what the hell you want."

Hadley made a show of walking around the office checking out Dixon's personal effects on the shelves, mostly medals and other badges acknowledging his successes before he replied.

"Well my good captain, I want you to do exactly as I say," Hadley eventually uttered. "You are about to receive a report from the admiral indicating that there may be alien viruses that can threaten our very existence and that we may be exposed to them. He will then order you to quarantine the ship until they figure out a way to scan for them."

"He has already ordered us to do that."

"Ah, yes he has. But what he has not yet shared with you is that this alien virus isn't really a virus, but instead a form of microbots, similar to what you'd call nanites that are actually able to take control of the host and control them to make them do as they are ordered."

"You sound insane."

"Oh hush, Captain, it'll all make sense soon. What Admiral Drake does not yet know is that the nanites that worked so well to herd the Hrum population have not yet been evolved to be able to pass between human hosts by the air."

"What's this have to do with me? How do *you* know, and why are you telling me this?"

"I am telling you this because they may not be airborne, but we have figured out a way to transfer them to an individual intravenously and very soon you are going to have no recollection of this conversation."

"We?"

Before Dixon could react, Hadley pulled out an injector and jabbed him in the shoulder with it.

"Good night, Captain, I really hate to do this to you, but the grand progress must go on!"

Dixon tried to call out, but found that his muscles weren't responding to his commands. He watched in horror as his limbs appeared to be moving of their own accord, and he was soon standing at the desk. He heard his own voice say out loud, "The grand progress must go on." Then Dixon heard Hadley chuckle and reply, "Yes indeed, Captain, it must," before turning and leaving the room.

Commander Taylor was just returning to the bridge when she saw Agent Hadley leaving her captain's ready room. She found that odd, and walked over to poke her head inside. She saw Captain Dixon sitting at his desk apparently composing a report.

"Everything alright, sir?

"Oh... yes... everything is very good, Commander. Just enjoying some relaxing moments and now ready to oversee the ordered quarantine. Have all of the captains on all of the other ships been notified?"

"Aye, sir." Taylor's brow furrowed at her captain's tone. She'd been deployed with him for years now. Dixon wasn't one to use unnecessary words in a casual conversation. Something felt off, but she couldn't put her finger on it.

"Sir, what was Agent Hadley doing in your office?"

"Don't worry about it, Commander. I was just expressing to him how very sorry we are that we were unable to recover any more data from the big alien space station."

She stood in his doorway for another moment, brow still furrowed before replying. "Aye, sir, I will return to the bridge," she finally said, her eyes squinted with a hint of confusion.

Taylor turned and walked back to the bridge. Captain Dixon was typically very concise in his statements and he was typically also incredibly polite, sometimes annoyingly so. He hadn't been rude, but maybe a little bit abrupt, and he had added unnecessary adjectives to his statements which also wasn't like him. Maybe Taylor was overthinking it, but something seemed wrong with the captain.

As she sat down at her station on the bridge, she received reports that all quarantine measures had been implemented. In addition, she had received numerous inquiries from the department heads asking what was going on. She had already prepared a message as she'd been expecting this, so she went ahead and sent it. She gave a very loose explanation of what the report contained and indicated that it was a precautionary measure. She had also decided that the engineering team and Lt. Drake should both be quarantined as a precaution, so they had been ordered to report to the med bay. Taylor thought it better to be safe than sorry when it came to an alien virus.

Down in the med bay, Lieutenant Natalie Drake, Ensign Mateo, and the other engineering officers who had boarded the scout ship were together in a quarantine area. They had gotten the message that everyone was being quarantined, but had not been told anything else.

"What the hell's going on?" Ensign Mateo snapped. "We already went through a decontamination process when we boarded the ship after the operation. How could we have picked up an *alien virus*?"

Nat just shrugged and laid back on one of the hospital beds they'd been provided with as furniture.

"I am not sure, Ensign," she said, staring up at the ceiling. But I'm sure they'll tell us as soon as they can."

"Yeah, maybe," Mateo quipped back.

"For now, I think I am overdue for a nap."

She made a show of folding her arms across her stomach and closing her eyes, but it wasn't long until she heard a commotion from the other end of the med bay. All NIS ships were equipped with modular med bays that could be converted for different uses. The current setup had half the bay turned into half a dozen, fourteen by fourteen-meter rooms divided by sealed clear plastic dividers. They didn't afford a whole lot of privacy, but they were all individually isolated. She saw a commotion in one of the rooms that the scout crews were occupying.

The scout captain, who until this point had been unresponsive, had suddenly sat up and began screaming loudly while scratching his body like it was covered in fire ants. He was alone in a room, but as the medical crews came running over, the man began pounding on the walls and yelling incoherent things. It was close to five minutes before the suited-up medical staff finally managed to enter the room and sedate the man, but he had been screaming about "not injecting me with those monsters" or "Why are you doing this to me?" and most interestingly "Please, I can't become one of them!" None of what he said really made sense, but it caused Nat to begin to worry that maybe there was somehow an alien virus on the loose.

As the only lieutenant in the room, she was the only person who had been allowed to bring her fully functional tab with into the quarantine. She had been permitted to share limited details with the other occupants to appease them, but she took another look at the report. *It didn't actually say there was an alien virus on the loose*, Nat thought. *What if it's not a virus, but rather a weapon of some sort? I hope that Commander Taylor sees fit to share the updated report with me when they receive it.*

She glanced around the room at the other occupants who now looked worried. "Relax everyone," she said. "We never took off our vac suits, and never went near any of the scout ship spacers. Enjoy your time off from duties and get some rest."

She made another show of kicking back in her bed and forcing herself to look like she was relaxing, but she doubted she would be getting any sleep herself—mind was still processing words that the scout ship captain had been screaming.

Coming to a decision, nonchalantly as possible, she grabbed her tab to shoot a message to the commander. It may have been nothing, but her instincts told her that what the quarantined captain was shouting wasn't really nonsense, not altogether nonsense anyway. She reported everything he had yelled as best she could from memory, even the parts that did not really make sense. After she sent that off, she finally decided that she should try and get some sleep.

Chapter X

On St. George at Summer Camp
Year 3326

It had been two days since Ryan and his men had arrived at the "summer camp," and he was getting antsy. His men had been busy scouting the surrounding area and fortifying it as best they could. They had also secured some inconspicuous transports as he was sure that any military vehicles traveling on the roads were an immediate red flag to the Hrum ships in orbit. In addition, he'd sent two men to attempt to make contact with Marvin and his men who he expected were holed up in one of their many fallback sites prepared in case of an attack. Ryan was not able to warn them of their new destination before they left the bunker, so he felt that Marvin and the men he brought with him would likely hole up in one of their designated spots. The men Ryan sent had strict orders to not let themselves get captured if they got into a fight.

Ryan was munching on a piece of peanut butter toast that one of his men had brought him in the cabin they'd converted into their command center. In addition to having a professional psychologist, he also had two recruits who had been cooks in luxury restaurants at one point in their lives. Apparently having militia and not regular troops had some benefits when it came to eating well, and rebuilding a dilapidated camp's generator. The few moments of peace he had while he was eating didn't alleviate the incredible amount of stress he had felt since he took command. They were currently all looking at him for answers, and he didn't really have any.

The Hrum in orbit were constantly blanketing most communication channels with a propagandic message demanding the surrender of the Grand Monarch, and her nobles while promising no harm would come to them. He couldn't imagine that a whole lot of them would willingly give themselves up to the Hrum, but on the other hand, most of those people were also so obsessed with their own survival, that they very likely would be willing to give up their own family if it guaranteed their safety. He was listening to one of his men who had just come back from scouting give his report when the door banged open and Izabella strode through the doorway. He hadn't seen much of her since the night they'd arrived, but it seemed she was done mourning the loss of her mentor.

She took a quick glance around before her eyes settled on Ryan, who was still holding his toast. She stormed over to him while he tried to determine the best course of action with his half-eaten breakfast. Before he'd made up his mind, she was standing in front of him and the other militia in the command center were beating a quick retreat, and he was still holding his toast.

"Am I interrupting something?"

"Uh... no... I was just...um." Ryan stammered, quickly setting the toast back on the plate on the table." No you were not."

"I see..."

"How can I help you, your majesty?"

She didn't reply, but fixed him with a cold eye.

"Izabella. How can I help you, Izabella?"

Holding his gaze for another moment she finally replied, "You can *help* me by telling me what your plan is to fight these monsters!"

"Ma'am, well, um... we are only a small group. My primary mission is to keep you out of harm's way."

"To hell with that!" she replied, raising her voice and poking her finger into his chest. "I should be out there. I'm a leader. I should be out there inspiring people to rise up against these bastards who dared to attack my home again! I put you in charge of my militia to fight against all threats to my planet, both human and alien."

"I sent Corporal Virgdomi...Virdogo....Corporal V and Private O'Leary to attempt to make contact with Marvin and the rest of my men. They should be back sometime in the next day or so." He held up a gentle hand to forestall her reply. "Once we establish contact, we can see if there are any other organized resistances around the planet."

"Oh yeah?"

"Um yes, your maj—"

"How will we do that?"

"Well, ma'am we—"

"We're back to *ma'am* then...?"

"Well, Izabella, for starters, we need to get an idea of where the Hrum have set up shop. There weren't nearly enough ships to invade all the major cities, let alone a planet. I assume they're entrenched in the capital and one or two of the other major population centers. I have no idea what their goals are, but that's the reality of the situation."

"What if more ships showed up?"

"It's possible, but I find that unlikely at least for now. Why would two separate fleets come to invade a planet one or two days apart? If more are coming, I doubt they are here yet."

Izabella nodded as if agreeing with his logic. "Well, what then?"

"Then, we begin observing them. I am not sure if you noticed, but these Hrum were different than the ones who attacked previously. They behaved much more in-line with how I would expect a space-faring intelligent species to behave. I want to see what they're doing. I also wish there was some way to contact more of the planetary militia, or even Commander Nord. I think it's important to the people of your planet to know that you are still alive. We don't have any equipment capable of punching through this jamming however."

"So how do you plan to do that?"

"I have no idea yet, but I will come up with something. Believe it or not, this is the first time I have had to protect a VIP and plan a guerrilla war at the same time." He fixed her with a crooked smile. "If I'm honest, I'm just making up most of this stuff as I go."

"I see, thank you for telling me."

"Don't tell the men," he said, putting a finger to his lips.

She buffeted him lightly on the arm, now wearing a small smile of her own.

"Well we were really scraping from the bottom of the barrel when we hired you in the first place. It was between you and a one-armed monkey for the job."

Ryan clutched his chest with mock hurt and gave a dramatic sigh.

"We figured you would eat less peanut butter than a monkey."

"You have deeply wounded me, my lady. Point me in the direction of that monkey and I will give him a call. You deserve the best!"

Much to his pleasure, that elicited a giggle out of Izabella. He decided at that moment he would do anything to make her laugh.

She reached forward and took hold of both of his hands. He marveled again at how small and dainty and perfect they appeared compared to his own scarred and meaty hooks. It reminded him again of the massive gap in their social status.

Before his thoughts could get too dark, she spoke. "I don't know what I would have done without you, Ryan. Thank you."

She released his hands and wrapped her arms around him. He found his own arms doing the same.

"You're welcome Izz." They stood there silently for several minutes just holding each other. He said nothing, just stood there enjoying her closeness and trying to control his heartbeat. He racked his brain for something else to say, but nothing came to mind.

Suddenly, she jumped away from him and yelled, "THE WREATHSBURG NETWORK!"

"What?"

"Of course! The Wreathsburg Network Station, of course!"

"Your maj... Izabella I have no idea what you're talking about."

"We can use the network station to broadcast whatever message we want to send. It was state-of-the-art when the Hrum first invaded and I know it was nearly operational. I was due to give my first yearly proclamation of independence as the leader of the planet next week."

"Ah… a broadcast station!" said Ryan, catching on.

"The most powerful broadcasting center on the planet…" she assured him.

Ryan had begun to understand what she was talking about. He had been briefed on the capabilities of that facility not too long ago. "That's an excellent idea!" he said. "If I recall correctly, Wreathsburg is only a few hours away. I can take a squad there to assess the condition of the station. We can record a message from you and broadcast it from there!"

"No."

"No..?"

"I need to be there. We have to go live so they can see my face."

"Izabella, we can record a video. They'll see you 'live' minus a few hours. You'd turn yourself into a massive target if you went there yourself. They could simply launch an orbital strike at the station and we'd all be nothing but a memory. We also don't have any way to escape quickly. We'd need a fast aerial transport"

"They've already shown that they want me alive. Do you really think they'd simply try and take me out?"

"I don't know, but I am not willing to risk your life on a guess."

"Everything's a guess! We are blind out here. Maybe we'll even be able to link up with more of the planet's military."

"With the Hrum ships in orbit, I just can't approve of you putting yourself into danger like that. Yellen would not agree to this."

"Don't you dare bring him into this!"

Ryan realized he'd made a mistake. Trying to leverage her into agreeing by bringing up her dead bodyguard was a low blow.

"Please, Izabella…" with a placating gesture, he continued, "let me send a few men to scout it out. We can come up with a firmer plan after we see what's going on over there. For all we know, the Hrum destroyed the station when they first invaded."

She took a breath to reply, but he cut her off—

"After we do that, we can discuss putting your beautiful face on the air to threaten the Hrum with eternal damnation."

Ryan had added that last comment in an attempt to break the tension that had been building and it seemed to work. Izabella seemed to noticeably deflate at that concession and she laid her head back on his chest.

"Flattery doesn't work on me you know."

"Of course not your majesty, of course not; I have no idea what I was thinking."

One of Ryan's men ducked his head into the room. "Sir… O'Leary and Virgo…Virgodomamamo have returned with Marvin and the rest of our men."

"Thank you, Corporal," Ryan acknowledged.

"They indicated they managed to fly that razorback gunship we liberated from Chomper in the cover of darkness and hide it a few miles from here."

Ryan smiled slightly as he thought about that memory. It seemed like it had been a lifetime ago, but it hadn't even been six months since that successful operation where they'd captured the wannabe warlord and stolen his gunship. It had been a risk to bring the gunship here, but he would welcome the extra firepower. Looking over at Izabella, he could see she was smiling broadly.

"Well that's a quick transport we can use."

Ryan purposely ignored her comment. "Your majesty, shall we greet the men?"

Nodding she looped her arm in his and steered him towards the door. "I'd love to. Let's go!"

Ryan ignored the amused look that his man was giving them as they walked past. Izabella apparently wasn't afraid to show her affection for him in public. Either that or she was messing with him in order to torture him for refusing to let her risk his life. He supposed that was something he would have to get used to if he was going to be guarding her for the foreseeable future.

Together, they walked towards the entrance of the camp where he saw the rest of his men greeting each other good-naturedly. Back slaps and insults were flying as the two groups came together. He spied his second-in-command in the crowd and headed in his direction.

Marvin, ever the inappropriate perverted-thinking man, spoke first. “Captain! I am in awe. It only took you two days to nab yourself a princess! I beg of you, teach me your ways!”

Ryan was relieved at the amused giggles that came from Izabella who released Ryan’s arm, moved forward and replied. “Chief Petty Officer Marvin, don’t think I forgot your dancing with Mistress Robinsby. She seemed quite taken with you. If you two had been any closer, you could have shared one skin!”

That brought a small smile to Ryan’s face. It was almost the exact thing Izabella had said to him when they first spotted Marvin dancing with the busty baroness only a few days prior.

Marvin, completely unabashed by her banter, gave a dramatic sigh and put his arm up in mock despair. “Ah yes, my future wife and love. We will yet finish our dance once we deal with these pesky buggers. She had the most perfect emerald-green eyes.”

“More like massive boobs,” Ryan muttered to himself.

Izabella moved forward and embraced Marvin in a hug which seemed to even catch him off guard. He locked eyes with Ryan and gave him a knowing wink.

Ryan, now desperate to steer this conversation in another direction, replied, “I heard you brought the gunship.”

Marvin grinned and nodded.

That was dangerous flying it to us. You could’ve been caught by the Hrum.”

Releasing Izabella, and turning towards Ryan, Marvin’s voice took on a more serious tone. “I agree, sir, but I decided the extra firepower and the quicker route of escape was worth it. I was hoping you’d agree, I didn’t have any way to contact you and we only flew at night.”

Ryan nodded thoughtfully. “No sweat, Marvin. I don’t disagree with your decision. I too like the idea of the firepower that machine will bring. Does it have a full loadout?”

“Aye sir. We have a nearly full loadout of both missiles and cannon ammunition, and we brought along extra fuel bladders.”

“Good job. You’re missing a few people though. Where are Luiz and his men? Perez is missing also, although that may be a blessing.”

"I had them stay in the capital. They are going to lay low and figure out the situation there. I told them where to go if they needed to contact us, but I felt it important to keep eyes and ears in the big city."

Ryan nodded, agreeing with his second-in-command. "Good thinking. Go ahead and tell your men they can have four hours to rest. I will be briefing them on our new plan in the command center." Turning to Corporal Virgadamomo, he said, "Good job, Corporal. Please give the men a quick tour and show them to their lodging. We have four hours to recover before I want them in the command center. We have a new mission."

"Aye, sir. Thank you, sir."

The young man turned and barked orders to the newly arrived men and women and they turned to follow him into the camp. Izabella gave Ryan a small wave and turned to follow them. She had made it a point to talk to each and every one of the militia and learn their names and she clearly didn't have any plans to change that.

Marvin stayed with Ryan and watched as they walked away. "A nice ass too."

Ryan shook his head in disgust. "Do you ever say anything that's not totally inappropriate?"

"No, sir!" Marvin said happily. "It's why you like having me around so much. In comparison, you look like a saint."

Ryan snorted in amusement. "You've got me there."

They said nothing for another long, simply taking in the surroundings before Marvin finally spoke again. "Hey, how do you say that kid's name? Corporal Virgo Virgin—"

"No fricking idea!" Ryan chuckled, "I've resorted to calling him Corporal V or Virgo."

"I myself prefer to call him Corporal Virgomama, but I suppose I can call him Corporal V. He told me on the journey back about Commander Yellen and how you're in charge now. It's a good thing you stepped up, kid's very green."

"That's true, but he's got potential. I like what I've seen in him so far. I might make him a squad leader, and that reminds me... I'm now technically a commander, so I am hereby drafting you into the armed services of St. George and rewarding you with the rank of captain. I'm not sure I have the authority to officially do that, but calling yourself Captain Marvin carries more weight than Sergeant or Petty Officer and I need you to manage the men while I manage Izabella's security."

"You seemed to be managing Izabella just….."

"Not what I meant," Ryan said, cutting Marvin off. "I trust nobody more than you and I need your help."

"You can count on me, sir. While you're at it, you should probably promote individuals as the squad leaders. Give them a little bit of weight to throw around themselves. We hadn't officially named anyone yet, a little structure would do them good."

"Agreed, Captain Inappropriate. Can you draw it up? Put Corporal V in charge of the Monarch's remaining men, keep them all together. He's shown potential. You can pick the rest, have the names ready to go for our planning session."

Marvin straightened up, clicked his heels, and mockingly saluted. "Yes sir, Commander Drake. Right away, sir." He turned on his heel and strutted away.

Ryan knew that Marvin would do as he ordered, but the man couldn't help but act like a child when no one was around. Ryan's stomach gave a grumble reminding him that he hadn't finished his breakfast, so he decided to do just that. He thought again of his family. It occurred to him that he was unofficially on the same level or had even surpassed his older brother rank-wise, which made him chuckle. Just check one more box to add to the things that would likely amuse his father and make him say, "Told ya so."

Chapter XI

In Twilight of Moon System on Hrum Ship
Year 3326

Jaxton and Dr. Casey were walking along the passageways of the small corvette-sized ship that they were temporarily confined to until Revalius' people showed Jaxton's how to utilize the scanning equipment they used for nanite detection. It was very similar in layout to the Hrum ships he'd boarded in the past, albeit much smaller. Major Stevens had proposed that they set up a quarantine in the hangar bay of their own ship, but Jaxton did not want to take a risk no matter how small that they'd bring back any sort of nanite infection to their ship. After working with several of the scientists and engineers from Jaxton's ship, Revalius' subordinate seemed confident that they'd be able to utilize the same scanning tools they used on themselves to scan the humans for traces of nanites. Major Stevens, ever the paranoid marine, ordered that they bring a corpse from one of the Hrum ships they destroyed to test the machine. He felt that the aliens were being far too helpful. Jaxton thought it was more they had nothing to lose in helping them, but Steven had just grunted and ended the conversation.

Dr. Casey and Jaxton had been discussing the implications of what Revalius had revealed. Revalius had said as much, but she also felt fairly certain that the nanites that infected the Hrum were not able to infect humans. That being said, if the Karathians were obviously aware of humans, and it was likely that they had developed or were in the process of developing nanites that could infect humans. It was all just speculation until they managed to get some working scanners, but that was her hypothesis. One of the marines who had been shadowing them cocked his head, for a moment before waving to get Jaxton's attention. "Sir, we are preparing to breach the chamber on the damaged Hrum cruiser. Commander Bradley is asking if you'd like to have the feed shared with you.

"Thank you, soldier. Yes I would. Please have everyone gather back in the conference room. We will watch it together."

"Aye sir." He jogged off, leaving Casey and Jaxton to make their way to the room at their own more sedate pace. By the time they made it back to the room, everyone else had gathered and were waiting for him. He sat down in the same seat as earlier. He thought it was funny how similar the chairs on an alien ship were to that of humans. Some of his smaller crewmembers were slightly dwarfed by the chairs, but him being a rather large man himself fit in it comfortably. He nodded to Major Stevens who was ready to give the go order. Stevens, a man of few words, simply said into the mic.

"Go!"

On the viewscreen that his technicians had managed to rig up, they saw the footage from half a dozen marines all standing outside the room, maglocked to the floor. With Stevens' order, they jumped into action, igniting the small breaching charge that they had preemptively placed on the hatchway. They had pressurized the entire corridor of the ship so that if the occupants were still alive, they would in theory not be killed by the resulting decompression.

As soon as the charge burned its way through the latch securing the door, it toppled inward with a bang. Two marines then hurled flash-bang grenades through the now gaping hole and briefly took cover for them to go off. They charged through, guns pointed straight ahead. Much to their disappointment, inside were the corpses of two ornately dressed aliens. The entire room was decorated in a fashion that Jaxton could only describe as ostentatious. Red and purple drapes all around with other decorations scattered around the room. One of the aliens had no apparent wound, but was dead as a doornail. The other had appeared to have been impaled by a small statue of some sort. It had probably been sitting on the desk or shelves and had rocketed across the room before embedding itself as shrapnel in the chest of the alien.

Everyone in the room watched intently as the marines took a closer look at the dead aliens. The only word that Jaxton could use to describe them was *skeletal*. Long pale, almost beak-like faces, stuck up from bony frames. The skin was an incredibly pallid, flat white. He guessed they were slightly shorter than the average human, but it was hard to tell from just looking at them lying there dead.

"If you put some feathers on them instead of those robes, they'd look like bird-human hybrids," Jaxton muttered.

"That's one ugly bird," he heard Dr. Casey reply, which brought a small smile to his face.

Jaxton was disappointed that the aliens were dead. The amount of intel they could have acquired from them could have proved a game-changer. Even in death they'd be useful. They were very likely the first key to determining why this war on the Hrum had happened in the first place.

Turning to Revalius, he said, "So these are the Karathian who your people have been at war with for close to a hundred years?"

"Yes, those are likely the puppeteers that I spoke of earlier. They alone likely controlled the entire fleet which you destroyed."

"Just these two, or would there have been more of them?"

"The ship likely had up to a dozen Karathian who were in command of their own specialties. It's hard to explain, but they can dip into the beings they control to an extent to maintain the various systems."

"I'm not sure I understand."

"Think of it like this, Admiral... you are an expert at space travel, your warrior commander an expert on fighting on the ground. You both have a limited knowledge of each other's specialties. If either of you were the puppeteers of the engineering crew of a ship, you'd be able to utilize their knowledge to an extent to maintain the systems. You wouldn't do it as proficiently as someone trained in engineering, but you'd be able to leverage some of what they know. If your warrior commander and you both commanded a hundred equally trained soldiers with the buggavites, he'd likely win, because he used both the knowledge of the troops he had control of as well as his own knowledge."

"I see. So being infected could actually make them worse at fighting?"

"It depends, but generally yes. They don't have the ability to react like a free-thinking being would in a similar situation. Especially if he has to deal with five, ten or even more puppets, so to speak, at the same time."

"That's good information to have," said Drake.

"Aye, I just wish we'd known all this far earlier than we did," added Bradley.

"It's also horrible. I'm sorry for the loss of your people, Revalius."

"Thank you, Admiral. I just hope that you have more success against them than we did."

The conversation died down as they focused on the marines' cameras. They did a thorough sweep of the room, and gathered everything that could be considered useful. Drake inspected a large safe in the wall of the room, which they also managed to open. Inside were several small cases that when opened appeared to contain several test tube-like vials and a dispenser of some sort.

When Revalius saw this, he jumped to his feet and exclaimed, "Admiral! I believe those are dormant nanites! We never managed to secure an unreleased dose of them. This is extraordinary!"

Before Jaxton could respond, Dr. Casey jumped in. "Are you saying those vials contain dormant nanites ready to be deployed into a host? Is that gun-shaped object in the case a dispenser?"

"I have never seen something like that, but I would say that's a safe guess. It appears to be some sort of injection device."

"Do you believe it's possible they're adapted for human use?" Drake asked. "Would there be any reason they have unreleased vials to infect more Hrum?"

"I do not find it likely that those are for my people. Once they infect the general population, they are easily spread. I find it likely that Dr. Casey's guess is more likely."

Dr. Casey's eyes widened in both excitement and fear. "Admiral Drake, it's of utmost importance that we get those samples to our lab as soon as possible."

"Hold your horses, Doctor. I will not bring anything onto my ship that has the possibility of endangering the entire crew. Once we determine it's safe or at least safe *to contain*, I'll see what we can do, but not before that moment when I can guarantee the safety of everyone aboard. I will not permit it." Turning to Stevens, Drake continued, "Major, please order the marines to keep that case off my ship. Secure it however you wish, but make sure it's under twenty-four-hour guard, and that nobody comes into contact with it."

"Yes, Admiral."

"Very good. Now let's see what our science team has come up with so far." Jaxton nodded his head towards Revalius' subordinate and one of his science team who entered the room shortly before Revalius' outburst.

"Admiral, with Arama's assistance, we have managed to use their scanning tools to detect the presence of nanites. We tested it on several of the corpses that we brought aboard.

"You brought aboard bodies infected with nanites?!?"

"Sir, we took all safety precautions. It was the only way to test if the tool was working." Turning to Arama, the science-tech continued, "Arama indicated that nanites die when the body dies as they are its source of sustenance. We kept the bay in vacuum and were fully suited just to be safe, but it did successfully detect the nanites in the fallen Hrum's body. We can say that we're confident it will detect any presence of nanites on all of us here."

Jaxton nodded as he digested the news. "Can we make more of them?"

"Yes sir, I believe so. They aren't so different from some of our medical scanning equipment. They should be easy enough to replicate."

"Excellent, I want every ship in our fleet equipped with them."

"Yes, of course, sir."

"In addition, work with the medical team to scan every crewmember in the fleet."

"Sir, we, I mean—"

"What is it?"

"We don't have a way to scale it up that fast. I mean not yet."

"Well get on the planning of it, please."

"Yes sir, we have already contacted them and they're putting together a plan as we speak. In the meantime, we can begin to clear our people to head back to the ship.

"Excellent, get it done. Revalius, walk with me please."

The meeting broke as the scientists scurried off, excited to play with their new toy, while the others prepared to return to the ship. Jaxton and Revalius, flanked by two marines, walked through the passageways slowly.

"Is there something you wish to talk about that you don't want your subordinates to hear, Admiral?"

"That's observant of you, Revalius."

"I am at your mercy, please ask whatever you would like."

Jaxton hesitated for a second—what he was about to do would probably get him in trouble if the alien refused. He sighed and finally laid it out. "Once my people clear us to return to my ship, I will ask that you come with us. We're not your enemy, and I will not force you to, but I believe it's in both of our interests. I'm in charge in this system, of these ships, but I'm not in charge of the entire military. I cannot say for certain what will happen to you once you disembark from my ship, but I'll promise to make sure you'll be treated fairly. If you say no, and wish to return to your asteroid base, we'll not stop you."

"I thank you, Admiral. In my culture, the one at the mercy of the other has no say in where he or she goes. Given this choice, I would still like to stay with you. If there's even a chance I can prevent these Karathians from doing to your people what they did to mine, I will take it."

"Glad to hear it, good sir."

"One thing though, Admiral..."

"Yes?"

"Why do you call my people *Hrum*? I know that you have translated my language and know that that's a unit designator, and not my species name."

Jax laughed at that. He was sure that the alien was quite confused by the crew constantly calling him a Hrum. In the Hrum language, H.R.U.M. was actually a combination of numbers and letters. It just so happened this combination similar to the English letters of H-R-U-M that the name had stuck.

"It's a long story, but yes we are aware it's not your species name. Let me explain it to you as we walk."

Jaxton was sipping from a coffee bulb in his command chair. The scans on Arcon went by without an issue, everyone, including the aliens were cleared of any nanites. Revalius and Arama were both in the medical bay working with his science and medical teams working to implement the scanning equipment and sharing all the knowledge they could with his staff. Revalius was both mortified by what his people did to the humans as well as amused by the reason they called him Hrum. Jaxton couldn't help but think it was slightly morbidly funny as well. It turned out that the H-R-U-M soldiers that had invaded St. George were actually from a special HRUM battalion that Revalius was actually very familiar with. He told Jaxton that he had been a starship captain many years ago, but had reached retirement age during the Karathian war. Unfortunately, due to the way the war was going, he'd agreed to take a less demanding post while still being able to serve his people. While he was a ship captain, he often shuttled battalions of troops between targets, and one of the more humorous stories of his career sprang from the time he transported one of the H-R-U-M battalions. Revalius had been very light on some details, which made Jaxton a little bit suspicious, but he told Jaxton that his people had long worked on attempting to biologically modify Hrum soldiers to encompass more traits that would make them the ultimate soldiers. He discussed how early tests were a failure, as the soldiers were uncontrollable and oftentimes unable to be reintroduced to Hrum society when they retired, or simply would not take orders, but as time went on, they had fine-tuned it. The most recent and successful batch of the enhancements their scientists had come up with were called *IAN11* in the Hrum language. In English it looked like the letters H-R-U-M. All enhanced soldiers bore that symbol. The enhancements—

if what Revalius claimed was true—were impressive, and accomplished all the goals their inventors had desired. Unfortunately, some downsides existed that could be pretty severe if not managed correctly. Immediately after their enhancements before they had time to regulate and become accumulated to them, the soldiers tended to fight anyone, anywhere, either for no reason at all, or for something super minor like wanting snacks. A staple in the Hrum diet, especially aboard their starships, was a sort of soda cracker with relish that sounded disgusting to Jaxton, but was apparently like candy to the Hrum. Revalius had been transporting one of the newly enhanced battalions aboard his ship when all hell had broken loose. It was roughly a month after their enhancements, so they were given the green light to integrate with their duty stations, but it was a long journey, and even un-enhanced hotheaded male aliens when in close proximity to each other occasionally got into fights. A simple argument that had started when one of the soldiers accused another of stealing his homemade relish, which he'd been saving for a special occasion, turned into a battalion-wide brawl requiring Revalius to slowly reduce the oxygen content in the Hrum grunt country until the fighters were rendered unconscious. Once he'd managed to bring them to order, he'd punished them by forcing them to clean his ship by hand with their toothbrushes, which were more like toenail brushes because the enhanced Hrum didn't really have teeth. He told Jaxton that he swore the ship was cleaner than any of his service crew, or automated cleaning bots could have made it.

The Hrum laugh, which to Jaxton sounded kind of like a barking cough, had initially scared Jaxton, but it was clear that Revalius had been amused by the story. Jaxton also shared some of his funny experiences and after a few good laughs, Revalius had given his permission for Jaxton and his people to continue calling them Hrum.

As he sat in his chair on the bridge, Jaxton was tapping a few notes into his tab. Dr. Casey had requested that he provide her with any and all observations of the retired Hrum captain that he could. He was no expert on alien body language, but even while telling the stories about his time as a captain, Jaxton felt that Revalius was not telling the entire truth about some things. He didn't really blame the alien, but he was still a part of the species that the NIS was at war with, even if they weren't in control of their own actions. With a sigh, and a final tap he sent off the message. Jaxton felt he had been MIA for too long and his other captains were sure to be getting antsy, so he scheduled a meeting with them to discuss what they would do next. He put the tab down at his side and took a final moment to compose himself and digest the past several hours before he jumped back into it. Interrupting his reverie, Commander Bradley walked out of Jaxton's ready room where he'd set up the meeting and gave Jaxton a nod that everyone was ready. Sighing, Jaxton rose to his feet and gave his XO a nod of thanks before walking in and settling himself at his desk.

When he observed the screen, he saw that per his orders, the only people in the meetings were his captains, and their XOs.

"Thank you all for coming, captains," Admiral Drake began. "I appreciate your patience. We have some new developments we need to discuss. For starters, excellent job in destroying the Hrum ships. Everyone performed flawlessly, and I am extending my congratulations."

He paused for a moment before continuing.

"The first new development is that we have come into contact with Hrum delegates and have spoken with them."

This caused a stir, as to this point, nobody had spoken with Hrum and received any sort of response. Jaxton continued, cutting off any forthcoming questions. "During this conference, we received new information as to why the Hrum have never communicated with us in the past. This is the second development we need to discuss. All Hrum we've come into contact with to this point, with the exception of these five, have been infected with what the Hrum call *buggavites* and we are calling *nanites*. These nanites, once they enter the subject's body, multiply and eventually take control of all bodily functions, essentially making a controllable pawn that will do what they are ordered to do. Think of it like a marionette doll, but on the larger scale with the ability to control multiple beings at once. Captain Mitchell was predictably the first one to respond and—"

"Admiral, you're talking about alien mind-control bugs?"

"To put it simply, yes that's what I'm talking about. We've confirmed the existence of these nanites in the bodies of the defeated Hrum and we are working to implement security and scanning measures that we'll share with each and every one of you shortly. We're putting in place a protocol and procuring equipment for you to test yourselves and your crews. You will all be expected to scan your entire crew for the presence of nanites.

It was Captain Dixon who responded next. "Sir, it feels like you're pulling on our pant legs. Mind control bugs?"

Jaxton brought his attention to Dixon's screen. He didn't miss the slight frown that Commander Taylor had on her face, but he dismissed it.

"Who's *controlling* the... *bugs*?" Mitchell asked, cutting back into the conversation.

"Excellent question, Captain, which we'll address is due course." Jaxton replied.

"This brings us to our third development," Drake continued the briefing with all the captains. "The Hrum have been at war with another alien race for close to one hundred of our years. The Hrum name for their enemy is Karathians and they are the ones responsible for these nanites."

He paused for a moment to share the pictures his marines took of the dead ornately dressed aliens.

"The Hrum word for them essentially translates to *Puppeteers* in English. These puppeteer Karathians are in charge of controlling these subverted Hrum."

Jaxton saw the looks of doubt on the faces of his captains, but he knew he had to push forward. "Look, I know this sounds crazy, and I don't want to hash this all out now, but trust me, it's real and I will share all the pertinent data with you after this."

He paused for a moment to see if any of the captains had any questions. Nothing came from the blank faces, not even Dixon who looked blankest.

"This brings me to the last thing we need to discuss. We're returning to NIS space as soon as we finish cleanup operations. We've accomplished our mission and now we need to return home. I think we can say with a fairly high level of certainty that these ships we destroyed were not heading to JOS for a Sunday picnic or a friendly chat.

"I'll be sending you the information on the nanites that I promised for you to review. I also expect you to implement all scanning and security procedures that my medical staff comes up with. That's your number one priority.

"If there are no other questions, we can end the meeting here. I'll speak with all of you soon, thank you all for attending. Admiral Drake out."

Jaxton sighed as he sat back in his chair. He knew that what was saying seemed far-fetched, and he wasn't even sure if he completely believed what had happened over the past day. He also knew the private video chats sprang up immediately after he signed off, with all the captains confabulating among themselves about all this new information. He took a moment to wonder what his brother was up to. As far as he knew, Ryan was on the surface of St. George when it was attacked. Knowing his brother, he was sure he was still alive. He also took a moment to pull open Captain Dixon's report of their assault on the space station to review it again. He was still a little bit peeved at how his sister somehow ended up right in the middle of the action. His gut said he should scold Captain Dixon, but then he would be playing favorites, figuring a bird forever under a wing never learns to fly, he decided to leave Nat hands-off for now. He was sure that she was there for a reason and that Dixon did not just send her onto the station to annoy him. He felt that the other captain had come to respect him, or at least acknowledge that he sometimes knew what he was doing. The same could not have been said prior to the past couple of months.

With his moment of self-reflection over, he switched gears. He stood and stretched his back. It was time to plan for what was to come. As far as he knew, JOS was still under NIS control and there had been no attack on the system. The ships he destroyed were very likely the ones that would have done just that. Checking the time, he decided that he had time for a quick shower and a nap. He hadn't slept in over a day and he was wiped.

Chapter XII

In Twilight of Moon System on Captain Dixon's Battlecruiser
Year 3326

Commander Taylor listened as Jaxton signed off and watched her captain out of the corner of her eye. She was still not sure if she was just going crazy, or something was seriously wrong with him. These nanites that Jaxton had mentioned were another unforeseen twist and she was eager to dig into the report that Jaxton said he was sending over. She watched as Dixon sat back in his chair as if deep in thought while she stood there awkwardly.

"Sir, would you like me to forward the data packet to the department heads?"

Dixon said nothing for a few moments. "No, mark it for my eyes only," he eventually grumbled. "I'll review it and then send it out after I have looked through it."

"But sir, shouldn't the infirmary know what to expect? They have to implement quarantine procedures."

"Commander, this was not a suggestion, do as I order," Dixon snapped with an exasperated sigh. "I'll send it out shortly."

"Aye aye, sir," Taylor replied, managing to hide any sarcastic indignation in her tone.

"Now if you would please return to the bridge. Fall in with the rest of the ship fleet."

She knew a dismissal when she heard one, so she simply saluted and left the room. Dixon did like to keep things close to his chest, but he usually had a reason for it. She could not fathom his current logic. Again she was conflicted. She had seen the message from Nat, but had yet to reply. Nat was still stuck in quarantine in the infirmary, so she was out of the loop for the most part.

Taylor was still weighing what to do when she reached the bridge. She repeated the order to fall in with the rest of the fleet, and sent a note to the infirmary to expect new orders regarding the quarantine. Dixon might scold her for that, but she wasn't quite stepping outside of her orders, just toeing the line.

Captain Dixon sat quietly at his desk with his eyes closed. His body language didn't show the fierce battle he was fighting. He felt completely detached from his body. It was like he was fighting an invisible force that was so completely overpowering that he was unable to resist. The only time it seemed to subside even slightly was when the entity that was controlling him was speaking. He watched as his body opened up the report that detailed out the alien nanites that had so effectively neutered the Hrum and now himself. As soon as the admiral had said it, he knew that the nanites were what Hadley had injected him with. It was strange hearing another voice in his head that was not his own. He was an observer in his own body and it was maddening. No matter how hard he pushed, he could not overpower the new occupant inside of him. He wasn't even sure if his thoughts were safe from the nanites, but he supposed there was no way to know for certain. He had seen the uncomfortable look that Commander Taylor flashed him when the puppeteer spoke through him and when he gave what he felt were incorrect orders. He was not sure if it was the pushing he did that caused it, or if the entity controlling them did not have a perfect grasp of the English language, but he heard extra words being used in his conversations and he was pretty sure Taylor had picked up on it. He just hoped that it was enough that she'd be able to put it together that he was compromised.

He watched and grimaced as his body modified the report. His puppeteer, so to speak, changed the orders to indicate that himself and a list of eight other crewmembers had already been cleared before forwarding the orders on directly to the medical team with orders not to share the information with anyone, including his XO. If she continued to push, he would have to do something about her. The one and only perk of his current situation was that he got a look into the mind of the enemy. He swore that if he managed to break free from this, he would make them regret that.

Lieutenant Drake laid quietly on her bunk as several suited-up marines brought in some crates and quickly left the infirmary. The medical staff quickly unboxed and began setting up what appeared to be a scanner of some sort. It only took a few minutes, but her guess that it was a scanner was confirmed as the attendees each one by one went through the machine and returned back to their duties.

Nat waved to one of the orderlies who she had been chatting with earlier over, and she pressed the button to communicate with her inside of her quarantined room. The others in there with her were also standing there curiously watching.

"What's going on?"

"We have received orders from the admiral. These scanners should be able to detect the alien bug that he was worried about. Apparently there was a meeting with a real live Hrum and the admiral and the Hrum talked!"

That was a revelation Nat had not expected. Hrum never talked with humans. She wondered what her brother and the alien had talked about.

"We all going to be put through that machine?" Nat asked.

"Yes, ma'am. Once we're done with all medical staffers, you're first on the list. The captain ordered us to scan everyone on the ship."

Nat simply nodded and thanked the young woman who turned and returned to her duties.

It was about twenty minutes later when the same orderly with four other fully suited staffers entered their chamber with the scanning device. Nat watched as each of the people with her were carefully scanned and cleared until it was only her remaining. She nervously stepped forward and let the machine do its work. Before she even realized it, it flashed green and she was ushered out of the quarantine pod and promptly ignored. The staff would be busy if they were to scan everyone on the ship in a fashion that would prevent the recently scanned spacers from coming back into contact with those who weren't cleared. She was glad that headache was not something she'd have to figure out.

Since she was in quarantine, she was not scheduled to be on duty, so she had some time to kill. Making up her mind, she decided to grab a cup of coffee from the galley, when suddenly there was a commotion from the direction of the quarantine pod that the scout ship crew were being held in. The device that had just cleared her and the others was flashing a bright orange. It had been scanning the comatose captain of the ship. As soon as it had done that, he'd jumped up from the bed and was attempting to strangle one of the orderlies. Luckily, it appeared that they had been ready for that and the two large, suited figures who were obviously marines managed to pull him off of her. They attempted to jab the man with a sizable injector, but one of the other scout ship crewmembers jumped into the fray and began brawling with the marines. Luckily for them, the two crewmembers were not trained in hand-to-hand combat, and they were held off until more suited marines arrived to help subdue them.

Nat was not surprised when the scanner was waved over the second crewmember and it also blinked the bright orange. Apparently that indicated that they were infected. The other crewmembers cowered and almost had to be dragged to the machine. Luckily, they were soon cleared and they were separated from the two that were not. Nat stood there for a moment before deciding to head up to the bridge to speak with Commander Taylor or the captain. She was hoping that they'd share more information with her than the orderly was able to.

It only took her a few minutes to reach the bridge where she saw Commander Taylor sitting in the command chair. She quickly walked over, saluted and said, "Lieutenant Drake reporting for duty."

"Thought you were in sick bay, Nat," Taylor said.

"I was just cleared by the medical staff."

Taylor gave her a small nod. "That's great news! I will rotate you back into your regular shift. Have you read our new orders yet?"

"No ma'am. I only had time to glance at them. I came straight here from the infirmary."

"Well that explains the smell," Taylor replied, waving her hand in front of her nose.

Nat was briefly mortified before she realized the commander was smiling. Playing along, she replied, "I actually came up here to use the captain's shower. I heard the water pressure is better." She noticed a small frown from Taylor at the mention of the captain. Thinking she'd said something wrong, she began to apologize. "Sorry, that was—"

"No, no, you're fine, Nat. It was inappropriate for me to make a joke. Thank you for letting me know that you are cleared for duty. Your next shift begins in two hours, please relax until then. We should be heading towards the Albion point by the time you return to duty to head back to JOS."

"Yes, ma'am." She saluted, turned on her heel and rushed off the bridge.

She was puzzled by the commander's sudden discomfort at the mention of the captain. She was nearly back to her quarters when she heard a noise from a storage closet behind her. Cautiously, she turned to see what it was. Standing there in the darkness was Lt. Carn clandestinely waving for her to join him in the small room. Carn had been oddly quiet since that lunch they had before they deployed. He had barely reacted when she jokingly told him she was holding his hot sauce hostage and had not joined them for lunch since that day. She hesitated, but walked past him into the closet and he carefully closed the door behind him after checking the hallway for anyone else.

"Thank goodness you're alright. I was worried when you—"

"Worried? Why?"

"I'm sorry for being so distant the past few weeks, but I promise you I have a good reason for it."

"Go on…"

"I'm here at the behest of your father."

"My father!" Nat felt her face flush in embarrassment—her dad was trying to protect her by sending out a babysitter. "You better start talking real fast, Carn."

"I'm sorry, Nat. Let me clarify. Your father, along with some of the other senior admiralty he trusts, believes that there is some sort of coup or cell within NISI and some other senior members of the government. It might even extend to the senior admiralty itself. The reason I've made myself scarce is I recognized some of the so-called xenobiologists that were aboard the ship and I couldn't risk them noticing me."

"So you hid?"

"Yes."

"But we've had several meetings that they were involved in, they had to have seen your face by now."

"That's where this gets strange. I was leaving the hangar bay after running an errand for Commander Taylor when I ran into them in the hallway. They walked right by me, didn't recognize me, or say anything. It's like I did not exist. Until this recent revelation with the nanites, I couldn't imagine why they would have done that."

"What nanites?"

"I forgot." He quickly tapped away on his tab for a second. "You probably haven't had time to review this yet," he whispered before turning the tab and handing her an unredacted version of the report that Jaxton had sent over. She took the tab from him and began to read.

"How did you have time?"

"I have my sources," he replied cryptically.

Nat side-eyed him warily. Carn was showing a deceptive side that she had never seen before. She continued to review the report before pulling out her own tab and pulling up the version she had in her inbox. They were very clearly edited and a lot of the information contained was missing. That in itself wasn't that odd, but the captain was the only one who had access to it before the rest of the crew.

Suddenly, she had a thought. "How do they know you?"

"How does who know me?"

"The xenobiologists," Nat replied, beginning to get irritated.

"Oh...I have been lying to you slightly. I was not just a marine prior to this job. I was actually a Ghost for nearly ten years, but I got too old and worn down for the day-to-day rigors of the job, so I transferred to the intelligence side of things where I met your father. I've worked for him for nearly three years, working to dismantle the rogue cell within Nissy."

"That doesn't answer my question."

"I arrested them for conspiracy," he finally admitted.

"What?"

"Yup. Along with several other senior government officials. They were the hired muscle and as far as I know, they should have still been rotting away in prison."

"So they're *not* Xenobiologists?"

"No, no they are not," he said, leveling his gaze straight into Nat's eyes. "Not by a longshot."

Nat took a few moments to digest this. "So why exactly are you here?" she finally asked. "You said you didn't expect to see them, but it doesn't explain why you are on this ship in the first place."

"Believe it or not, I wasn't sent here because of you. I was sent here by your father to be his eyes and ears in the fleet and to report to your older brother if I found anything that needed to be reported. You being here just let me keep an eye on the daughter of a man I deeply respect. Sort of two birds with one—"

"Just you? and does Jaxton know you are here?"

"I can't answer for sure, but I don't believe so. I think your father wanted to keep this as close to his chest as possible."

"I'm going to assume that means *yes* to my first question. So why are you coming to me now?"

"Because things got kicked up a notch."

"Why's that?"

"I think the nanites are related to this coup or splinter cell somehow. Some of the people we arrested or took down over the past few years would seemingly turn evil for no rhyme or reason. People who never showed any indication they're greedy or power-hungry suddenly became just that. It made no sense."

Nat's eyes widened as the implication of what Carn was saying set in. "You think that the Karathians could be behind this?" she asked. "Using their nanites, they are already attempting to infiltrate our leaders?"

"That's *exactly* what I'm saying. None of it made sense at first and I didn't feel the risk of bringing you in was warranted until this happened. We need to get in touch with your brother as soon as possible."

"Why not send him a message?"

"I can't risk it being intercepted. I have no way of knowing for sure, but I believe those five xenos were infected and who knows who else might be. Who runs into a burning lab, and completely ignores orders like they did? They were ordered by whoever was controlling the nanites to do it. I would not be surprised if they survived and are reporting to whoever is in that system what they've learned. I also find it likely there've been others on this ship and in this fleet who've been infected. The second I saw the redacted version of this report, it made me think that it's possible that the captain has been subverted."

"I bet Hadley is on that list. He was quite chummy with those five. He didn't even react when the captain gave him his condolences for the loss of the men."

Carn nodded. "Exactly my thought."

"What makes you think the captain is involved? Outside of this report?" Nat asked, squinting her eyes, playing devil's advocate. "I mean he *is* permitted to control what he shows us."

"I think whoever's in charge of infecting people with nanites only has a limited supply. I don't think they can spread them like they did with the Hrum. When I was leaving the bridge after one of my shift changes, I spotted Hadley coming out of the captain's ready room. I sat in the shadows and watched as Commander Taylor went in there shortly after, and when she left, she seemed almost distraught or concerned. Call it a hunch, or maybe intuition, but I find it too coincidental this happened right before a report arrived dictating quarantine protocols for an alien bug."

Nat digested this for a little while. "We need help, Carn," she finally resolved to say. "If you're afraid we can't even send my brother a private message from me, then we need someone with more sway on this ship."

"Have someone in mind?"

"I think we need Commander Taylor."

Carn looked unsure as if weighing his options. "Hmmm... I don't know..."

"Trust me, Carn. I trust no one on this ship more than her, and she and my brother go way back. I even watched the medical staff scan her for nanites, so she should be clear."

"You think those infected couldn't have figured out a way around getting scanned?" he replied glumly.

"I think we have to take the risk. If everyone is infected and we tell no one, we're doing basically the same thing as us sitting and doing nothing."

Carn nodded as if making up his mind. "Okay, but you'll have to make contact," he declared, searching Nat's eyes for confidence. "You have a more personal relationship with her than I do. It'll look less strange if you talk with her privately."

"Agreed."

Carn felt a weight lift as he saw the confidence in Nat he needed.

"Now let's get out of here before someone sees us and wonders what we're up to," Nat said.

"Let's plan to meet here after our shifts, during quiet hours," Carn said.

"Be safe and I'll talk to you soon."

Chapter XIII

On St. George at Summer Camp
Year 3326

Four hours after Ryan finally finished his breakfast, he had his entire command gathered in their makeshift command center at the campground. It wasn't saying a whole lot because in total, they only had about four complete squads of men with a few stragglers, like the razorback pilots and the few men Marvin had designated as his ghostees. Ryan wasn't about to complain because it was more than they had originally. In addition, they had plenty of ammunition, half a dozen vehicles, and even a heavily armored gunship at their disposal for their mission. He looked around the room, counting heads, his eyes briefly locking on Izabella's. Unsurprisingly, the stubborn monarch had insisted that she be invited to the briefing. He smiled faintly at the thought of what she'd do if he'd tried and stopped her from coming.

"Afternoon everyone, I hope you have gotten settled in, because we have a mission." Ryan paused for a moment before continuing. "Our target is the Wreathsburg Broadcasting Center. We decided we have run for long enough and we're now ready to fight back. I don't know about you, but I'm sick and tired of hearing the Hrum broadcasting their message of surrender over and over. I think it's time we sent them a message of our own and here's how we plan to do it."

Ryan had already briefed Marvin on the plan, so he was ready for Ryan when he gestured over to the large viewscreen that had been commandeered from one of the guest rooms and brought out into the lobby. Marvin was tapping away on his tab and had projected a topographical overlay of the broadcast center and the surrounding area for everyone to see.

"Ready, sir."

"Thank you Marvin. Now as I said, we're going to be assaulting the Wreathsburg Broadcasting Center. We will not know for sure what to expect until we get there. Captain Marvin and his ghostees will be our advance team. Under the cover of darkness, they'll take the gunship as close as they can safely, and then scout the area ahead." He gestured to a group of three of the militia who'd began calling themselves *Marvin's ghostees* who had been working with Marvin on additional scouting, camouflage, and other covert tactics. "They'll scout and report back. We have no idea what the military situation on the ground is, all of the military channels have been silent. They could just have rotated codes and we have no access to them, or they could be compromised. Until we have better intel and recon, we'll stay off them. Shortwave radios only."

He continued his briefing for nearly an hour before dismissing the men to get ready. The ghostees and Marvin would be moving out as soon as it got dark and he would follow a few hours behind in their trucks. Luckily for them, most of this part of the countryside was heavily wooded, and very private. There was little vehicle traffic and a lot of cover should they need to get off the road. Wreathsburg was a fairly large city with a prewar population of close to 300,000, but now, less than half of that. The broadcast center was outside the city limits due to the powerful signals it emitted and was mostly spared in the invasion, and the fighting that followed. It had been repaired and modernized in the time since the NIS liberated the planet. It was responsible for handling nearly all civilian and even some military communications. Ryan was sure that the Hrum had set up shop there. It made sense if you wanted to speak with the people you were attempting to subdue and also explained how they managed to broadcast to so many places on the planet.

Marvin and his ghostees piled into an old van they'd found in the small motor pool at the campground. Dusty windows, moldy seats, an ominous rattling from the motor… the van had seen better days for sure, but it would get them to where they stashed the gunship. It also helped that the vehicle wasn't military, so on the off chance of a Hrum flyby, they would hopefully not suspect it was a threat. Most people only kept a few days worth of supplies in their homes. Ryan had to imagine that there were some people venturing out to get supplies and hopefully distracting the Hrum. These weren't the same mindless beasts who had attacked them previously, so he suspected that the Hrum left most civilians alone.

The van puttered away and Ryan's men were loading supplies into their own vehicles. There was no way to hide what their convoy was. He had debated acquiring their own civilian vans, but he decided he'd rather have the firepower that came with their military trucks. Because of this, however, they had to wait until it was fully dark before they left.

Marvin and his ghostees had reached the gunship, fired it up, and took off without incident. Unless the Hrum were actively scanning the area, it would be incredibly hard to spot the small ship. They would only be airborne for a little bit over an hour. They could have gotten there quicker, but stealth was the name of the game now. Marvin had really enjoyed the past few months as an instructor. The joy of imparting knowledge on someone so willing was a new experience. He always found joy in torturing new Ghosts during his time in their ranks. Some would call it hazing, but he thought of it as tradition. It was different with these recruits. They were like a fresh block of clay that he could mold into whatever he wanted. It was a lot less fun to haze people who were relying on him so heavily to help them succeed. He made a mental note not to mention that to any of his buddies back on the ghost teams. They'd definitely ridicule him for it.

"Captain, we are ten minutes out. The skies seem clear. You should only have a few klick's hike. Assuming we get down undetected, we'll camouflage the ship as best we can and wait for your order."

"Roger. You heard the man, ladies. Ten minutes till boots on the ground and then a nice hike in the woods to follow.

Remember your training, we are shadows. Only engage if it's your only option, we want to get in and get out without incident or detection."

"Yessir!" they quickly responded.

Their tone caught Marvin's ear. The more he worked with Ryan, the more he found himself learning from the man. He was a natural-born leader, people followed him without complaint, and on top of it all, he was fair. Even though Marvin was a few years older than him, he looked up to Ryan.

"It must run in the family," Marvin mumbled to himself.

It was incredibly obvious that Ryan looked up to his older brother, and couldn't hide the pride in his face when talking about how well his sister had done. The only thing he didn't appear to realize is that he himself was also something special.

What would Ryan do to break the tension? Marvin thought to himself. Probably say something emotionally stirring or inspiring to get their minds off this, but that's not my style.

"Hey ghostees, does anyone know if Commander Drake's sister is single?" He smiled inwardly at the looks of confusion they gave him before continuing. "Way I see it is that with all her brothers and father being so busy trying to save the NIS, she's gonna need somebody to take care of her. I cannot think of a better man than myself to do the job!" This brought smiles and even a few small chuckles to the faces of his men.

The pilot who had been listening in was the first to reply. "I don't know, Captain. I heard she's kind of a badass. I think she'd be the one taking care of you."

"Well that doesn't sound so bad. I could use a good foot rub."

The men were now laughing at the exchange of banter and the atmosphere in the shuttle which could have been described as *heavy* had lightened up considerably. *Mission accomplished,* Marvin thought to himself.

The shuttle soon banked and began its descent. They had been hugging the treeline, so it was only a few seconds before the landing gear hit the ground and the ramp deployed. Quietly, just as they'd been trained, his men disembarked from the shuttle and hustled to the treeline. This was the most dangerous moment in the mission. A few minutes later, it was clear that they'd managed to land undetected. They quickly assisted the pilots to secure and camouflage their shuttle. They had practiced this several times back in the training grounds over the past few months, so it went smoothly. They were on their way to the broadcast station less than fifteen minutes after they landed.

Marvin checked his watch and saw they were on schedule. They only had about five kilometers to hike to get to the radio station, but they were going to be forced to move slowly. It would take a few hours to get there. As they walked, they dodged a few suburban areas with houses, some clearly occupied, and continued on. He didn't think it was worth announcing their arrival, even if it was likely just locals hiding out in their homes. It was best to not advertise their presence.

Once they arrived at the broadcast center, it became clear that it too was occupied. Unfortunately, these occupants were considerably less friendly looking. There were armed guards patrolling the perimeter, and a few Hrum shuttles in the parking lot. Using his helmet, he zoomed in on the shuttles and saw that their ramps were open and a few armored beings were unloading something. He saw his men snapping pictures and taking notes on what they saw. What Marvin found interesting was that there didn't appear to be any signs of fighting anywhere on the grounds. The Grand Monarch had insisted that there were always several squads of soldiers stationed here. It was a high value asset and they needed to protect it.

Maybe they fled when the Hrum arrived? That didn't make sense though. He'd seen nothing but bravery in the people on this planet. They had survived hell, and were willing to fight tooth and nail for every bit of their home.

Speaking softly he ordered, "Make sure to get a count on the guards." He looked around at the men to ensure they understood. "We aren't going to risk entering the facility, but the number of them patrolling may give us some clues to how many we have to deal with. See if you can see what's being unloaded from that shuttle."

His men simply clicked the channel in acknowledgement before two of them melted away into the darkness. Marvin continued to observe the guards. They looked a little bit short. Hrum were typically at least two meters tall, and Marvin was willing to bet that none of the ones that he'd seen so far fit that description. Turning to the last man near him, he said. "Let's get a closer look at those guards." Marvin always trusted his instincts, and they screamed that something was off, but he couldn't put his finger on it.

Silently, they crept closer to the towering gate surrounding the facility. The patrols were roving in pairs, but they seemed to be following a fixed circuit.

Marvin observed them for several minutes, timing them, before he whispered, "They're patrolling in almost perfectly fixed intervals. Who does that? and better yet, who does it exactly three minutes apart. Someone always needs a bathroom break, or to scratch an itch. This seems almost robotic."

Before he could say anything else, there was a disturbance near the main gate. A covered truck drove up the road, approaching the gate. The two guards in front of it barely reacted, simply opening the gate as the truck approached. The truck rolled through and pulled up to the main doors.

To Marvin's great shock, humans started hopping out of it! Human beings! They moved almost robotically, just like the guards who Marvin now expected were also human.

"What the hell is going on," the ghostee next to him said.

Marvin didn't respond, only shook his head. When the truck was nearly empty, another figure stepped out. This one was heavily robed and much smaller, nearly a head shorter than any of the humans in the truck. When it pulled back its hood, the face was not Hrum or human, but something else entirely. It looked almost skeletal. Sort of like a bipedal vulture. It turned as if scanning the areas, its creepy glowing eyes appearing to linger on Marvin as if seeing him, but eventually it turned its head back towards the facility and followed in the other truck occupants. Marvin was incredibly weirded out at this point and had decided that he'd seen enough.

"Let's get back to the rally point. The commander needs to see this."

He couldn't see the face of the man across from him, but he was sure it was as pale as his. *Humans working with the Hrum? What was that strange alien, and how does he play into this?*

They met back up with the other two ghostees before starting their trek back towards the designated meeting spot. They hardly spoke, it was clear that the other two had also seen the humans and the strange alien. They were all clearly distracted by what they had seen, because they missed the warning signs as they approached their shuttle. Before they knew it, a swift blow brought Marvin to his knees. Cursing his lack of focus, he rolled and struck out with his leg, feeling a satisfying crunch as he kicked out the legs of his assailant. He tried to roll to his feet, but a large military rifle was hovering in front of his face, only inches away. He put his hands up in surrender, and saw that all three of his men had also been subdued.

"Speak! Who are ya, what're ya doin' here?" a gravelly voice said from the other end of the rifle.

"My name is Captain Marvin, I am an NIS Ghost," Marvin replied with some force to show he was not cowed. "Who the hell are you?"

"That's none a your damn business. Now tell me, who's the admiral who single-handedly squashed the Hrum at Jewel of Sunlight?"

"Um… what?"

"Answer the damn question. Or die. Your choice."

"Umm, Admiral Jaxton Drake."

He kept the gun in front of Marvin's face for a moment before pulling back and pointing at the ground. The face of an older man, likely in his late fifties or sixties, appeared. He offered a hand for Marvin to grab. Still reeling from what had happened, the fallen captain took it, and was helped to his feet.

"Apologies for the rough introduction. We can't trust anyone 'round these parts anymore, not even other people."

Marvin, still dazed, managed to squeak out, "Does this have something to do with the broadcast center?"

"Aye, it does. Here…" He dusted Marvin off with a few pats, while continuing, "The Hrum landed here the day they arrived and began kidnappin' people by the dozens. They've been takin' em somewhere, and then when they return, they're changed."

"Changed?"

"Aye."

"Changed, how?"

"You saw the broadcast center, correct?"

Marvin nodded.

"And you saw the guards were too small to be Hrum?"

"You're saying that hostile humans are working with the Hrum to guard the center?"

"I'm sayin', people like my son were taken away, and when they return, they're just like the Hrum!"

Marvin saw a tear form in the old man's eye at the mention of his son. He simply gestured for him to continue.

"My son and grandson were taken on the first day. Dem sons-of-Hrum whores! I managed to escape with his wife. Three days later, we seen my son, carrying a Hrum weapon and walkin' down the street in Hrum armor. She ran out to him, shoutin' his name. He shot her. His own wife. He shot her dead."

The old man was now crying freely. Tears running down his face. One of the other men with him put a comforting hand on his shoulder.

"I'm sorry if this is hard for you. Please take a minute, I'll wait."

"No, I'm okay. It's just hard. I stayed hidden and once she had fallen, he simply kept on walkin'. Like he didn't even know her or know he killed her. I followed him and the other man with him back to where they came from. They led us to the university hospital and when they went inside, I hung around and watched for a couple of hours. They brought in truckloads of people, oftentimes they's kickin' and screamin' or fightin' to escape, but when they left, they were almost like zombies or robots. Just like my son."

"Something's changed them," one of Marvin's men who had been let up and was standing behind him replied.

The older gentleman nodded.

"Sir, we have to tell the commander and the—"

Marvin cut him off before he could presumably say the *Grand Monarch.* "My man is right," Marvin told the old man, "Our commander needs to hear about this. Have you had any communication with the military?"

"No, but nothin' outside of short-range communication devices has been workin'. Even those don't always work. I think they are doin' something at the broadcast center that's jamming our gadgets."

"We've noticed the same." Stepping forward, Marvin stuck out his hand for a formal greeting and said, "I already told you my name, but it's Captain Marvin. It's a pleasure to meet you."

The grizzled older man hesitated briefly before replying, "Nice ta meet-cha, youngster You can call me Dale."

There was a few moments of chatter as everyone introduced themselves.

"Dale, would you be open to coming with us? I need to get this information to my commander, and we are due to meet with him."

"What're your intentions?"

"That I cannot tell you. Not right now. I'll leave that up to my commander to speak to, but I can promise you that we are here to help."

"What's your commander's name?"

"Believe it or not, it's Drake. Ryan Drake."

"Drake? As in the younger brother of Jaxton?"

"Affirmative."

"Well let's hope he's half as good as his brother. Lead the way, young soldier."

Without another word, they fell into line behind Marvin who walked the remaining distance to their shuttle. Once inside, they found their two pilots tied to their seats with two more men standing guard over them.

"Oh, I shoulda told ya..." Dale said.

Marvin took a look back at Dale, who nodded to the men.

They cut the two pilots loose before stepping out of the razorback.

Before the two freed pilots could complain, Marvin ordered, "Give the commander the green light. He's waiting to hear from us."

"Aye sir," the sullen pilot said.

He nodded to his copilot and they moved towards the front of the ship. Ryan was waiting for them a short distance away. They had a prearranged signal that gave him the green light to meet them and another that told them to run. He felt that the operation should still go on ahead, or at least they should still have the commander take a look.

Ryan and his men had pulled into the shadows of the woods several kilometers from where Marvin and his men landed the razorback. They had decided that they would have two prearranged signals indicating what Ryan should do. If Marvin didn't respond by a certain time, or sent the second signal, Ryan and his men would bug out. Head away from the city and find somewhere to hole up.

Just before he was starting to get antsy, his driver spoke, "Sir! we received the green light from the captain."

"Very good, let's go in slowly. Stay alert just in case..."

"Aye, sir."

The trucks hopped back on the road for a couple of kilometers before pulling into the clearing where Marvin had landed the razorback. They were greeted with more than double the amount of men than Marvin had landed with, and that put everyone on edge.

Ryan opened a comm channel. "Marvin, who are these people?"

"It's alright, sir," Marvin said. "They're locals. They have some intel I think that you should hear."

Ryan was still on edge, but that made sense. He stepped out of the armored truck and walked towards the group standing in front of the razorback. They were armed with a variety of hunting and military weapons. Ryan spotted Marvin who waved him over and introduced him.

"Dale, our Commander, Ryan Drake. He's in charge of this mess."

"Pleased to meet ya. How you plan to help us?"

Ryan was slightly taken aback at the older gentleman's abrupt demeanor. He looked over at Marvin who just shrugged before jumping in. "He's worried about his son," Marvin said. "He was taken by the Hrum when they landed here on the invasion day."

Ryan nodded thoughtfully before replying. "Mr. Dale, I will need my man to apprise me of the situation. Is that alright with you?"

The old man just grunted.

"So what's going on, Captain?"

"Not good, Commander, not good," Marvin said, looking over the hills with a wince then back at Ryan. "The Hrum are using the broadcast center, which we suspected, but they also seem to be working on several other things here."

Over the next twenty minutes, Marvin shared all the pictures and information his men had gathered and Dale had shared. Dale occasionally jumped in and added some detail. By the time they were done, Ryan was pale. They'd come here originally planning on sending a message to the people of St. George to motivate them to fight, and to show that their leader was alive, but now his gut said that he had to go save those people and stop whatever was going on. That being said, a few squads of partially trained militia weren't going to be enough to simultaneously assault two separate targets. He needed more men. Pausing and taking a minute to look around, he again took note of the firearms and trucks that the locals had brought with them. He realized nearly everything they were equipped with was military grade, some of it looked almost brand new.

"Mr. Dale, how many men did you say that you had?"

"I didn't."

Ryan gave him an exasperated look before continuing. "Well would you mind telling me, man?"

"I would."

Marvin, sensing Ryan's temper flaring, interjected in an attempt to keep the peace. "Sir, what my commanding officer is trying to say is we want to help, but we don't have enough troops to assault both facilities. In the spirit of cooperation, we want to know if you'd be willing to provide fire support."

Dale said nothing for several long moments, as if weighing the options before replying. "Well, why didn't ya put it like that in the first place?" the old man growled. "An officer should really communicate better when asking for help."

Marvin was sure he could hear Ryan's teeth creaking as he ground them.

"I do got one question though. What do *we* get outta this?"

"You get your son back!" Ryan replied, nearly shouting, his usually slow temper flaring. "I can count a few other obvious benefits to not having a hostile alien race in your backyard."

Marvin cut in to curtail a fight, "Sir, if we could just—"

"We're trying to help you, you great old buffoon." Turning to Marvin, Ryan continued. "They'll just be a liability. We'll handle this on our own."

And with that, Ryan stormed off towards the trucks, leaving Marvin and Dale standing there.

"Well, that was rude," Dale said deliberately, all while still holding a straight face and showing little to no emotion. "I don't see how people like to serve under someone who gets angry so easily."

Marvin, who actually found himself liking the crotchety old man, chuckled. "He isn't always so prone to anger. He's just under a lot of stress these days."

"Stress?"

"We can't say everything, but yes, stress. A whole armored truck full of it."

He patted Dale on the shoulder before following Ryan to where he stormed off to.

Ryan hadn't gone far, and Marvin found him resting his head against the cold metal of one of the trucks. "I've never seen you blow up like that before."

"It's just these idiot locals. They don't seem to care about the fact that their planet is under attack again."

"Did you really give them a chance? You blew up on the man pretty quick."

"He didn't want to answer my questions."

"Can you blame him?"

"Whose side you on, Marvin?"

"Yours," Marvin said without hesitation. "And his. *Ours*." Marvin turned away to look at the old man, then back at his leader. "Look, he's seen his family and friends turned into some sort of mindless drones controlled by the Hrum."

Ryan took a breath, his rage dissipating as he processed Marvin's words. "I suppose not," he finally conceded.

"Sir?"

"I didn't really give him a chance, I mean it's the Grand Mon—"

"They also can't be sure why we're here. They're just as suspicious of you. For all they know, we're more intruders in their town, maybe trying to trick them into showing where the rest of them are hiding. We have no way of proving who we really are, and they sure as hell don't know about that hot piece of ass you have hidden away in the truck."

Marvin's words forced a chuckle from Ryan's lips. "I'm not sure Izabella would appreciate you referring to her as that, but I see your point." Nodding his head, he turned as if he'd made a decision. "Thank you, Captain."

"Of course, sir."

"For once you've given me some good advice."

Ryan walked towards their command truck and opened the back. He spared a glance around and saw that the locals were focusing intently on what he was doing.

"Your majesty, would you mind coming out here for a moment?" Ryan said.

He heard muttering from behind him as what he said was processed by those listening. A few moments later, Izabella, with a haughty look on her face that most nobles appeared to possess, pushed her way out of the truck and into the clearing.

"What is it, Captain…"

"Would you mind lending a few words to some of your loyal subjects?"

All around him, the locals and even some of his own men dropped to their knees and bowed their heads. Izabella looked around the clearing, spotting Dale, who like the rest had dropped to his knees. She walked over to him. She gently took his arms and guided him to his feet.

"Please don't kneel, I am sorry about your son. My name is Izabella, what is yours?"

The old man trembled, clearly taken aback by the casual tone she took. "Dale, your majesty," he replied.

"Dale. My granddad's name was Dale… Dalphert actually, but he hated it, so he went by Dale.

"It's an excellent name."

"Thank you, your grace."

Izabella took a moment to look around at the clearing. "Everyone, please get up," she said, lifting her hands in front of her. "This is not the time or place to stand on ceremony.

Right now, I'm just one of you and we need to work together to kick these bastards off our planet. We didn't invite them here, and they sure as hell aren't welcome to stay. We already fought them off once, please, I beg you. Help my men give them the butt-whooping they deserve!"

Ryan, standing passively over her shoulder, couldn't help but smile at her unconventional speech. Nobles prided themself on using grandiose language and not resorting to swear words. She seemed to understand that in order for them to trust her, she'd have to sound more like them. He also could see his men were smiling and he could tell the locals were getting fired up. He tuned back in as she continued to speak.

"So please... give this man, my protector, all the help he needs. He's the reason I'm still alive, and I owe him my life. He has been here helping me rebuild our planet and has fought harder than anyone I know to save it."

Ryan found himself blushing slightly in embarrassment. Why did he keep ending up in the crosshairs of people looking to him for advice or leadership? Again he thought of how his father would have reacted.

The mood in the clearing had lifted, and the people were now cheering and going around introducing themselves to one another. Ryan was a little concerned at the noise, but it was a large planet, and the Hrum couldn't be everywhere. He assumed the locals he couldn't see were keeping an eye out. After the introductions had died down a bit, he looked over at Izabella, who gave him a subtle nod and a smile. He found a convenient tree stump to stand atop of to speak.

"Thank you everyone, I appreciate your faith in me," Ryan said. "We're going to have a tough road ahead of us, and the Grand Monarch needs each and every one of you to help. In order to do this, I'm going to ask you some tough questions. Questions that will be putting a lot of trust into me and my men. In return, I give you this promise: I will not rest until each and every one of these Hrum bastards are six feet under and not a single living soul will doubt that this is your planet. Well... I'm glad we've teamed up. Let's get to work!"

Chapter XIV

In Jewel of Sunlight System on Captain Dixon's Battlecruiser
Year 3326

Much to Nat's annoyance, it took nearly two days and they'd already arrived back in the Jewel of Sunlight system, but she finally managed to arrange a time to talk with Commander Taylor in private. She had asked her if she wanted to spar in the rec center after their shifts. When asked why, Nat replied that Lt. Chen, her usual partner, was sick and she didn't want to miss a workout. Nat had convinced Carn to bring Chen into their confidence, so she had agreed to skip her shift to play sick. Taylor also seemed to understand that Nat had something she wanted to talk about. In order to make sure the commander didn't order Nat to talk to the ship's psychologist, she hinted that the issue was personal. She was almost certain that Taylor was aware of her and Brewster's *relationship*—if you could call it that—and she knew how close her brother, Taylor, and Brewster all were. Nat had a feeling that Taylor would be more open to talk to Nat herself if it wasn't about trauma from the operation or some other issue.

She had arrived at the gym early and had intentionally picked an odd time to workout in the hopes that the fitness center would be empty. Her wish was granted, and with the exception of one or two crewmembers who were running on the track, it was a ghost town. She sat by herself stretching until Commander Taylor arrived. When she did, Nat simply waved her over where she also sat down to stretch.

"Evening Commander, thanks for joining me."

"Glad for the invite, it's been a while since I've boxed."

Nat smiled. "My brother Ryan actually got me into it. You probably heard that he was a very good wrestler back in school, but he also liked to box. He used to test his moves on me and made me hold the pads even though I was way smaller and scared at first. He says it made me tougher, but I think he just wanted to watch me suffer."

"As all brothers do," Taylor replied.

"Yep! Eventually he taught me a few moves and I began to like it." She sat back smiling. She missed her brother at that moment and hoped that he was all right.

"Well, you'd best take it easy on me," Taylor said, cracking a smile. "I've taken a few self-defense courses, but never any real boxing."

"Of course, Commander Tay—"

"Let's cut to the chase though, Nat."

"Okay..."

"That's not why you called me down here. I checked with the infirmary. Chen's fine, although I can't imagine what you said to her to make her agree to this."

Nat looked down, embarrassed. She did hate lying to her boss. "I'm sorry, Commander. I just didn't know how else to talk to you privately."

Taylor nodded. "Is this about your relationship with Major Brewster?"

"I had a feeling you knew about that, but no it's not."

Taylor just sat there quietly, waiting for her to continue.

Nat sat there as if struggling internally with something before finally spitting it out. "Have you noticed the captain acting strangely at all?" Taylor, who had been leaning back to stretch, jerked forward suddenly.

"Act strangely how?"

"He redacted a large portion of the report the admiral sent us, and he's been talking a little bit weird."

Alarm bells were ringing in Taylor's mind. She too had noticed the captain's new peculiarities, and how he'd begun to interject unnecessary words into the conversation when he spoke.

"Lieutenant, I think you better tell me what's going on right now."

"Carn and..."

"*Carn*? What does *Carn* have to do with this," Taylor snapped.

Nat knew Carn would be annoyed, but she decided to lay her cards on the table for the commander. If they couldn't trust Taylor, their plan was doomed to fail anyways.

"Carn and I think the captain has been subverted by these nanites that the Karathian infected the Hrum with...."

Nat spent the next twenty minutes laying out her case to the commander whose expression went from neutral, to nervous, to scared. Taylor had almost convinced herself that she was just seeing things and that the captain was just playing his cards close to his chest, but this put a whole new spin on things. She cursed softly. She had been in the meeting where the captain discussed the nanites, so she knew more than most, but the captain had given her the redacted report as well, so when Nat shared the un-redacted report with her, it all but convinced her that the captain was working with the enemy.

"We have to figure out who is controlling the nanites."

"How do you plan to do that?" Nat inquired.

"Let's think about this for a minute. If there really are nanites on this ship, they'd have to have already been on the ship prior to our last operation in the Twilight of Moon system. We may have picked up some stragglers, but I find it highly unlikely that there wasn't already a presence."

Looking back at the un-redacted version of the report, she continued to read. One of the things that Dixon had deleted indicated that an implant of some sort controlled the nanites. Revalius wasn't able to confirm whether or not they were implantable in Hrum, or just in the Karathians, so they had to run with the assumption that they could be implanted in anyone as far as they were aware. Revalius said the root of the problem when it came to those was that they never managed to get ahold of one because as soon as the host died, the device destroyed itself. Revalius was convinced that there were Hrum who were implanted with it in order to blend in and further infiltrate their population.

"If I were trying to infiltrate a secure ship, I'd make sure they knew of every communication going in and out. It would be a good way to gather intelligence." Taylor mused. "Your logic that the infiltrators have a limited supply of nanites makes sense. They'd be quite hard to hide if there were a lot of the injectors all over the ship. I think our best chance is tomorrow morning when the captains all gather to discuss the plan moving forward."

"Where are we going next?"

"Don't know yet, but with the intelligence we have gathered, I expect it will be somewhere where we can communicate with the rest of the fleet. The existence of these nanites is too important to not be the number one priority."

Nat nodded at that. "Do you think that my brother has been infected?" Nat asked suddenly.

Taylor digested that for a moment before replying carefully. "I do think that's likely an enemy goal, but I don't think so. Not yet."

"Why do you say that, commander?"

"I think that someone or something gave the orders to begin infecting our officers in the Twilight of Moon system. The ones aboard our ship may have just been tasked with infiltrating and waiting for further orders, which would make sense why they are just making their moves now. Even if there is someone here with an implant who can give orders, I don't think they'd act outside the scope of what they were initially put here for, which is likely surveillance."

That made sense to Nat. She hoped that Taylor was right. "So what do we do about the captain, and how do we get a message to Jaxton?"

"Well...we have to assume that our regular lines of communication are not secured, and we don't want to tip our hand, so I think we have to try to speak with him in person."

"Is there any chance you are invited to the meeting tomorrow?"

"No, which is uncommon for Dixon, but not unheard of. A lot of captains leave their XOs on the ship for meetings such as this. Jaxton won't think anything of it.

Suddenly blushing, Nat replied, "I can talk to Major Brewster."

"Maybe. I do have the ability to approve day passes to leave the ship, but you'd have to find a reason and convince him to get one and get approved."

"I can ask. It's worth a shot. He should be able to talk to Jaxton in private. It shouldn't raise any eyebrows since they're good friends."

"Do it. I'll push the approval through. Hopefully we hang around here long enough that you can see him. We can't exactly have you arrange a stay at a seedy motel on the planet." Taylor said that last part with a wicked grin, causing Nat's already deep blush to get darker.

"I don't think the Hrum hotels would accommodate you two." She paused for a few moments to think.

"I can request approval to visit one of the shipyards we salvaged when we attacked JOS. We cleared all the Hrum out of them and have been slowly re-pressurizing them. I don't see why that would raise any red flags. Lots of officers make field trips to see other weapons and ships."

"That's a great idea!" Nat jumped to her feet, and helped Taylor to hers. "I'll put in the request right away."

"Sounds good. If all else fails, we have to come up with another contingency. I hesitate to say it aloud because it leaves a bad taste in my mouth, but we may have to figure out a way to remove the captain once we confirm that he's infected."

"How do you plan to do that?"

"We only have a slim chance, I don't know how we can remove him, but they're going to scan all newcomers headed to the Arcon. I will figure out a way to watch and see what he does. It's not foolproof, but it may help me ease my conscience that currently says we are doing something bad."

"You're doing the right thing, Commander."

"I hope so."

With that she walked out of the gym, leaving Nat to her thoughts.

Nat just hoped that Brewster hadn't lost interest in her. They'd only been able to exchange occasional messages since they'd left the Trinity system. Chen was going to find this absolutely hilarious.

Commander Gemma Taylor considered herself an upstanding and loyal officer. She knew she was good at her job, and always dreamed of one day commanding a ship of her own. After she talked with Nat, for the first time, she was considering doing something underhanded and what could be considered mutinous. In her mind, the puzzle pieces that Nat had provided her with fit together too nicely for it all to be made up, fanciful musings of a junior officer with a fleet admiral for a brother. A lot of things clicked in her mind that were jumbled before this, and she was almost certain that that NIS spook Hadley had something to do with it. It made sense that he was infected. If a hostile alien race wanted to infiltrate a species, why not start with the intelligence agencies. What better way to stick your tendrils into an organization than taking over the group dedicated to operating in the shadows with the highest security clearances, and having their finger in almost every pie so to speak.

She hoped that whatever Hadley had done to the captain wasn't permanent, and that he could be saved. She respected Dixon, who had fought for her promotion and assignment on his ship, and even considered him a friend. The best way to save him, she thought, was to get him caught. Her perfect opportunity was coming up in just a few short hours. All of the captains were gathering on the admiral's battleship and, luckily for her, Jaxton had implemented strict scanning protocols for everyone boarding the ship. For a moment, she considered trying to warn another captain, but quickly dismissed the thought. There was no way she'd be able to convince one of them with a message. In addition, it could get easily intercepted, reducing a slim chance to none.

In her head, she was trying to figure out the most likely people subverted. If it was her, she'd have made sure that she knew of all communications, both in and out of the ship. That would take more than just one or two people to monitor and intercept, so she found it likely that the communications officers and their staff were likely infected. If that were the case, however, it likely also meant that a large portion of the medical staff and maybe even some of the marines were in the same boat.

She shook her head, there was no use in speculation. She and Nat both agreed that the best course of action was to get someone who they trusted the information and let them present it to Jaxton. Her shift was over, but she was walking as if on autopilot and her feet took her to the bridge. When she walked through the armored doors, she came face to face with fear.

"Very good evening, Commander," Captain Dixon said, wearing a neutral expression. "Your shift is over, is it not?"

"Um, yes sir, sorry sir—I just forgot something," Taylor replied, cursing herself internally for getting lost in her thoughts and not paying attention to where she was going.

"Well, very very well then," Dixon replied, moving out of her path. "Do not let me stop you then."

"Um—thank you, sir. Have a good night, sir."

"You also."

She walked past him, glancing over her shoulder. He was still standing in the same spot, unmoving, he didn't so much as turn to look. This odd behavior and speech helped her reaffirm that she was doing the right thing. She knew Dixon well and had worked with him for a long time. She was positive that he was not himself. She relaxed and kept walking.

"Commander," Dixon called out suddenly.

"Sir?" she replied, jerking in surprise.

"Tomorrow, when I am visiting with the other captains, I want you to go ahead and organize ship wide drills on fire suppression techniques. The crew's times in their past two have been repugnant."

"Aye, sir," Taylor replied, stifling her anxiety.

The Captain nodded and walked away stiffly.

Fire suppression drills? what could he possibly want that for? she thought to herself.

Walking quickly to her station, and grabbing some random items to make it look like she was there for a reason, she hustled off the bridge towards her quarters while pulling up the data from their past drills on her tab. It didn't make sense. The ship had their fastest two times during the drills they'd run last week. The captain was meticulous in reviewing the scores from their drills and would never assign unnecessary work for the crew if it didn't warrant it. Her pulse was suddenly pounding in her ears. Was he trying to send her a message? Was Dixon fighting a battle against whatever was inside of him? Had to be. She was positive now that he wasn't in complete control of his faculties. The new wrinkle in things was that she also believed that Dixon was in there somewhere fighting.

"Hold on, captain, we're coming to help you," she muttered.

The entity controlling Dixon had gotten stronger. The more he fought, the more ground it felt like he had to give up in order to score even the smallest victory. It was an odd feeling—fighting for control of your own body. He found that he could steer the entity towards certain lines of discussion, but he couldn't push it too hard or it would see what he was trying to do. At this point, he was pretty sure that his thoughts were his own, but that was where it ended. He just hoped that Taylor had picked up on his odd request and realized something was wrong. In addition he prayed that the admiral's medical teams would be able to intercept him before he did something bad on Jaxton's ship.

Chapter XV

In Jewel of Sunlight System on Battleship Arcon
Year 3326

Outside of the bumpy transition, the twenty-six hours that Jaxton and his fleet spent in Albion was uneventful. He made a mental note to ask Revalius if he knew why this Albion lane was so long, but hadn't gotten around to doing it yet. The scanning for nanites had also been completed and everyone aboard Arcon cleared. The science and medical teams found and used scanners on the rest of the ships of his fleet and they were deemed clear of nanites with the exception of two of the scout crewmembers, one of which who'd apparently snapped when the scanner had been brought to him. He even got a confirmation from Captain Dixon that said Hadley had been scanned. If anyone was infected Jaxton had hoped it would have been that scoundrel.

Dr. Casey had been very insistent that she be able to examine the crew as well as the two dead aliens, but relented and agreed to settle with just samples of their blood taken from them and carefully transported to their ship. Jaxton felt it wasn't worth the risk even though both he and his science team were almost certain that these nanites were not able to be transferred through the air. When asked by Jaxton why it was possible for the nanites infecting the Hrum to do so, she speculated that it was likely that something in human immune system prevented them from being infected the same way that the Hrum were, but she admitted that it was only a hypothesis, and it was one that could change as the enemy developed new nanites. That thought chilled Jaxton. He felt that getting that information up the ladder was of the utmost importance so that the NIS could plan accordingly and also work on developing a cure or other preventative measures. He had begun to think of the nanites as a sort of virus. Human history back to the early days of civilization were riddled with instances where a sickness caused utter panic among the general populace. Entire empires had collapsed, nations rioted, and other horrible things followed some of these events

As the viewscreen cleared and his ships arrived in the JOS system, Jaxton began to listen to the various stations give their reports. All seemed quiet and routine. Very little had changed from the time they had left until now. The only differences were a few additional ships outside of the original picket force were stationed strategically to block the Albion lanes.

"Sir, we're being hailed by the Battlecruiser Rubicon." Reported Lt. Johnson from her station. "Their captain is requesting a call with you."

"Thank you, Lieutenant. I'll take the call in my ready room."

Jaxton took one more look around the bridge to make sure there was nothing else that needed his immediate attention before unbuckling his harness and gesturing for Commander Bradley to come with him. They walked together to his office and booted up the screen. The face of a captain, not much younger than Jaxton, appeared on the screen. He thought the younger man looked familiar, but he could not place where he knew him from. He was the first to speak.

"Good morning, Admiral. I am Captain Pierce. Thank you for taking my call. I hope that your journey was uneventful, it's been anything but that here."

Jaxton figured the man was talking about the new attack on St. George, but they'd been out of the loop for a while now, so he wasn't entirely sure what the captain was talking about.

"Good morning, captain, it was nothing that we couldn't handle. We have some information to share with the NIS admiralty that is of the utmost importance, but we can talk about that after. What do you mean it's been eventful here? I didn't see any evidence of space combat or damaged ships when I arrived."

"Sir, sorry for the confusion. You'd be mostly correct about that. We had a small skirmish with a corvette size ship that entered the system about two days ago."

"Unfortunate, Captain, I trust that your—"

That's not what has been strange though. Since that time, the Hrum on the planet have been acting strangely."

"Strange how?" Drake asked.

The captain paused for a moment as if trying to gather his thoughts. "Sir, it's hard to explain," he said. "But it's almost like a switch flipped and they're suddenly almost *On* again."

"Go on..."

"As you are well aware, on Hrum planets, once we achieve all our strategic objectives, we leave and mostly leave the Hrum on the planet alone."

"Because they attack any humans they see, so we deemed it an unnecessary risk to leave troops stationed there..." Jaxton finished the captain's thought.

"Yes. Right, sir. They don't react to our ships in orbit, it's almost like they aren't even aware they're there, but we stay and observe them just in case."

"I'm still waiting for the other shoe to drop over here, Captain."

"Sorry, sir, right. Shortly after we destroyed that ship, it's like a switch was flipped and the Hrum all over the planet suddenly had somewhere to be. We have had to perform several airstrikes and even a small bombardment from space to keep Hrum away from areas we deemed as sensitive or a potential risk to us. They're returning to the military installations, the factories, and basically all the areas we leveled as a part of the demilitarization of the planet. In addition, a large number of them have disappeared into the forests and we haven't seen them since. It's nearly impossible to track them all with the resources we have on station." Jaxton shared a look with his XO, they too would have been confused if they hadn't known what they knew now.

"Captain, please hold for one moment," Jaxton said before muting his screen and turning to his commander. "Chris, please bring Revalius up here. I think he'll be able to fill in the blanks on a few of these behaviors."

"Yes, sir," Commander Bradley said as he walked out of the room speaking into his communicator.

Jaxton turned back towards his screen at the patiently waiting captain and unmuted him.

"Sorry for that, I called for someone who may be able to fill you in better. While we're waiting though, what do you mean by some *disappeared* into the forests?"

Captain Pierce looked a little confused, but replied anyway. "Large numbers of Hrum civilians marched into the forests. As you know this planet is heavily wooded and as a result we were concerned of hidden threats when we first assaulted the planet. Nothing materialized when we invaded, but if you recall from the briefings, it was one of the things of concern."

Jaxton nodded at that. He did recall that from the briefings that seemed like they had happened a long time ago. The way Pierce spoke of it, made it seem like he was there.

"I do recall that," Jaxton replied. "Have you sent a team to investigate?"

"We did, but they never returned. They were ambushed. We weren't able to retrieve them due to the heavy woods and they barely had time to say what was attacking them before they were all killed. They said they were being attacked by Hrum. I don't have enough marines to monitor a whole planet, so outside of a few additional flyby scouting missions and some drone fly-throughs, I haven't been able to focus on it."

"You did the right thing. The Hrum are definitely behaving oddly, but I think I can provide some clarity to that. Before I go any further, I would like you to keep an open mind with who I will be bringing in here to talk with you. You may be... well shocked by him."

A confusion clouded Captain Pierce's face, but he simply nodded.

They settled into an amicable silence for several moments before Captain Pierce spoke again.

"Sir, I would also just like to thank you."

"Thank *me*?"

"Yes sir, I don't know if you remember, but I was the captain on one of the cruisers from Admiral Kape's task force who survived the Hrum ambush. Admiral Bowden recommended me for promotion after the battle, and I was given command of this battlecruiser." The younger man puffed up slightly as he said it. He was clearly proud of his promotion. Cruisers weren't the most powerful or challenging of ships to operate. A promotion to a battlecruiser billet was a highly sought-after post.

Jaxton's face cleared as he recognized the man on the screen. "Oh, right!" Drake exclaimed. "You grew a beard."

"Aye, sir."

"I thought I recognized you, but I couldn't put my finger on it. Congratulations Captain on your promotion. I believe that Bowden made the correct decision in recommending you. You did your ship proud in the JOS operation."

"Thank you, sir. But we couldn't have done it without you."

Jaxton only nodded at that. He had heard the same thing so many times at this point that he had given up trying to argue that it wasn't all him who saved them.

Before anyone could say anything else, Commander Bradley arrived with Revalius flanked by two marines. Jaxton smiled slightly at the look of surprise on Pierce's face when Revalius walked into the picture.

"Um, sir...?"

"Relax, Captain."

"But, sir, that's a—he's a—"

This is Revalius. As you can tell, he's a Hrum, but he's not like the others who we've fought with over the past years. It's a bit much to explain all at once, but it will become clear in time."

Pierce opened his mouth several times, but no words came out.

Revalius, seemingly unperturbed by this, introduced himself through the translator, "I am Revalius Je, it is my pleasure to meet you."

Pierce pulled himself together after a moment. "It—um it's an honor to meet you as well..." he replied, before resorting back to his goldfish-like silence.

"Relax, Captain," Jaxton interjected. "Revalius, this is Captain Pierce. I invited Revalius here to make sense of some of the odd things you've been seeing in the forests on the planet. Please fill him in on what we just talked about."

"Aye sir."

Over the next fifteen minutes, Pierce brought up images of Hrum civilians disappearing into the forests in large swathes. Revalius' face showed mixed emotions, but Jaxton, who was unfamiliar with Hrum biology, wasn't sure what to make of the looks.

"Revalius, do you know what they're doing?" Jaxton asked.

Revalius didn't reply for a moment. "Admiral, I believe they are heading towards the stasis bunkers," he finally said in a measured tone. "We scattered them throughout some of our planets."

"Stasis bunkers?"

"Yes, so my crew was able to maintain a watch in the system where we met you. Via a form of stasis where we sleep and it slows—"

"I know what stasis is. I'm asking why you have stasis bunkers on the surface of a planet."

"When the war with the Karathians got bad, we began implementing doomsday protocols where we built bunkers that we could essentially hide in and hopefully remain safe from nanites."

"Yet we see clearly infected Hrum heading straight to them? What's that mean?"

"I do not know, Captain. Very few were aware of these bunkers' existence, and those who were informed or found out were put into stasis and not allowed to leave."

Captain Pierce jumped back into the conversation.

"So these…Karrr…r*athians*, what are they?"

Jaxton quickly replied. "Essentially, those in control of the Hrum on the planet."

"In control?"

"Yes, in control. I don't want to spend the next few hours explaining this to you, but essentially the Hrum, like Revalius, were… or *are* at war with another alien race they call the Karathians. They infected a vast majority of the Hrum population with a form of nanites who essentially turn them into the Hrum that we have fought with for the past five years. Pierce nodded at that, but said nothing.

Revalius continued, "Admiral, I believe that the most likely thing that happened is that the Karathian recently learned of the bunkers and a Karathian puppeteer ordered the civilians to attack or infect them."

"Are they protected?"

"Yes, it's unlikely civilians or even trained soldiers would be able to successfully assault the bunkers. I believe that it means that there is a good chance that there might still be uninfected Hrum on the planet! The only thing that doesn't make sense is why are they going after them now?"

"Revalius, what does a Karathian ship look like?" Captain Pierce asked. "We destroyed a small ship, roughly corvette class, that entered the system before all of this kicked off."

"They look largely like our ships. We traded heavily with them before they attacked my people and we sold many ships to them—" Revalius looked at the slightly grainy image that Pierce had pulled up and continued. "Ah, that's a luxury transport. It's very possible there was a Karathian puppeteer onboard. He must have sent orders before you destroyed it."

Jaxton nodded thoughtfully. "This's all very interesting news and we are going to have to investigate eventually, but if the bunkers are safe for now, I think we need to focus on the Karathian attacking St. George."

"Actually sir, there are several other attacks across NIS space," Captain Pierce replied. "At least five. I received a report that Sapporo was under assault. There was a dreadnought in orbit there, so I believe it's unlikely it has fallen, but I don't think we'll be receiving any more messages for the time being. The last message said we had seven more ships including a battleship en-route to us, but they've not made an appearance yet."

"When were they supposed to arrive?"

"Today, sir."

"Well let's not panic yet. Even if they were attacked, seven NIS ships are no pushover when it comes to a fight. Have you had any news regarding St. George?"

"Only that the initial NIS response was rebuffed. After that, nothing."

"No orders for us? Has anything come through outside of the initial message?"

"No sir. After not hearing from you, I believe that command thought you were missing."

"That makes sense. I think it's time for us to get back into the fight. I can tell you for sure that one fleet that was on its way here to attack you is no longer a threat. We made sure of that." Jaxton's face split with a wolfish grin before he continued. "I find it unlikely there will be many more, so I think we have an opportunity to counter."

Pierce, who was now also smiling, replied, "I like the sound of that, sir."

The next morning, Jaxton found himself in a conference room with all the captains from his fleet as well as the ones from the picket forces over JOS. His medical staff had run each of them through the scanner that Revalius' second-in-command had helped develop and they all came back clean from any nanites.

He was about to begin the meeting when Captain Dixon hustled into the room. "Sorry I'm late, sir. Had one and two administrative tasks to go ahead and finish."

A frown clouded Jaxton's face with Dixon's statement, but he waved the tardy captain to his seat.

"No worries, we're just getting started. Latest intelligence indicates that besides St. George, there are at least five other NIS or Hrum planets under assault. We only have confirmation on those five, but I find it highly likely more abound and they were just not able to alert us. I retain confidence in the strength of our people, we'll hold the line from the invaders. Before I go any further, I want to address the elephant in the room." He gestured to Revalius who was standing over his shoulder. "I already shared our intelligence briefings with each of you, so you at least should be familiar with who this is. Let me introduce you to Revalius. He is both Hrum and not our enemy. I invited him here because he can provide us with valuable intelligence when it comes to dealing with the Karathians"

Murmuring arose around the room as the assembled captains eyed the alien suspiciously. Was this really the hated enemy they fought so hard against all these years? Right here in front of them? Sitting here now like some VIP or something....

Jaxton let it go on for several moments before quieting them down and continuing. “As I was saying, I believe we're relatively safe here. My fleet utterly destroyed the force that was coming to assault this system. Due to this, I believe we have an opportunity to set up the Karathians with a surprise of our own. The question becomes, which system do we assist? I want to open the floor to discussion now.”

The room, which had been quiet, quickly transformed into several loud conversations and the noise level filled the space. The various captains shouted their opinions and discussed what they thought they should do. They were relatively isolated on JOS as they had mostly empty systems or other Hrum planets in between them and NIS planets. It was pretty quickly decided that nobody wanted to go protect a Hrum planet, so the consensus seemed to be leaning towards returning to Sapporo to regroup. Jaxton was racking his brain in an attempt to make an argument for returning to St. George, but in order to do that, he'd be traveling through several NIS and occupied Hrum worlds that very likely could be under attack, or even in enemy control again.

Revalius, who remained quiet during most of this, suddenly spoke. “Admiral, I know this is a lot to ask, but may I see your star maps of the Albion lanes overlaid with the planets?”

The room went completely silent, the entire room staring at the alien, like he was an... alien. It felt wrong to share their star maps with an alien, even one who claimed to be friendly.

Dixon was the first to speak up. “Sir, that is not a very good idea. How do we know he can be trusted?”

Several other captains, including Captain Pierce and Mitchell, shouted their agreement with Dixon. Jaxton didn't particularly like the idea either, but he raised his hands to quiet the assembled group.

“Why do you want that?” the admiral asked.

“I know it is a lot to ask, but I believe that you are not using all known Albion lanes. You said it yourself to me when we talked in the system you found me in. The route in which your planet of St. George was attacked from my species in the first place was occurred through an Albion lane that you were not aware of. It is my understanding that your people were caught off guard because you were unaware an Albion lane even existed from that direction."

"That's true, but we have upgraded our drives since then," Jaxton replied. "We can detect them better than before."

"I acknowledge that, Admiral. You asked why the Albion lane to the Twilight of Moon system was special. I told you it was not, which appeared to confuse you. It made me think that your species is not aware of any other lanes that are that long of which there are many. There is nothing special to my knowledge of these because we detect them the same way we detect the rest of them. I believe Arama, my second, can point out more of these lanes you have not yet discovered."

"Or he can use the information he sees to report to his people so they know where we might attack from!" yelled Dixon from near the back of the room, which again erupted into conversation.

Jaxton and Revalius held eye contact for a long time without saying anything. He had no idea what the alien was thinking, but the potential of learning new routes was enticing to him.

"Quiet! I can barely hear myself think!" yelled Jaxton. "Speak one at a time or not at all. Anyone who speaks out of turn will be removed from the meeting." The room instantly went quiet. "Now… who wants to speak first?"

Several of the assembled captains raised their hands, Jaxton picked on Captain Mitchell.

"Sir, I understand you don't want to return to Sapporo, but how can we risk our ships by traveling through unsurveyed routes, if they even exist?" Mitchell asked. "And I must say, I don't feel comfortable taking the advice of an alien, especially one who's the same species as the ones we are currently at war with."

Several other captains echoed his sentiments with nods and grunts. Jaxton only nodded and selected another captain who had her hand raised.

"Sir, is there any way we can limit what he sees? Pick several of the systems around JOS and ask him where there are Albion lanes. We could also test if he's telling the truth with what's currently there."

There was some agreement to that idea as well from around the room.

"What's your name, Captain?" Jaxton replied.

"Winters, sir."

"Winters?"

"Captain *Joy* Winters, sir."

"Any relation to Admiral Winters?"

"Aye, sir. My uncle, sir."

"Then I'm sorry for your loss, but I really like your idea. Anybody else?"

There was more conversation around the room for nearly an hour. It ranged from giving Revalius their complete trust, to removing him from the meeting altogether, to bringing him up on war crimes. Eventually Jaxton, being the one in charge, made the executive decision and went with Captain Winter's idea. He called up Dr. Casey and her team had them prepare the star maps for Revalius and his second's eyes. Because Revalius was in the meeting, when his second-in-command Arama arrived, he simply asked her to give Jaxton whatever he required.

Dr. Casey presented Arama with a star map that showed four Albion lanes out of the system and not much else. Jaxton gave control of the screen to Revalius and asked him to identify where each of the lanes went. Without a word, he turned to his second, Arama, and let her manipulate the screen. The first thing she did, after scrunching her face, was add the fifth Albion lane to the JOS system. Jaxton had asked Dr. Casey to hide it initially as a sort of test. It didn't guarantee that the Hrum were being honest, but it was a start. Arama clearly knew the Albion lanes as well as they, perhaps better. The assembled captains watched as she consulted her own tablet and populated the star map of the systems surrounding them. One thing that Jaxton did that raised some eyebrows was that he added the location of St. George and instructed her to navigate to the system to the best of her abilities. They watched as she built the map. They closely matched the NIS maps that Dr. Casey was showing only to Jaxton, but included several additional lanes. It seemed the technology that the NIS had developed during the Hrum war to detect Albion lanes wasn't quite as good as they thought it was.

Roughly thirty minutes later, a complicated star map emerged that would have looked like a confusing spiderweb to most, but to seasoned spacers, it was just another map. One thing it did show that excited Jaxton was that they only needed four jumps to go to St. George and most of them were very short jumps. The only occupied system that it required they go through was the Water of Twilight system. In fact, they would actually be traveling to St. George through the very lane that the Hrum attacked them through in the first place—a sort of amusing twist on the situation that Jaxton appreciated.

Arama indicated that there was an additional Albion lane connecting them to WOT in the same system that Jaxton had first been promoted in when Admiral Bannon had lost his life to the Hrum ambush. Dr. Casey had indicated that they had no knowledge of such a lane, but the more Jaxton thought about it, the more it made sense to him. They had been ambushed in a system that should have been empty and the NIS had not bothered to do a super detailed scan of the otherwise empty system. Simply put, the Hrum should not have been in a position to ambush them if there was no other way in or out of that system. Jaxton had not taken the time to think about it before as it was a chaotic time.

"Dr. Casey, Is it possible?" Jaxton asked.

"Yes, sir. Very possible. We tend to focus our detection equipment on systems that actually contain a habitable planet or have some other use. That system is a dead and empty system with few minerals, so it's likely we only did a cursory investigation when we explored it."

"Well, Captains, what are your thoughts? One at a time, no more yelling please."

Captain Dixon was the first to raise his hand. "Sir, I still believe this is not a very good idea. Even if the alien's words are completely true, do you really want to risk an entire task force jumping through an Albion lane that we have not scanned or sent probes through?"

Jaxton nodded and replied, "A valid concern. What are the chances that the Albion lane is dangerous to our ships, Dr. Casey?"

"Honestly sir, near zero. The worst that will likely happen is the system doesn't go where Arama claims and we have to turn around. I don't want to spend a long time talking about it, but essentially the existence of Albion lanes nearly guarantees that it goes somewhere. It's just a matter of where. The biggest threat would be planets that had some sort of catastrophic event, or black holes forming, neither of which are particularly likely."

"Thank you, Doctor. Anybody else?"

Captain Pierce was the next to raise his hand. "Sir, I'm with you. You have not steered me or my crew wrong yet. If you believe returning to St. George is the correct course of action, then I'm in agreement."

The young captain's faith in Jaxton was quite touching, even if in Jaxton's opinion it was not earned. The volume in the room rose as more captains muttered their agreement with Pierce. It seemed that he wasn't the only one with total faith in Jaxton. As he scanned the room, he saw that Dixon was one of the few holdouts. He thought that he'd earned Dixon's respect by this point, but he was still willing to disagree with Jaxton which was probably a good thing. The last thing admiral needed when crafting a complex mission plan was a bunch of yes men, or women. Although, he did notice that Dixon's behavior had been a little bit odd since the operation in the unknown system. Jaxton was wondering if he was fighting some demons from losing crewmembers or if something else had happened. As much as he hated it, he thought that it might be a good idea to chat with Dixon about it. He made another mental note to talk with the captain at the next opportunity.

"Thank you everyone, I appreciate the support," Drake said to wrap up the meeting. "We will move forward with the plan to liberate St. George by traveling through the WOT Albion lane. There was a picket force in the WOT, but if St. George was attacked, I find it likely that WOT is also under Karathian control. We'll need a plan for that system as well." He checked his watch before continuing. We will spend the next three hours resupplying and organizing before moving out. We'll only be leaving a single destroyer here to monitor the system. I don't know what to expect, but I'm willing to take the risk that this system will be left alone in the near future. Any questions?"

He looked around the room for a few seconds.

"Very good. Thank you all for coming. You are dismissed."

Chapter XVI

On St. George near Wreathsburg
Year 3326

After Ryan had given his speech to the locals, it didn't take long for them to pack up and move to a new location. They camouflaged their trucks and the gunship and walked several miles to where the locals had holed up. The region of the planet they were on was heavily forested and mountainous, and as such, there were many caves and mines that dotted the countryside. One of these many mines was where the locals had taken shelter.

The main entrance was not all that impressive. It looked dilapidated, like one strong breeze away from caving in, but the locals marched through without hesitation. Once inside, Ryan's opinion changed completely. The cave was lit up and had high ceilings, the opposite of what he expected. Ryan was convinced they could have stored an entire wing of gunships in the room. It was enormous.

As if he was expecting Ryan's next question, Dale spoke. "This mine was used by the resistance during the first invasion. After we kicked the scumsucking Hrum off the first time, we continued to build on it, added amenities, stored food and weapons, and prepared. Turns out that was a good idea, we just needed it sooner than we thought."

Ryan saw that they even had a motor pool of sorts. They had a couple of old, but serviceable shuttles, and some armored trucks.

"How'd you get those in here?" Ryan asked, pointing at the vehicles.

"Oh those. Well after the first war, we collapsed the old main entrance and excavated a larger one on the south face of this mountain. It's very well-hidden and we only use it in an emergency. We figured it'd be best to not advertise our presence any more'n we hafta."

"What about the power?"

"The mine had one of them old fusion generators that we got runnin'. We're afraid to push 'er too heavy, so we don't run any more than we got to, but it's enough to power the lights and charge power cells for our vehicles."

"This is incredible," Izabella said, jumping into the conversation. "You have done your people proud."

Ryan nodded in agreement.

Dale showed them the rest of the cavern before escorting them to an area with several large tables, maps of the area spread around. He had sent several of his men ahead to prepare an area for them to brainstorm ideas. Ryan took a good long look at the maps. They were much more detailed than what his men had. A lot of the lines he assumed weren't marked roads, but rather local trails and game paths. This would be incredibly useful when it came time to get into position. They could keep their forces off the main roads until they were nearly at their destination which would allow for them to surprise the enemy.

Ryan listened to a couple of the local men who had introduced themselves as woodsmen explain the surrounding area in great detail, giving Ryan a better picture of what he was looking at. They worked together to tally what forces, weapons, and other tools they had in order to figure out how they would assault the two targets.

Based on Marvin's recon, the radio tower was the more sparsely guarded facility, while the hospital held more unknown factors. They couldn't predict what sort of welcome they'd get from the captured men and women, and whether or not they could treat them as hostiles. They also weren't sure how many Hrum were inside, or even what parts of the hospital they were utilizing. The locals begrudgingly agreed that Marvin and Ryan should lead the two assaults. What they lacked in knowledge of the surrounding area, they more than made up for in experience in combat.

They agreed to essentially split their militia in half, with Ryan taking Corporal V and Kim, while Marvin took the newly promoted Sgt. O'Leary and Veron squads along with his ghostees. Dale and his close circle of men were also with Marvin. They were taking two different tactics when it came to the assaults. In an attempt to draw away extra Hrum from the broadcast center, they were going to attack the hospital first. The militia not directly involved in the assault were going to attempt to ambush any Hrum that tried to reinforce the hospital by laying in wait between the two targets. The terrain of the region again worked in their favor as there were plenty of locations to conduct their ambush. Ryan left those details up to the locals who seemed excited at the idea. He did instruct Corporal Kim to give them pointers as he had shown a devious streak when it came to planning ambushes during their training. Ryan had forgotten once again to ask Kim about his past, but he was too busy at the moment to take the time now to do it. He was far too knowledgeable to be a simple corporal.

Marvin and Dale planned to attack in two separate groups. Extensive underground tunnels connected the hospital to the university for the wintertime when the weather got dangerous to be outside. It allowed for back and forth transit for students and staff alike without going outside. Dale was convinced that these tunnels would be mostly unguarded as they were closed off due to some flooding and collapses that had not yet been repaired since the first invasion. If they could get eyes inside the facility quietly, it would greatly benefit the rest of their men during their attack.

Marvin unhappily agreed that as the commander of the assault, he should not be included as one of the men infiltrating the facility, and that one of the local woodsmen would go in his stead. They had no idea what sorts of signals the Hrum could intercept, but they did know that their military comm sets did work within a few miles of each other, so they'd at least be able to communicate in an emergency. Ryan was hopeful that they'd be able to disable or destroy whatever was doing such a good job blanketing comms all over the planet when they assaulted the station.

The hospital and university existed at the end of a long valley. The rear of it was guarded by a fierce river too dangerous to cross unless you happened to have a guide who had been crossing it in secret for years. Ryan had pegged the man as a smuggler of some sort, but this was not the time or place to worry *what* he was smuggling. Marvin's ghostees and their guide would cross there, and were preparing to leave right away as they had a much longer journey that was not accessible using a vehicle.

There was only one main road into the valley, but it was possible to sneak in using the old dug roads. Marvin and Dale would lead their men down these until they were only about 100 meters from the main entrance where they'd begin their assault. The Hrum, while showing more intuition and tactical awareness than before, were still arrayed in a fairly predictable layout that Marvin believed would allow them to take out a significant number before they'd even be able to return fire. The facility was not built to keep people in or out, which was useful for them. They'd be able to take down many of the Hrum from the cover of the woods before they had to expose themselves to cross into the facility. They projected that there were at least fifty Hrum, but they had no idea how many humans, or if they were even friendly. Marvin made sure that all his men were wearing some sort of identifier so that they'd not accidentally shoot their own men if things went bad.

Once inside, they'd scour the facility for clues to what the Hrum were doing and hopefully put a stop to it. Then they'd attempt to release the prisoners, and send them through the tunnels to the university where they'd hole up and attempt to make a stand for any Hrum that came their way. Their smuggler was arranging for them to escape out the back way, but it would take time as it wasn't the easiest of treks and there were sure to be injured civilians. These Hrum hadn't shown an inclination to simply bombard their targets before, so Marvin was hoping that remained the case. If it came down to it and more Hrum showed up to come after them, he would order a retreat to the university which was a heavily built building that he felt they could hole up in fairly well.

The plan was that shortly after Marvin began his attack, Ryan and his men would commence one of their own. If any of the Hrum stationed in the broadcast center left, they would wait until the ambush was tripped before beginning the assault. It wouldn't be ideal if the Hrum just simply turned around and headed back in their direction when they got alerted of an attack. The fence around the facility would be easy to cut, and the station itself was a fairly normal commercial-type building that had a large ground-level presence, before the center jutted towards the sky, built around the large antenna. The broadcast center itself was near the top of the building and that was Ryan's ultimate target. Izabella, who still refused to be left behind, was to stay with Ryan who planned to stay near the back of the assault. The locals would be conducting an assault from the West, while Ryan and his militia would be coming from the East. Corporal V and Ryan would be acting as the bodyguards, while Kim's and Corporal V's men along with the a few other select locals would be in the lead. About one hundred local militia would be conducting the assault to the east while Ryan and his thirty or so men snuck in from the east. The plan was largely similar to that when Ryan infiltrated Chomper's estate not that long ago. He was well aware his only casualties on that mission came from the role the locals were playing which made him unhappy, but his men were much more suited to the task of infiltrating the facility, and he was not willing to let Izzy out of his sight or significantly reduce the number of men guarding her.

The plan called for the festivities to begin the following evening as that gave them the best opportunity to flee if everything went to hell. The razorback would be on standby to support if any Hrum shuttles or other aircraft crashed the party. It was also there to evacuate Izabella if need be. Ryan always hated planning, because it could go wrong in an instant and everything that they planned became irrelevant. At least plans put everyone on the same page, if only momentarily.

The locals had built some modular housing within the cavern, and Ryan, due to his elevated status as the monarch's bodyguard and commander, was given his own room directly next to Izabella's. He was completely exhausted. They had spent hours going over every detail and possible scenario that they could think of, and he was just hoping that what they were doing was enough. Even his most experienced militia were relatively untested in the field of battle and that made him nervous. His feelings for Izabella were also making all of this more difficult. He just wanted to keep her safe, and protect her. The responsibility of trying to do that and lead his men at the same time was getting to him. He wanted to go over to her room, sweep her into his arms, and kiss her. He wanted to tell her that she was like no woman he had ever met before, and that he was in love with her. Unfortunately for him, in his mind, there was no way that a simple grunt like himself would ever live up to the standards expected of the monarch's consort. He settled moodily onto his bunk when he heard a light tap at the door.

"Come in."

Almost as if she knew he was thinking about her, Izabella carefully opened the door to his room, stepped inside, and closed it behind her. She looked beautiful, even wearing a rough spun nightgown that one of the kind local housewives had given her. Ryan's hands practically twitched with desire to scoop her into his arms.

"Your Maj… Izzy, is something wrong?" he inquired.

"No, it's just—I wanted to talk to you." she replied. "May I sit?"

"Of course," Ryan said as he sat up on the bunk.

There were no chairs, so he patted the spot next to him on the bunk. She sat down next to him, her leg lightly touching him as she got comfortable. He was far too aware of that contact, and he felt his heart begin to pound. *She's the leader of a nation, she wants nothing to do with you,* he thought as she said nothing. They sat there for several minutes, and said nothing before she leaned her head onto his shoulder and wrapped her arm around his waist. He found himself doing the same.

"How do you deal with ordering people to do something that you know could very well get them killed?" she finally asked.

Ryan had this very same thought many times, and it was actually his father who had finally given him a piece of advice that had gotten him through it. "I moved up quickly once I joined the marines," he told her. "I dropped onto Okuraha during the uprisings as a private, and left as a sergeant. It started with a promotion to corporal when my squad's corporal was killed, and then eventually sergeant when my men and I did some pretty stupid stuff that saved some people."

"Stupid stuff?"

"Yeah sometimes the craziest action in battle, stuff that would be seen as insane in regular life, gets you medals and promotions. I was fairly lucky at first. I had lost friends, and comrades, but nobody I actually was in charge of. I had never ordered them to do something that got them killed."

"So glad you were always lucky," the monarch whispered, nuzzling in closer.

"Well that all changed near the end of the uprisings, only days before we were sent home. I lost two soldiers who I had ordered to go and scout a position that we knew the enemy was likely occupying. When they radioed for help, I told them we would do our best to get to them, but we were overwhelmed, and they were captured, and then eventually killed. Their deaths weighed on me for a long time."

He stopped for a moment. It had been a long time since he'd thought about that and it was tough to speak about. Izabella straightened up, then took her hands and cupped his face. A look of concern and caring. He sighed again, and gently took her hands into his own before continuing.

"I did what I had to. There was nothing else I could have done in the situation. I began to spiral. We were sent home shortly after and I began to drink too much, and get into fights for no real reason. Overall, I was just being a piss-poor example for the rest of my men. My father is actually the one who saved me from my own self-pity. At that point my father and I hadn't spoken in several years. He was disappointed in my choice to join the marines, and thought I was throwing away my opportunity to excel at the academy. He found me at a bar while I was on leave and was deep into the cups. He sat down next to me and I barely acknowledged his presence. He said nothing, but ordered a beer. For a long time we just sat there, quietly, me ignoring him and him saying nothing.

"He finally said, 'Son, I know we aren't on the best of terms, but let me tell you a story.'

"Over the next hour, he told me about how he'd lost several thousand men and women under his command during the Pekanee Uprisings. He told me how his XO had gotten speared by a piece of shrapnel, pinning him to his station and he'd watched the life fade from his eyes as the man died. He talked about the fighter pilots he'd ordered to their death in an attempt to disable the AA gun emplacements mutilating his fleet. He stopped counting the deaths under his command as he'd reached a thousand. He said it took him a long time, but he got through it by knowing he'd done his best to honor their sacrifices by fighting as hard as he possibly could to keep them alive even when he knew it was impossible to save everyone. He gave his absolute heart and soul into everything he did, because he could not live with himself if he didn't. Essentially, he can live with the decisions, because he knows if he makes the hard decisions, he'll be saving someone else from having to make them and that was enough for him."

"So what did you do next?" Izabella said as tears flowed freely down her face, the emotions of the story getting to her.

Ryan, smiling slightly at the memory, replied, "I told him to go to hell, and then I stormed out of the bar."

Izabella's eyes widened at that, but before she could say anything, he continued.

"The next morning, I called him and asked if he and mom would mind if I came home for dinner that evening. It was the first time I'd been home and only the second time I'd seen either of my parents since dropping out of the academy. My relationship with my dad isn't where we were before all of that happened, but the massive chasm that had grown between us has begun to heal. He has mostly accepted, I think, that I was not cut out for the academy, and I've accepted, mostly, that he may have been right about my abilities to lead people. Although I'll be damned if I admit that to him."

Izabella giggled at that. Ryan never got tired of hearing her laugh.

She held his gaze, her beautiful auburn hair and green eyes were positively captivating. Before his brain could tell him otherwise, he leaned forward and kissed her. She enthusiastically returned the kiss, and he pulled her close. For a few moments, the only thing that mattered was their embrace. Unfortunately, his brain regained control and he realized what he was doing. He jumped up from the bed as if he was being scalded.

"Izz—I'm sorry, I can't. *You* can't. I'm not worthy of you. You're a noble, leader of a planet. I'm just… me. It wasn't appropriate for me to kiss you."

"We've kissed before," she said, a lopsided grin on her lips and blush in her cheeks. "You reacted in a very similar manner if I recall."

"Yes, but… that's different," he replied unconvincingly.

She just sat there unmoving. "You should be with a nobleman. Someone of royal blood, with ties to this planet. Not a foreigner who is nothing more than a ground pounder."

"By your own words, that's selling yourself a bit short don't ya think? What if I don't care about any of that."

"You should."

"Telling me what to do now?" she said teasingly. "What if I want to hear you say what I think you want to say."

"Your majesty…"

"Izabella."

"Izabella….I—"

"Don't make me order you to do it," she replied with a mischievous look on her face. "I am sorta your boss now after all."

The tension deflated from Ryan's shoulders as she said that and an exasperated laugh escaped him. She held his eyes for several moments, giving him a gesture as if saying "I'm waiting."

He stomped around back and forth in the small room for a minute or two before relenting.

"I love you. I have loved you from the moment I met you. You're like nobody I have ever met before. You're strong, determined, and you continue to amaze me every day with your mind and beauty."

"I meant order you to kiss me, not rant at me…" she said, holding back a giggle.

"I want to tell you everything about my past, my family, my friends, and I want you to be my future… Is that… is that what you wanted to hear?"

Izabella said nothing, she simply stood up and turned as if to leave. Ryan thought he'd done something wrong when she stopped when she reached the door.

She paused, let her nightgown fall to the floor, and replied simply, "Yes," before locking the door.

The next morning, nobody said anything when Ryan and Izabella left his quarters together. Ryan refused to make eye contact with Marvin because it was too early to deal with any of his lewd humor. If anything, the wonderful night he'd spent with Izabella only made it harder for him to deal with the risks of taking her into danger, but he knew that there'd be no convincing her otherwise.

Checking his watch, they had a few hours before they had to move out. Ryan sat alone as Izabella had gone to talk to some of the locals and wish them luck. Ryan had tasked Corporal V to keep an eye on her as he got his breakfast. Marvin finally made his appearance and sat down next to him and quietly began eating. Ryan was perplexed. He was braced for the onslaught of lewd jokes, but it seemed that none were forthcoming. Could it be he had matured overnight? Ryan eyed Marvin, who seemed totally unaware of Ryan's gaze and was happily munching away on his breakfast. Ryan looked around to make sure he wasn't being pranked, before finally turning back towards Marvin.

"No jokes? No lewd comments? Nothing?"

In very un-Marvin-like fashion, he slowly lifted his gaze away from his food and calmly replied, "You've found a good one, Commander," before returning to his food.

Ryan still couldn't figure out if Marvin was messing with him or not, perhaps teeing him up for a mammoth zinger, but before he could dwell on it for much longer, Dale and several of the other locals walked up to them.

"We're locked and loaded, boss," Dale said. "Our scouts came back last night, and it looks like nothin's really changed."

Ryan nodded at that, bringing his focus back on the mission. "Excellent, hopefully it stays that way and we can pull this off without a hitch."

"Hopes for the lucky who can afford it," Dale replied in his monotone drawl before turning and walking away.

Ryan hadn't really been able to get a read on the man, but Marvin seemed to like him, which was obvious by the massive grin on his face.

"Shut up, Captain. Don't you have somewhere to be?"

Marvin said nothing, but stood up, saluted and walked away with his overly formal mocking strut.

I think I need to discipline him for that sometime. He's been doing that a lot lately. Ryan thought before getting up and heading towards his own command. There was still quite a bit to do and he had to check over his and Izabella's kit to make sure it wasn't missing anything. It was going to be a long day....

Marvin and his men were waiting just inside the treeline outside the university hospital. It looked just as Dale's men had said, with two roving patrols around the building and several groups of guards situated around the facility exterior. What he didn't mention but was painfully obvious to Marvin, the guards weren't positioned by someone who was an expert on guarding a target. Had they more time and Marvin had been able to look for himself, he'd have likely changed the plan of attack to take out small groups quietly in an attempt to sneak into the facility without being noticed. He currently had no idea whether or not his ghostees and their guide made it into the facility, and they would not be contacting him until after the fireworks kicked off.

Checking his watch, the marine captain saw that it was almost time. They'd start by trying to simultaneously take out all the roving patrols and guards, which he thought was very doable, considering there were over seventy rifles pointed at what amounted to about sixteen targets. They estimated that there were around fifty additional Hrum in and around the facility, so they had them outnumbered, but many of his "soldiers" weren't even wearing body armor and had little to no military training. Normally, with a group of fully trained troops, he'd be very confident, and the benefit of surprise couldn't be overstated. What made him nervous was that he had no idea how his mostly untrained troops would hold up when something went wrong and they had to adjust on the fly.

Checking his watch again, he saw that his sniper teams would be making contact any moment now, and he prepared his own rifle. He was relegated towards the rear of the formation as their commander, so he didn't have any targets that were an easy shot, but it still paid to be ready. When he was about to start wondering if they were going to shoot, a booming report from a high-caliber rifle rang out. It was closely followed by a heavy weight of fire from his other men who were waiting for the first shot. He saw that at least ten of the Hrum that were in plain sight were down, and the few that were remaining were seeking cover in a panic.

"All units advance," he ordered. "Don't outrun your support."

Marvin hadn't had time to teach the finer points of infantry warfare, but he stressed the importance of fighting as a team, which the locals and his own militia seemed to understand quite well. He watched proudly for a moment as Veron and O'Leary advanced smoothly with their squads. He'd also decided against splitting his teams up as they had worked together and he felt it would be more effective than attempting to integrate some of the locals into their teams.

In short order, the remaining six Hrum were neutralized and his teams were making ingress into the facility. There were three main entrances that they were targeting. Marvin followed his militia through the central doorway into a massive lobby absolutely covered in marble. The hospital had been donated to the people by one of the local nobles, and he'd apparently spared no expense in making it overly grandiose. Their target was the basement as he came to the conclusion that the most likely place for them to store prisoners would be there, so it was best they attempt to save them as quickly as possible.

Over the mic, he suddenly heard the voice of one of his ghostees. "Sir, we made it through the tunnels."

"Outstanding."

"They were mostly blocked, but we managed to slip through. We set charges in case we need to xfil through there more quickly. We haven't run into any of the enemy yet."

"Roger that, good job. Stay put and hold the tunnel entrance. If we end up going that way, we'll have you blow it."

"Aye, sir."

The short-range comms were apparently choosing to work, which was good Marvin thought. They'd been spotty since the Hrum had arrived. There were a few scattered firefights, but no major engagements until they reached one of the three sets of stairs leading down to the basement. One of his other teams had indicated that they had seen several Hrum troops running down the stairs and they were currently holding position.

Being in the northern outskirts of the planet, the hospital was only three stories tall, but there were three additional levels below the ground floor. Most of the upstairs was reserved for patient rooms and recovery wards, while the downstairs held most of the science labs and surgery centers. Marvin ordered his men to stay put until the other teams finished their sweep of the upstairs. He was very disappointed that they didn't have any sort of surveillance equipment or spy drones that would help him take a look without risking the lives of one of his men. He'd just received the all clear from the upstairs, which was nearly empty, when he heard the sound of automatic gunfire, and then shortly thereafter, a panicked voice over his comm set.

"Captain, they're coming up!"

"Head them off," Marvin ordered.

"They're coming…"

"Stand your ground, solider—" Marvin growled.

"There's hundreds of them, sir!" the soldier yelled over comms. "They're everywhere."

Marvin was just about to ask what he meant, when suddenly the men guarding his own staircase began shooting. He peeked into the hallway where the stairs were situated and was shocked to see armored Hrum soldiers waving forward smaller unarmored figures carrying rifles. They began firing wildly the instant they saw Marvin's men. He quickly realized the horror: humans!

They were fighting humans.

Another cry arose over the comms where it appeared his third team also was engaging the targets billowing up from below. He felt a momentary pang of guilt, but they had discussed the possibility of hostile humans, so it hadn't caught him completely by surprise. He only hoped that his other teams, who were likely firing upon their family and friends, would be able to fight.

Bullets whizzed and whistled over his head as more of the unarmored humans poured up the stairs. For now it seemed like they were able to hold their own, as there was no apparent strategy outside of their blind charge. He knew ammo would be an issue at some point, but they had brought as much as they could carry in case they had to hole up somewhere. He saw one of his men go down, and get quickly dragged back into cover by his teammate. Looking over at Sgt. O'Leary, he saw that she was preparing to pull out an HE grenade. She briefly looked over toward him as if asking permission before arming it, and hucking it towards the staircase. It took one hop and exploded, scattering body parts all around. The flow was only momentarily abated before it picked up again. Marvin tried to catch a glance of the armored Hrum, but he didn't see them. Just like the Hrum he'd fought in the past, they charged forward mindlessly, making him wonder if there was something or someone controlling them. The only thing that made sense to him was that the humans were being controlled in some way. The more he thought about it, the more it made sense that the armored Hrum were in control. They had been waving the humans forward before they disappeared.

Opening a channel to his entire command, he said, "If you see anything not human, make it your first target. I think the humans are being controlled by the Hrum soldiers."

Nobody replied, as they were too busy attempting to hold their positions, but he hoped they'd take his words into account.

From his left, Corporal Veron spoke up. "Sir, I think the two coming up the stairs first managed to make it into the room directly to the east of the stairs."

Marvin nodded, it made sense.

"O'Leary..."

"Sir..."

"Got any more of those HEs?"

She had been listening in and quickly picked up on what he wanted and nodded. Getting into position, she and one of the members of her squad armed and threw two grenades into the room closest to the stop of the stairwell. Marvin watched with interest as one bounced off the corner and missed, while the other deflected directly into the open doorway. There was a slightly muted thump as they went off and almost as if a switch was flipped, the flow of enemy fighters abated and all gunfire from their staircase subsided and it was momentarily quiet.

"Sir, it looks like we killed 'em all," Veron said, peering over his cover, scanning for more threats.

"Yes it does," Marvin mused. "Nice throw, O'Leary."

"Mine missed, sir," she replied. "Old Dale's the one who nailed the throw."

Marvin turned. He hadn't even seen the old man. He'd been a part of one of the teams sweeping the upstairs due to their familiarity with the building, apparently they'd joined them at some point. Marvin nodded his head; Christoper winked, nodded, and two-finger saluted back.

"Veron, check out that room."

"Roger, sir," Veron said.

"See if anything remains of those two Hrum we blew up."

Veron nodded and waved his men forward. Keeping a close eye on the stairs, he carefully advanced into the room.

Only a few seconds in, he said, "It's clear, sir, but you're gonna want to see this."

Marvin and Dale hustled their way into the room, which appeared to be a waiting area of some sort. Inside sprawled a handful of dead humans as well as the dead armored Hrum. The other thing he saw was also alien, but clearly not Hrum. In fact it looked very similar to the thing he'd seen outside of the broadcast center. Its eyes, which had appeared to be glowing red last time, stared dull and lifeless. Marvin looked around at his other men who were just as puzzled as he was.

"Dale, you seen anything like this?"

"Nope," he replied. "Looks like a giant dead bird."

Marvin made sure to capture plenty of pictures of the creature. There'd be time to analyze it later, but they still had a mission.

"Snap some photos," Marvin commanded. "If we have time, we'll bring it with us later. Let's see what's downstairs."

While O'Leary lined up the camera on her headgear and tapped the shutter a few times, Marvin checked in with the other teams, who all indicated that the enemy had stopped pouring up from the basement not long after Marvin's men had blown up the mysterious alien. He confirmed with them, but none of them had seen any sort of birdlike alien though.

Carefully, Veron and O'Leary's teams made their way down the stairs into the sublevels of the hospital. In the hallways huddled a few dozen unarmored humans, who'd apparently dropped their weapons and stood in place unmoving. After quickly securing them, the marines moved on. They were responsible for the first level, while the other teams were going to the other two lower levels. As soon as they opened the large double doors, they were greeted with a barrage of gunfire and some very angry Hrum soldiers who charged them immediately. Luckily, the fire was inaccurate and the hostiles were quickly taken down.

"Those Hrum behaved much more like I expected Hrum to behave," O'Leary said. "Never thought I'd see the day where I missed that."

Marvin only nodded and gestured for them to continue their advance. This floor was where most of the surgery centers were located. His unit entered the first room, and recoiled in horror. Inside lay at least half a dozen heavily mutilated human corpses. Several of his men collapsed to the floor and he heard them retching. It looked like whoever was cutting on them was performing a science experiment of some sort.

They found much more of the same until they reached the end of the hall. Inside, they found about a dozen, nearly naked comatose humans. Leery of what they'd seen, they slowly advanced, the naked men and women not reacting to their arrival. They didn't even react when the marines reached out to grab them. They just lay there unmoving. Marvin had never seen anything like this.

"What the hell's going on here?"

Everyone just shook their heads and stared.

"See if you can find something for these people to wear. I have no idea what's wrong with them, but they deserve their dignity."

Luckily it was a hospital and they managed to find some loose-fitting gowns, which they slipped over the heads of their unresponsive comrades.

They searched the rest of the floor without incident, they didn't find any more aliens or live humans. Marvin opened a comms channel to attempt to contact the units on the floor below, but found he was unable to. He hadn't heard any gunfire, but the floors were thick, so it wasn't impossible that they just didn't hear anything. Concerned, he had his soldiers secure the room that the live humans were in before regrouping and making their own way downstairs.

Cautiously, his teams made their way into the second lower level. This floor was poorly lit, and it had an all-around spooky and sterile vibe to it. As they crept their way in, each step timed with rusty water that dripped the ceiling, they were suddenly greeted with another grisly sight. What appeared to be the entire team that was responsible for securing this floor were scattered around the room, their faces distorted in pain. Now on high alert, his team furiously scanned the room, trying to see what had taken out twelve of their men. They found nothing. They carefully cleared the floor, checking each room, but found nothing. Most of the rooms appeared as if they'd been unoccupied for a long time, although a few of them appeared full of alien computers and tablets of some sort.

"Sir, the floor is clear, but we haven't heard from our team on the third level," Veron reported, his voice shaky. He was just as spooked as Marvin was.

"These folk have no injuries," Dale suddenly said.

Marvin turned to see Dale removing the helmet from one of the fallen men and investigating him.

"I see no injuries of any kind; it just appears they fell over and died."

Marvin realized he was right. While the team was scattered around the room, and locked in grisly poses of death, none of them appeared to have any sort of physical injury.

"I don't like this, sir," O'Leary chimed in.

"That makes two of us, Corporal," Marvin replied. He took another long look at the area around him and noticed that there were a few spherical canisters scattered around. Cautiously, he picked it up and saw that it had Hrum symbols on it. "I think they were gassed."

"It must've dissipated, or we'd be feeling it ourselves," Veron noted.

Several of his unit covered their faces as if hoping to avoid breathing in whatever it was that killed the others. Marvin took a moment to think.

"Say, Dale..."

"Yeah boss...

"What are the odds this hospital has rebreathers and masks for dealing with infectious diseases?"

"Likely," he said, picking up on what Marvin was asking for. "They'd likely be stored on the first floor with all the other supply rooms. This's the largest hospital in the region. They'd have all sorts of specialty protective gear."

"O'Leary, you and your team go up and get enough masks for all of us."

"Yessir!" she snapped before turning and running upstairs with her team.

"Dale, please show her where to go."

"You bet, boss."

Marvin did a quick assessment. Of the nearly seventy-five people he'd started with, at least thirty were dead, wounded, or missing. He only had two squads with him. Luckily most of the troops in his group were the best trained, but the vast majority of the teams that investigated the other two floors were civilians. The rest of the men he hadn't sent down to the lowest level were tasked with overwatch, or were helping the wounded. Being in a hospital did have some advantages, Marvin supposed.

Just over thirty minutes later, his two squads were geared up and ready to make their way downstairs. They decided to task half a dozen men with guarding the opposite staircase, while the rest of them made their way down. The bottom floor was just as dark and they saw nothing as they entered. This was the largest of the floors, having been expanded into the bedrock as the hospital grew. They weaved their way cautiously through the large hallways, which were big enough to drive a truck through, clearing rooms as they went. They saw nothing until a light glared at them from ahead. Slowly they advanced until they spotted their missing teams. These also appeared to have suffered the same fate as the soldiers on the floor above. Marvin motioned for them to leave the bodies and they continued to move forward. Whatever it was that was down here was trapped, and it was their job to find it and kill it.

They continued to advance until they reached a large amphitheater room. In it was a solitary figure standing near the front, tapping away on a large console that dominated the front stage. The figure looked just like the one that they'd blown up on the ground floor. It turned as they entered, but did nothing else. Marvin scanned the room as he walked forward. Suddenly, the being made a coughing noise, and ducked down behind the console. At least a dozen Hrum suddenly erupted from hidden areas and began to fire. Marvin fired off a few shots, nailing one of the Hrum before ducking down. Luckily, the room was filled with heavily built rows of desks that seemed to be doing a good job at stopping the projectiles. Not all of his soldiers were so lucky as he saw a few of them get stitched by enemy fire and fall.

Suddenly angry, Marvin stood and yelled as he switched his rifle to full auto. He nailed two more Hrum before he felt a burning sensation in his side, but he did not stop. He continued to yell as his men rallied. Before long, the only things standing were what remained of his team and the lone purple figure in the front of the room. It stood impassively with its hands at its side. Marvin, whose side was burning, carefully advanced and his team cautiously surrounded it. The alien then reached into its robe and attempted to pull something out, but Marvin didn't hesitate and dropped it with a quick shot to the head from his sidearm. Something billowed out of the creature's robes, briefly blinding everyone as it swirled around for a couple of seconds before it dissipated and just as quickly disappeared. The area now appeared to be covered in a light gray dust. After a quick search, Marvin saw that the being had released another of those canisters that they'd discovered on the floor above. Apparently their rebreathers did the trick in preventing it from getting at them.

They spent the next hour searching the rest of the floor and tending to their injured. The numbers were grim. They'd lost another six men and ten had wounds of differing severity. The only good news came when they found where the Hrum had been keeping their human prisoners, close to two hundred of them.

Most of them were malnourished and scared, but unharmed. Some of them were even doctors or nurses, so once they had their immediate needs tended to, they were able to help out with the other injured. Marvin's ghostees met back up with them and they finished their sweep of the hospital. It was at that point that Marvin realized that Dale was nowhere to be found. It took him nearly twenty minutes to find him sitting on the floor, cradling the head of a younger man in his lap, crying. It was apparently his son. Marvin hated everything about these aliens. He had no idea what their end goal was here, but the amount of anger he felt at what they'd been doing to these poor people boiled his blood and lit a fire in his heart.

"I'm sorry, Dale," Marvin said, attempting to comfort the older man. "I'm sure he was a good man."

Dale didn't reply, just remained sitting there quietly sobbing.

Marvin, not knowing what else to do, went out to the roof of the building to try and get another message out. After hearing only static again, he sighed and sat heavily on the gravely roof, his back against the wall. The doctors said the shot that had hit him missed anything vital, and after patching him up, said he was good to go, but at that moment, all the bumps and bruises he'd acquired that day had caught up to him and he was exhausted. He watched as the sky continued to brighten as the sun continued to rise, and he closed his eyes. He hoped that Ryan was alright.

"To any NIS or planetary forces listening, this is NIS Ghost Commander Nord calling. Anyone copy? Please respond."

Marvin's eyes snapped open as the communicator sitting next to him suddenly spat out a message.

"If you're listening, anyone in the city limits of Wreathsburg. I don't know what you did, but communications have cleared all over the planet. You have an incoming assault of Hrum from orbit. I repeat, inbound Hrum forces. I count nearly three-dozen shuttlecraft converging on your position. Get out now!"

"Shit."

Checking his watch for the hundredth time, Ryan sat uncomfortably in the woods outside the broadcast center perimeter. It felt like he'd been sitting there for hours, but in reality, it hadn't even been thirty minutes. He tried to stay calm, but the presence of the woman he loved next to him, willingly putting herself into danger, worried him more than he cared to admit. Even with a too-large set of armor on, he thought she looked adorable. To his surprise, she'd been very familiar with firearms and had laughed at him when he tried to teach her. Apparently Commander Yellen had made sure she could defend herself and had encouraged her to train with weapons several times a month. It made sense he supposed, especially when you are considering the safety of the most powerful person on the planet.

Keeping his voice low, he turned to Izabella. "Are you ready?" he asked.

She only nodded, apparently just as nervous.

Ryan warmed her with a quick smile and an arm squeeze before turning back towards the broadcast center.

"Come on Marvin, what's the holdup?" he muttered to himself.

As if the man were listening, a flurry of activity burst alive and several squads of Hrum and the smaller human soldiers marched out of the center and loaded quickly up into trucks. With them traipsed another of those purple birdlike aliens. It was only a few minutes when they roared out the gate and down the road.

"Kim, send the locals a message. They have a party headed their way."

"Aye, sir," he replied easily.

The locals were close enough that their communicators should work, but he knew they'd be on lookout regardless of the warning. It was only a few minutes later when there was a large boom that shook the ground slightly. Ryan turned towards Kim who nodded excitedly.

"Time to move people. Wreathsburg Team. Commence your assault."

Ryan didn't get a response, but he knew his message was received as a smattering of gunfire rattled through the air, and even the sound of some heavier weapons that came from the west. He waited for several minutes, before ordering his own team to advance. They quickly made their way into the facility, uncontested. They had decided that speed was more important than fully clearing the facility, so they moved as quickly as they could, only clearing what they passed in hopes that the Hrum were fully engaged in defending the assault.

They quickly made their way up from the ground floor, having seen nobody outside of a few decaying human corpses that were probably still lying there from when the Hrum arrived. In fact, they saw no one until they reached their target, which was the control center of the entire building. Outside of shutting down the power at the source, this was their best bet at taking control of the station. Even though he had intended to stay near the back, by the time that they'd reached the room. Ryan was in front with Kim following. There was no commander here to scold him and Marvin would not find out. The way he saw it was that he was best suited to lead, as he'd done this many times before.

As quietly as a couple dozen men could move, they poured out onto the broadcast floor where a surprised group of six purple-clad aliens awaited them. The two groups stood quietly for a moment, staring at each other.

"Put your hand's up and don't move," Ryan finally said.

He had no idea if they understood him, but it was the best he could do. As he'd expected, they didn't reply, but one of them began to reach for something in its vest. Before that could happen, Ryan mowed him down. The others sat completely still and raised their hands, which surprised Ryan.

"Can you understand me?"

One of the creatures nodded. It pointed at a small box that Ryan recognized as a translator.

"Don't move. Keep your hands where I can see them."

The creature only nodded.

"Kim, search them."

"Aye, sir."

"Also see what the dead one over there was reaching for."

Kim and his men moved in, and roughly searched the aliens. They pulled several things from their pockets, and the one who was dead was clutching a small silver orb. Ryan looked at it carefully before setting it on a table.

"What was he reaching for?"

The aliens didn't respond.

Not willing to play games with the sick aliens who had murdered hundreds of innocent civilians, he stepped forward, raised his sidearm, and shot the alien next to the one who had spoken.

Then asked again, "What was he reaching for?"

The alien wore a look Ryan could not read, but said nothing.

Ryan repeated the sequence until there were only two aliens alive before he decided to change tactics. Instead of threatening the alien next to the one who had spoken, he made eye contact with the one who had yet to speak and pointed the gun at the other.

"Last chance, what was he reaching for?"

"A buggavite," the alien who hadn't yet spoken quickly replied. "It's a buggavite dispersal ball."

The other alien waved his arms as if to shush the speaker.

Kim quickly pistol whipped him on the back of the head and he fell to the ground. Ryan only spared him a quick glance. Hopefully Kim hadn't killed him.

"Go on," Ryan replied. "What does it do?"

"It spreads buggavites through the air to eliminate threats. It's for defending oneself."

"What are buggavites?"

"They are how we maintain order. Without order is chaos, with chaos is destruction."

Ryan was thoroughly confused.

It was Izabella who stepped forward and spoke up. "Are they what you use to control my people?"

The alien gave what looked like a nod. "They bring order to the world. We will bring order to all."

"This dude's a whack job," Corporal V replied.

Ryan found himself nodding in agreement. "How do they bring order?" he inquired.

"They allow the almighty to lead us all on the path. The chosen are honored with his wisdom to bring order."

"*Chosen*? Who are the chosen?" Ryan said, starting to lose his temper. Even though the alien was his prisoner, Ryan got the impression the alien was talking down to him.

"We are," the alien said.

"Um, pardon me?" said Izabella.

"*We* are the chosen," the alien replied, seemingly getting excited. "We control the destiny of those who are dirty and unworthy of the path. The almighty has ordered it."

Ryan was getting sick of the alien's attitude and was trying to figure out what to do next when Izabella suddenly took out her pistol and repeatedly shot the alien in the chest until her gun ran dry. Everyone in the room looked at her with a stunned silence. Ryan carefully extracted the gun from her shaking hands and pulled her in close for a hug. She had tears running down her face and was sobbing.

"You can't talk to the Grand Monarch like that."

Ryan and a few of the others in the room chuckled.

"And I am sure it never will again," Ryan mused. "Now, let's see if we can let the planet know you're alive."

There was a commotion at the base of the stairs as several wild-haired locals hurried into the room.

"Sir, the aliens just charged us," one rattled off in a huff. "At first they fought as you said they would, but then they just went berserk and rushed us. It was like shooting fish in a barrel."

Kim was the first to reply. "Did they go nuts about ten minutes ago?"

"Aye."

"Commander, do you know what this means?"

Ryan shook his head confused.

"Well I believe that these aliens controlled more than just the humans they captured," said Kim. "I think they also use it on the Hrum."

Kim hurried over to the dead aliens, checking each of them before he pushed back the cloak of the one that was just unconscious. He pushed its hood back and gave it a close look.

"Sir, look. It seems like there's an implant of some sort in the side of this one's head."

Everyone else in the room crowded around and took a look. It did appear to have a metallic looking device implanted in the side of its head.

"So that's what it meant when it said he was one of the chosen. I bet these implants allow them to order those infected with these buggavites."

One of the locals from the back spoke up. "So why didn't we see any of these creatures when the planet was attacked for the first time?"

Ryan looked at Kim who just shook his head. "I don't know, it's just a theory, but it seems too coincidental the second we shot a few of these aliens, the Hrum went crazy."

Ryan decided that the conversation had gone on long enough and they'd wasted enough time theorizing. "We can let the scientists figure this out," he said. "We still have a mission." Turning to one of the locals Ryan asked, "Have any of you worked here? Do you know how this all works?"

The local nodded and shouted down the stairs. A few moments later, two women and a young man came running.

"They can help."

With only a moment's hesitation, they ran to the console, flinching slightly at the sight of alien guts everywhere, but they tapped away at the screens. They had been informed what Izabella intended to do, so they quickly prepared a studio on the other side of a glass wall for her.

One local woman turned to Ryan. "Commander, it appears that the broadcast the aliens have been sending all over the planet is originating from the ship in orbit. They are beaming it here and it's being relayed all over."

"Can we shut it down?"

"Yessir, but they will know when we do it."

Ryan nodded thoughtfully. He had a feeling that would be the case. They were just going to have to get out of here as quickly as possible after Izabella's broadcast.

"The second the Grand Monarch is ready to speak, shut it down. Until then leave it. After she's done, put it back up."

"Um, okay, Commander."

"Maybe they won't notice a little glitch..."

The young tech didn't look convinced, but she did as he asked. It was only a few minutes later that Izabella indicated she was ready and they gave her a countdown.

"We're on in 3....2...1...." The tech pointed at Izabella as her count reached zero.

Ryan again marveled at her strength. So young to assume leadership of an entire planet and so soon to defend her planet against hostile alien forces. She was truly one of a kind.

"Brave citizens of St. George. This is your Grand Monarch Izabella speaking. Contrary to what these unwelcome invaders are claiming, I am very much alive and well, thanks to the valiant efforts of my brave bodyguards and the citizens of St. George's fighting spirit. They have tried multiple times to kill me. My brave protector, Commander Yellen gave his life to protect me so that I could come speak to you now. The enemy thinks of us as inferior, as cattle, as... below them. But they are wrong. They see themselves as superior, as conquerors. But I just see them as intergalactic bullies, bullies who have met their match. For all their bluster, these bullies still haven't managed to break the spirit of you people. *My* people. Our allies came and helped us once before, they will do it again. We just have to continue to show what we are made of. Some of them are already here. You may be familiar with the name Jaxton Drake, a true hero in our time. Luckily for us, his brother, Ryan Drake is just as much of a hero and is here fighting with us. He saved me when my commander fell, and he is the reason I am speaking to you now. He is here because he believes in us, he will help us rise as a people.... And rise we shall!"

Ryan shook his head as he heard Izabella bring him up. Comparing him to his brother was a stretch, but the speech did sound good. Who was he to argue with the leader of a planet? He tuned back in.

"I have asked a lot of you the past five years, but you have risen to the occasion. Let's give this one last effort and make it clear: Nobody invades our home!"

There was cheering in the room as everyone listened closely. Even Ryan found himself smiling. As Izabella wrapped up her message, Corporal Kim ran up to him and grabbed his arm.

"Sir, we are receiving a message from Nord!"

"The Commander? What did he say?"

"He said the Hrum ships in orbit dispatched a dozen or so shuttles and they're headed in our direction before they went to face our ships in the system. We only have thirty minutes until they arrive!"

"Our ships in the system?"

"Yessir, the NIS arrived and are fighting the Hrum in space."

Ryan cursed under his breath. The typical Hrum would have ignored them to face the fleet. These new ones did not appear to want to do that, however. The fact that they did not simply bombard them from space meant they wanted Izabella captured alive, which was something he would not let happen. He could still not entirely fathom what their goal was, but he had a feeling it had something to do with these buggavites.

"Transmit to him what we know regarding the aliens and the buggavites. If nothing else, this intelligence will make it to someone who will know what the hell to do with it."

"Aye, sir."

"Corporal V, Get all of our forces inside. We don't have time to flee, and the Hrum would find us before we got far."

Looking around the room, Ryan made eye contact with Izabella who had finished her address and was watching intently.

"Madam Monarch, great speech, but now I need you to do exactly as I say if I have any hope of keeping you safe."

She just nodded.

There was no way they'd be able to evacuate her using their gunship, it was just too slow and didn't have the range. The Hrum would easily be able to track it down. Thirty minutes was going to pass in the blink of an eye, but he would be damned if he didn't give these Hrum a warm reception.

Chapter XVII

In Jewel of Sunlight System on Captain Dixon's Battlecruiser
Year 3326

Nat, Taylor, Carn, and Chen were all gathered in the cramped closet that Carn had first pulled Nat into. They had unsuccessfully tried to get Captain Dixon caught up in scans with Jaxton's medical teams. They were not entirely sure how, but he had managed to get approval to enter the ship through another bay, and once aboard, he somehow talked his way out of getting scanned.

"You think someone on Jaxton's ship helped him?" Carn inquired.

"I just don't know," Taylor replied. "I hope at minimum he was late or some orderly flagged his reluctance to a scan, but I just don't know."

"So what should we do? I didn't end up having time to go visit Brewster. Between the drills and the admiral's urgency to leave, it just wasn't possible."

"I would be sad too if I missed out on a date with that man," Chen replied, a shameless grin across her face. "I do like myself a tall muscular fighter jock. He could carry me into his cockpit and—"

"At least we know you're clean, Chen," Nat said, interrupting and blushing furiously at her comment.

"Chen, the nanites would probably flee if they knew what was going on in your mind," Carn quipped.

"I was just sayin..."

"Anyways..." Taylor cut in. "What do we do *now*? Our shifts begin soon and we're already on our way to WOT and then St. George."

"Can we incapacitate the captain in his ready room?" Nat asked.

"I don't think we'd be able to get more than one or two of us in there without him getting suspicious," Taylor replied. "Even if we were quick, I don't know how we'd be able to take him quietly without the bridge guards hearing."

Nat was the next to jump in. "Carn, do you think you can take out the two marines on the bridge?"

"Two Marines? By myself?"

"I think that'd give us time to appeal to the rest of the bridge crew," Nat said, finishing her thought.

Taylor looked confused at that comment, looking in Nat's direction.

"Carn was a ghost for a long time."

Nat's response only slightly reduced Taylor's confusion.

"Why would a ghost reenlist and go to the academy?"

"That's a story for another time," Carn said pointedly, looking at Nat. "I just don't know. I would need weapons or armor of some kind. They are fully armored and carrying rifles, while we just have our vac-suits. I might be able to take down one of them, but there's no way I'd be able to get both."

"Well what about *their* suits?" Nat asked.

"What about them?"

"Can we disable their suits somehow?"

"We may be able to rig up something in engineering, but it would raise eyebrows," Carn replied.

"I might be able to get one of the engineering crew to rig me up something," Chen said. They all looked at her confused. "What? I don't have a hunking fighter pilot like Nat here does. At least the engineering boys know how to handle their tools."

Carn turned away, hiding a smile.

"How soon you think you can get him to do it?" Taylor replied.

"Well, I had plans with him after our next shift, so I think if you give me twenty-four hours, I can get you something. He'll keep his mouth shut. Especially if he wants to keep seeing me."

The group sat back and nodded thoughtfully.

"Typically at least one marine is roving the deck," Carn said. "If I call him over to my station, Chen or whoever has the device should be able to incapacitate the other and get his weapon. I should be able to at least distract the other one long enough for you to come help. Taylor, you'll probably have to be the one to bring it on the bridge."

"And how do you expect me to do that?"

"I don't know, bring a box of donuts or Christmas presents for us for our hard work."

"It's not Christmas..."

Carn waved her comment aside. "You'll think of something. The point is, you'll get less scrutiny carrying large objects onto the bridge than someone like myself or Nat would. It has to be you."

Taylor found herself nodding.

"You're right," Taylor finally agreed. "Okay, Chen, as soon as you get the device, get it into my hands." She checked her watch. "We have just over a day until we transition into the St. George system. I don't like the idea of a mutiny during an operation. It would put the lives of all our crew on the line."

"Leaving that man in charge puts all of our lives on the line," Chen replied glumly.

"Yes, that's true. It's up to us to stop him and to get a message to the admiral."

Chapter XVIII

In Unnamed System on Battleship Arcon
Year 3326

Upon leaving Jewel of Sunlight, Jaxton and his stealth fleet had been boosted by the majority of the picket force stationed there. Now in addition to the seven ships of his original task force, he boosted an additional eight ships. They'd left one destroyer in orbit around JOS whose job was to act as a scout who would run at the first sign of conflict. He'd also ordered a second to Sapporo to gauge the situation there. Of the eight ships, they had three cruisers, one destroyer, and four battlecruisers. As always, Jaxton wished he had more battleships due largely to the fighter wings they could carry. He'd had lunch with Major Brewster, who agreed to transfer over to their makeshift carrier and work on integrating the additional fighters they did pick up from Jewel of Sunlight into their tactics. They would operate independently of their stealth fighters, but he really wanted to hammer home that they would likely be facing Hrum fighters at some point during the upcoming operation.

Greg had been running nonstop training in the simulators since their battle in the Twilight of Moon system when the Hrum had shocked them with fighters of their own. He wanted to make sure that his pilots weren't rusty on the finer points of dogfighting, which had fallen largely to the wayside during this war with the Hrum. He had also shocked Jaxton with the news that he had gone on a date with his younger sister. Jaxton had no idea the two even talked, and to say he was shocked was an understatement. There were no rules or regulations that prevented them from seeing each other, but it was a strange thought that his sister was dating his best friend. He hadn't quite come to terms with it yet and he needed some downtime to think about it, but in all honesty there were very few men that he thought were worthy of his sister. His best friend was one of them. Thinking about that had made him chuckle at the sorry state of his own love life. Dr. Casey, the beautiful lead scientist on his ship, still made him nervous whenever she was around. Unfortunately, whenever he thought of making a move or asking her out, his father's words about the roles and responsibilities of an admiral came back to him. "The captain is the absolute authority on the ship. His word is gospel." Jax mockingly said aloud to himself. "Stop behaving like a horny eighteen-year-old." He shook his head. Whether he wanted to accept it or not, he knew his father was right, and his love life would have to wait.

As he walked onto the bridge, he was greeted by his XO Chris Bradley who saluted him and excitedly spoke. "Sir, more good news..."

"Well isn't this our lucky year," Jaxton said with a sarcastic smirk.

"We just made contact with the seven ships who were sent to reinforce Jewel of Sunlight. It seems they were a little delayed in leaving Sapporo, but when they left, it was no longer under attack."

"That *is* great news! I'll speak with them, but they'll be a major boost to our combat forces."

"Agreed, sir."

"While I'm doing that, I need you to do something."

"Whatever I can do, sir..."

"Can you talk with the crew about how we wish to integrate them into our forces,"

"Of course, Admiral."

"Also we need to dictate who will be in charge when we do get into it with the Hrum."

"Aye, sir. I was thinking of Captain Pierce, If I may suggest, sir."

Jaxton nodded thoughtfully. "Do we know who the captain of the battleship is?"

"Indeed, sir. It's Admiral Bowden."

"So the old bastard didn't retire…"

"Apparently not, sir."

"Well I trust the man. He'll understand the situation, and I think he'll accept Pierce as his CO for this operation as he's the one who nominated him for a promotion in the first place. I'll talk to him."

"Aye, sir," Bradley replied.

The XO hustled over to the command station and began barking commands.

Jaxton walked into his ready room and called up Admiral Bowden. As he'd suspected, Bowden willingly accepted his orders and the two fleets merged together. They did not know what to expect upon arrival in the St. George system. The one thing they did know, however, was that Jaxton's ships had to operate independently from the rest of the fleet due to their stealth capabilities. He had a feeling that Captain Pierce would initially decline and argue with him, but something in Jaxton's mind said that the man would make a good admiral someday, and that he had a good head on his shoulders.

The integration of the ships went off without a hitch. As Jaxton had expected, Pierce was reluctant, but eventually agreed to take charge of the ships in their fleet without stealth capabilities when the operation began. It helped that Admiral Bowden had readily agreed and spoke with the younger man privately. Jaxton was sure that he said something along the lines of he would be there to support him and advise.

They were preparing to transition into the WOT system. They did not know what to expect, nor had any NIS ship gone through this Albion lane before. The plan was simple. Jaxton's ships would transition first, utilizing their stealth to get a look at the system before Pierce and Bowden's fleet followed behind about two hours later.

According to Arama, the Albion lane was pretty close to the minimum transition length, so they'd only be in Albion for a little over five hours. Jaxton had sent a note to Dr. Casey to work with Arama to get a better picture of the Albion lane map. His reason was twofold. First was that they clearly needed a better way to detect the lanes. It would be interesting to see how many they missed. It was crucial for the defense of a system to know from where the enemy could attack from. The second was that he hoped that it would inspire some trust between the two races. He had already begun to think of the Hrum and the Karathians as two different entities, even though it was Hrum soldiers they were fighting, and he'd only met a handful of actual Hrum who would speak to him.

"Sir, all ships report they are ready for transition," Lt. Stephanie Johnson reported.

"Thank you, Lieutenant. I suppose there's no sense in waiting any longer. We're just going to have to trust Revalius.... Helm, you are clear to initiate Albion."

"Aye, sir," replied Lt. Booker. "Initiating jump, sir."

With the same bumpy transition as when they used the other Albion lane to the Twilight of Moon system, the ships jumped into Albion. Jaxton made a note and sent it off to their science team. It seemed all these lanes that were so well hidden all had the same bumpy effect when they used them. He had no idea what it meant, but it could be useful for his science team.

As usual, there was nothing to see while in Albion, but since the transition was so short, he didn't rotate his bridge crew out. They ran one or two more drills before taking a quick break for some coffee and snacks. Before long, they were all at their stations and preparing to arrive in the WOT system. They transitioned in with another jolt and the system screen began to populate.

"Sensor report."

"Nothing in the immediate vicinity, sir. Still waiting for data from the rest of the system."

"Very good. Update me when you find something."

"Aye, sir."

Jaxton waited patiently as the data flowed in. It would be a little while before the data from around the planet showed. In theory there should have been nearly a dozen NIS ships in the system, but there was no telling if they had been attacked.

"Sir, it appears there was a large battle here. I am seeing lots of wreckage, both Hrum and NIS."

"Anything living, Lieutenant?"

"Still looking, sir."

"Helm, take us in slowly. Signal the other ships to minimize emissions. We are going to stay as dark as possible."

"Aye, sir," Lt. Booker replied.

Jaxton pulled up the sensor officer's screen on his own station. He had been right—clearly a large battle took place here. He saw wreckage from at least ten individual ships.

"Sir, I'm detecting engine signatures from orbit around one of the planet's moons."

"When you find out who they—"

"They're Hrum!" Booked nearly yelled.

Grimly, Jaxton replied, "It appears they defeated the NIS ships stationed here. Any sign they've detected us?"

"No, sir, but I'm seeing at least twelve distinct energy signatures."

Turning to his XO, Jaxton asked, "The question then is: what do we do?"

"Sir…?"

"We could easily wipe them out using our stealth, but we'd be wasting valuable time clearing a planet that holds little tactical value to us."

"Agreed, sir. They'll see Captain Pierce's ships when they arrive though."

"Can we in good conscience let them face the Hrum alone?"

"Tough call, sir."

"Guess that's why I get the big bucks…" Jaxton scoffed.

Jaxton sat back in his command chair, scratching his chin and weighing his options.

"Commander…"

"Yes, sir...?"

"What are the odds the Hrum behave like we've seen in the past? You think they'll chase us into the St. George system if our other ships just blow by them?"

"I hesitate to guess sir, but my gut says yes."

Jaxton nodded, and then stood up, coming to a decision. "Leave a communication pod. When Pierce arrives, tell him to order his ships to full power. If they're quick enough, and the Hrum don't immediately react to their presence, they should be able to reach the Albion point into St. George before the Hrum can do anything."

"Sir, that's risky. We'd potentially have enemies both in front and behind us."

"I agree, Commander. I just don't see another way to fight them without wasting the better part of a day, if not more. You said it yourself, at the moment this system has little value to us."

"I did say that, sir."

"It's settled then. Tight beam message to the other captains. We're just passing through."

"Aye, sir." He did as he was ordered.

Jaxton sat back down and took a look at the map of the system. He hoped there weren't NIS survivors waiting for rescue. He had enough ghosts to haunt him, he didn't need any more coming his direction.

Chapter XIX

In Water of Twilight System on Captain Dixon's Battlecruiser
Year 3326

"Sir, the admiral's ordering us to ignore the Hrum ships in orbit of the main planet's moon. We're sneaking through."

"Thank you, Lieutenant," Captain Dixon replied. "Commander, take the conn. I will be over there in my ready room."

Commander Taylor did as ordered. She took the seat and watched her boss walk stiffly over to his office. Captain Dixon never left the bridge mid-operation, but she had no idea how to see what he was up to. She locked eyes with Nat who just shrugged slightly. They resumed their duties for several uneventful minutes before the bridge doors swooshed open, and Hadley walked through and made a beeline for the captain's quarters. Taylor made no move to stop him, as Dixon had ordered her to give Hadley unfettered access to the bridge. She watched the doors close behind him as she worried. Chen had indicated that she managed to get her engineering friend to make the device, but it wasn't ready yet. Unfortunately for them, the transition across the WOT system was short, as the Albion lanes were relatively close together. In addition, the transition to St. George was a shorter route as well.

There was nothing she could do but watch. Eventually, the captain and Hadley stepped out of the room and Hadley hurried off the bridge. Dixon reclaimed his seat and it was back to business as usual. This was one of those times that Taylor hated space travel, especially when in a hostile system where they couldn't afford to run drills or some other tasks to distract them from what was going on. They sneakily crossed the system right under the noses of the Hrum around WOT's moon.

The remaining fifteen ships of their fleet arrived in a series of bright flashes. It was nearly impossible to hide the arrival of that many ships, and it was not long before the Hrum reacted. Captain Pierce also apparently understood his new orders, as he commanded all the ships to full power and they blasted their way to the Albion lane. Jaxton had ordered the ships to maintain stealth, and they had a considerable distance advantage, but Pierce's ships would eventually catch up. To Jaxton, it was very important to not give away the presence of his stealthy ships, but eventually they'd have to burn their engines to keep from being overtaken. In order to minimize the chances of detection, he had charted a route that eventually put his fifteen ships that were not stealthy directly in between where he expected the Hrum to be in relation to his own ships. Once that happened, they'd go to full power. It was not a perfect solution, but he hoped it was enough to fool the Hrum.

With nothing to do but watch the ships close the distances, the bridge was quiet.

Eventually the ships were in position and the captain spoke. "Helm, put the engines at full power mode. Initiate burn."

The helmsman seemed caught off guard at the awkward sentence from the captain, but he did as ordered. Taylor watched as the other ships of their fleet also lit off their engines. Eventually, they reached the Albion point and transitioned. At that point, Dixon ordered the bridge crew to take a break. He said he wanted them fresh for their arrival in St. George. Taylor, who usually stuck around for a bit after the crew was dismissed, hurried off the bridge with Nat. She saw Chen and Carn hurry off towards engineering. Hopefully they were going to secure their makeshift device to disable the marines and the captain. When they finally reached the closet they'd chosen as a meeting place, Nat spoke.

"We're running out of time. Hadley and the captain are up to something."

"Hopefully Chen and Carn get that device. We'll have to make our move right before we exit Albion."

"Agreed. We can't afford to fail."

They sat in silence for several minutes until there was a tap at the door. Chen and Carn were waiting outside both wearing excited looks on their faces.

"We got it!" Chen said. "My friend promised to keep his mouth shut."

"That's great news!" Taylor replied. "Carn you might want to get situated on the bridge early. You know what you're gonna say to the marine?"

"Yeah, don't worry about me. I'll handle him."

The group settled into silence. Each of them mentally working through their portion of the plan. Chen and Nat would attempt to subdue the captain, while Taylor hopefully managed to incapacitate the marine guarding the door. Carn would chat up the other one and attempt to subdue him. It was a risk, as the only one who had ever trained for hand-to-hand combat was Carn, but what choice did they have? They couldn't let whatever Dixon and Hadley were planning come to fruition. The group broke apart and headed to their various stations.

Nat, Chen and Carn walked together to the bridge, attempting to act as casually as they could manage. Even so, Nat's hands quivered as she grabbed a coffee bulb from the dispenser. She cursed herself for being nervous. In engineering, Chen had also managed to secure some makeshift knives they could use to threaten the captain. It wasn't the same as a firearm, but the only ones allowed to carry guns on the ship—unless the captain ordered—were the marines. They were only allowed to carry them at certain times as well. The three of them settled into their stations and waited. Carn, who appeared much calmer than the others, also settled into his spot. As the roving marine passed by, Carn turned and cracked a joke that got his attention.

"Hey, you know how to put a spaceship to sleep?"

The marine cocked his head and drew a blank smirk.

"You rocket."

That teased a chuckle out of him.

The two began having an animated conversation that by all intents and purposes appeared friendly. Nat supposed the man had many years of pretending; it wasn't hard to fake anymore. Nat watched through her peripheral vision as the captain settled into his seat, counting down the moments until Taylor made her appearance.

The doors abruptly swooshed open, and Commander Taylor appeared, carrying a large bag cradling a festively wrapped package. She stopped in the doorway as the captain turned and looked at her.

"Commander, what—"

Before he could finish, Taylor quickly pulled the package out of the bag and lobbed it in the direction of the marine to her left. There was a sudden flash followed by a pop as the package exploded, stunning all those who were not prepared. Nat and Chen had taken cover the second she'd thrown it, so they were quickly on their feet. They rushed over to the captain, who was clearly stunned and shaking his head. They kicked him down and pulled out their makeshift weapons. Carn, who was also prepared, had somehow managed to sneak a large metal bar onto the bridge. He cracked the marine he had been talking to on the head. The man was wearing an armored helmet and did not go down immediately, but the combination of the improvised explosive and the impact had stunned him badly. The two dissolved into a wrestling match for the marine's weapon. Taylor, whose marine had been significantly closer to the blast, was unconscious. Taylor quickly secured his weapon and rushed over to help Carn.

"What... are you doing, Lieutenant?" a very groggy Captain Dixon asked.

"It's for your own good, sir. You are not yourself."

Creepily, the captain said nothing, just fixed Nat with a blank stare while she secured his arms as Chen threatened him with her knife. Eventually, with the assistance of Commander Taylor, Carn subdued the remaining marine and they had control of the bridge! The other bridge crewmembers had begun to shake off the effects of the explosive and had begun shouting questions. The only thing keeping them back at the moment were the two weapons that Taylor and Carn had liberated from the marines who were now neatly tied up with their own restraints.

Before the situation got out of hand, Taylor shouted. "Nat, go secure the hallway, make sure nobody else heard this. Listen up everybody. This was necessary. Captain Dixon is infected with the alien nanites. Haven't you noticed that he's been acting strangely lately?"

There was some murmuring as the crew talked among themselves. Taylor scanned the room. Some of the bridge crew still appeared to be in a daze from the explosion, but others were listening intently.

"I promise you, as soon as possible, we will contact the rest of our fleet and have Admiral Drake send over some marines to secure the captain, but until—" Taylor stopped as a smug-looking Hadley walked on the bridge, holding Nat at gunpoint.

"Well, well, well…" Hadley said with a sneer. "What do we have here?"

Carn and Taylor quickly pointed their rifles at Hadley, who was using Nat as a human shield. She appeared mostly unharmed, with the exception of a rapidly swelling black eye.

"I think I am going to have you two go ahead and drop those. Let's talk without guns pointed at each other, shall we?"

"So you're going to drop yours and let Nat go?" Carn inquired.

"Of course not, but what I *will* do is blow her brains all over this deck if you don't."

Carn did not so much as flinch, but Taylor began to lower her weapon.

"Commander, don't," Carn yelled. "We can't trust him to honor his word."

"I don't see another option, Carn. Do as he said."

Carn looked conflicted, but slowly did as she ordered.

Once the guns were on the ground, Hadley continued. "Tut tut, you've all been quite naughty. Lieutenant Chen, why don't you go ahead and let the captain up and walk over here with your friends."

She did as he ordered, cutting the restraints before dropping the knife. Dixon, wearing a blank expression, got to his feet, grabbed the two rifles and walked over to Hadley who continued to smile smugly. When he got there, Hadley shoved Nat over towards Carn, Chen, and Taylor, before handing Dixon the sidearm and taking a rifle.

"Commander, I am very disappointed in you," Dixon finally said. "A mutiny? What have I done to you to warrant such hate?"

"You aren't yourself, Captain, everyone knows it. But I know you're in there sir. Fight it!"

Hadley bellowed with laughter. "Oh he's in there alright, but you are correct, he isn't himself. In fact, he answers to me and me alone. In fact, I am impressed you figured it out. Your plan almost worked."

"What are you planning, Hadley?" Carn asked.

"The adults are speaking, Carn," Hadley hissed. "Shut your mouth or I'll shut it permanently. This is not some grand reveal where I tell you all my plans like a supervillain in a movie. Today, I will destroy this pitiful force you have put together on stolen technology. At this exact moment though I think we need to clean house." He looked over at the remaining bridge crew and nodded. Suddenly, nearly half of them sprang into action, jumping on their unsuspecting crewmembers and bludgeoning them to death. Nat watched in horror as men and women she considered friends and comrades, suddenly turned on each other in a show of horrifying violence. Tears streamed down her cheeks as she watched, unable to do anything but stare.

"Well now, that sure was refreshing," Hadley said, turning to Nat. "I do say, I have to applaud the innovation, you almost succeeded, but now you will watch me destroy everything you've worked so hard to build. I will take special joy in killing your brother too. His ability to escape impossible situations has been an inconvenience. A minor one, but an inconvenience nonetheless."

"Hadley, if there's any humanity left in you, you won't go through with this. Fight them!"

"*Fight* them? Why would I do that? The Karathians have shown me the true path. They don't control *me*, I control *them*."

He pulled at the side of his head where he peeled back what appeared to be skin, revealing a complicated spider-webbed device under the surface. They've given me a gift!"

Nat had nothing to say. She stood there numbly, unable to do anything.

"Your Captain has put up an admirable resistance to the nanites. Not many people can resist the nanites to the extent he has. But, like all things, it must come to an end… Captain?"

"Yes, sir." Dixon replied.

"Do me a favor and shoot Commander Taylor in the head."

"Yes, sir," Dixon replied.

Dixon carefully stepped forward and pointed the sidearm at his Commander's forehead. For her part, Taylor stood there impassively, making eye contact with Dixon. She glanced at Hadley and scoffed. Then she looked back at Dixon, her commanding officer all these years, hoping to see life in him, searching his eyes for the valiant commander and captain he once was.

"Sir, I'm sorry I let you down," she said, standing tall and saluting. "I am Commander Gemma Taylor, I did my duty and have no regrets of what I have done."

Taylor stared directly into Dixon's eyes where she thought she could see an internal battle going on. The gun appeared to waver for a moment, before with a loud bang! Dixon pulled the trigger. Commander Gemma Taylor dropped to the floor, her eyes slowly glazed over as life left her body.

"Noooooooooooo Nooo, no, no!" screamed Nat. "You bastard. You didn't have to do that."

"Of course I did," Hadley replied. "I want you to understand that I alone am in command here. Captain, please secure those three and get someone to clean up this… *mess*. We have a fleet to destroy." Hadley walked over to the captain's console and sat down.

"Aye, sir." Dixon replied.

Dixon had never fought harder than the moment that he'd pointed the gun at his Commander. He screamed, battered, fought, and eventually begged that the entity controlling him would stop. He felt his finger squeeze the trigger and watched in stunned disbelief as the woman he worked with for many years, his steady and honorable XO, fell to the ground, stone dead. He watched life fade from her eyes as his body ignored his every command. For a brief moment before he pulled the trigger, he'd felt his arm twitch as he'd fought. It was hopeless. He'd always considered himself a strong-willed and hardworking person, but despite all that, he'd just murdered his XO in cold blood. Now more than ever, he hated what had happened to him. *Gemma, I'm so so sorry.*

Chapter XX

In St. George System on Battleship Arcon
Year 3326

With a small jolt, Jaxton's battleship Arcon arrived at the St. George system. It had been many years since he'd first been here, a young lieutenant on a battlecruiser, going nowhere. His ship had not played a role in it, but they'd arrived shortly after the first liberation of the system. It was truly tragic. This system was once considered the jewel of human space and everybody and their mother wanted to live here. Jaxton promised to himself that they would make it that way again.

"Sensors, report."

"Sir, there are at least thirty Hrum ships in the system."

"Formations…?"

"Two groups of eight in orbit around St. George, and the rest scattered in the direction of the other two Albion Points."

"Seems to me we aren't dealing with our run-of-the-mill Hrum then," Jaxton grumbled, standing and pacing around. "Damn it. I've always said we'd regret the day the Hrum wise up."

XO Bradley chimed in, "We still have tactical advantages, and field experience over them, sir—"

"Yeah yeah, but this is going to be bloody now that we can't expect them to act like animals."

"You mean the Karathian, sir?" Bradley said.

"You're right, we should be calling the enemy by their actual name. Let's go with plan Bravo three. We are headed straight for the planet. Drop a comms buoy and order Pierce to stop and engage the Hrum that should be chasing him once he arrives. Even if they come through expecting a fight, the Karathian ships chasing him will still be at a disadvantage."

"Sir, that'll leave us deep in the system, exposed and very outnumbered once we engage the Hrum in orbit."

"I don't see another solution at the moment, Commander. The only force we can engage before Pierce gets here are the ones over St. George. Chances are once he arrives, they'll be actively scanning and will most likely raise their shields."

"Aye, sir. I suppose you are correct."

In the WOT system, they'd managed to maintain their two-hour head start to Pierce's ships. They'd also entered the Albion point with quite a bit of velocity, so they didn't need to burn their engines other than a few small course corrections in order to angle towards the planet. Jaxton assumed the only reason the Albion point they just entered through was unguarded was that the Karathians knew they controlled the other system. Jaxton smiled wickedly. He was about to give them a lesson in making assumptions.

Jaxton's ships were about fifteen minutes from engaging when his communications officer suddenly spoke up. "Sir, you've got to hear this!"

"Put it on the main screen, Lieutenant."

"Brave citizens of St. George. This is your Grand Monarch......." The voice of the leader of St. George, Izabella St. Claire was broadcasting through the bridge. Nobody on the bridge said a word as she continued to speak. "...his brother, Ryan Drake..." Jaxton couldn't help but smile. His brother was alive, and had apparently saved the monarch's life after the Hrum arrived. Ryan always gave him a hard time about all the so-called "heroic" things he'd done throughout the Hrum war. Looks like Jaxton would have a few things of his own to harass his little bro about.

"Sir... what do you want to—"

"You heard the lady!" Admiral Drake exclaimed, looking around at everyone on the bridge. "Let's give these bastards a surprise they won't forget."

The bridge erupted into cheers before everyone quickly resettled on their jobs. The plan was simple. Get as close as they could before blasting away with everything they had on the unsuspecting Karathians in orbit. They had a limited amount of time until the Karathians were aware the system was under attack, and Jaxton intended to make sure they took every advantage the aliens would give him. The distances closed until they were only a minutes from firing.

"Sir…" Lieutenant Chen said.

"Yes, Lieutenant..."

"The Hru…*Karath*ian ships are dispatching dozens of shuttles. It appears they're headed down towards the planet."

"Probably headed towards wherever the Grand Monarch was broadcasting from," Drake said, then mumbled, "Ryan probably shouldn't have let her do that."

"Have you ever been able to argue with a stubborn woman, Admiral?" Bradley said with a chuckle, having overheard his CO's mumble.

"Now that you mention it, I don't think I have," Jaxton replied, also laughing. "In fact, I pity what my brother has had to put up with, attempting to tell the leader of an entire planet that she can't try and do something that she wants to do must be a fun job."

"Exactly my thought, sir."

"Well, give them something else to focus on, people."

The crew commed with their teams and worked their stations.

"Gunnery, you are free to engage," Jaxton continued. "Comms, as soon as we open fire, relay to Brewster about those shuttles. They have a large head start, but let's see if he can do anything about it."

"Aye, sir," both Lieutenants Johnson and Lewis replied.

The powerplants on his ship hummed to full power as the weapons charged and missile silos opened and the missiles blasted off. His Evo cannons only took a few seconds to charge up for their initial volley, but they did pull an immense amount of power.

"Evos armed and ready and requesting permission to—"

"Yes, fire, Lieutenant!" Jaxton ordered.

"Firing…" reported Lt. Lewis.

Lewis tapped away as his gunnery team picked out their individual targets and bracketed them for the guns. Control of the ship was passed to them as it maneuvered to target the unlucky Karathian ships that were about to face annihilation. As before with their stealth technology, the first eight Karathian ships were caught completely off guard and the initial volley shredded all but one. That ship had managed to pull behind another of them and took off, running away from the fight towards the other eight on the other side of the planet. Before Jaxton's fleet could destroy it, a smaller ship, similar to the one that Pierce had described they destroyed in the JOS system, detached from the battlecruiser-class ship and blasted away at speeds much higher than any of Jaxton's ships could obtain. Jaxton cursed as he watched the ship flee. It was likely that ship held another one of the Karathian puppeteers he was keen to get his hands on. A few moments later, missiles fired from Dixon's ship took down the remaining Karathian battlecruiser. Now, in orbit over the planet, two almost evenly numbered fleets faced one another. While Jaxton's fleet's stealth was compromised and the Karathians knew he was there, the designers of the stealth technology claimed that their ships would be almost fifty percent harder to target, which should confuse the enemy targeting systems. On top of that, Jaxton thought they probably held a slight tonnage advantage. As a final ace up his sleeve, he had ordered the fighters to remain in their hangars initially, but now they were stealthily launching right under the noses of their enemy. They had over one hundred fighters between their makeshift carrier and what they had in their own hangars.

"Comms, order the carrier to dispatch all of their marines onto the planet and then sit at the rear of our formation. Have them coordinate with any military left on the planet."

"Aye, sir," Lt. Johnson replied.

"I don't want a single marine left aboard that carrier. If we get destroyed, at least they'll be able to fight on the surface."

Their carrier, while stealthy, was just a large cargo hauler they'd slapped bigger engines on. The ship's shields wouldn't survive a whole lot of abuse. True carriers were rare as they'd not been an important part of the fleet prior to the Hrum war.

"I know we expected they wouldn't behave like Hrum, but I was really hoping we were wrong," Commander Bradley said to Jaxton who nodded.

Their stealth technology may have made them hard to detect, but its usefulness was limited once they were exposed.

"I guess we're going to have to hope that our new weapons are good enough to turn the battle in our favor," Jaxton said, stopping and taking stock of the situation.

He cursed again that he let the Karathian ship escape and flee to deeper in the system. He should have expected there would be one or more of them in the enemy fleet and adjusted his strategy accordingly. If what Revalius said was true, the Karathian puppeteers valued their lives far above the average being, and would go to nearly any lengths to guarantee their survival.

"Sir, Captain Dixon's ship is falling back in the formation," Lt. Chen reported

"What's he doing?" Jaxton shouted. "Get Captain Dixon on the Comm now!"

Before Johnson could do that, however, Dixon's ship banked up and around slightly, aimed its spinal cannon directly at Jaxton's ship, and fired.

Captain Dixon watched, still completely powerless as Hadley commanded his ship. So far, the man was blending in, even firing on a Karathian ship when they sprung their initial ambush. If he'd been in Hadley's shoes, he'd have found a way to give away their presence sooner, but too late for Jaxton to disengage. A fake misfire on an engine or something that would show up on sensors made more sense, but it was clear that Hadley was not an expert on starship command. Dixon watched as his hands controlled his ship's weapons. The weapons officer was not one of the crew who Hadley had subverted, and he now laid in a pool of blood on the bridge next to his station, having been bludgeoned to death by his ex-comrades. Dixon listened as Jaxton ordered the fleet to meet the remaining eight ships in orbit head-on.

"This is our chance. Helm, gunnery. Fall back and target the admiral's ship."

"Aye, sir," said Dixon and the officer piloting the ship.

As the ship slowed, Dixon could do nothing but watch his hands tap the console, ignoring all the warnings about friendly fire, and other concerns. He had just about given up when he saw the pool of blood where his XO and someone who he'd considered a friend had lain after being murdered by Hadley using him as a vassal. A sudden burst of anger momentarily overcame the entity controlling him and Dixon managed to swing his hand to the dual firing levers and squeeze.

"What! What are you—" Hadley rushed to the viewscreen and glared, the lights of the screen projected on his face. "Nooooo…" shouted Hadley.

Dixon felt a brief moment of satisfaction as the spinal cannon fired early. It hit the battleship with a glancing blow, knocking down shields and tearing up the side of the ship, but missing the targeted engineering spaces. The entity regained control, and Dixon felt his body continue to fire upon the wounded, but now pissed-off battleship. As he felt his consciousness fade away, he found his thoughts focused on his fallen officer. *I'm sorry I couldn't do more, Gemma.*

The Arcon shuddered as it was struck by a glancing blow from Captain Dixon's battlecruiser. After the initial shock of the impact, it appeared the shot missed anything vital, but it had torn up some of their missile launcher tubes as well as one of their hangar entrances.

"What the hell's going on?" Bradley shouted.

"Helm, turn our damaged sections away from Dixon's ship. Can we return fire?" Jaxton yelled.

It was obvious that something had happened to Dixon. Luckily for Jaxton, the shot was inaccurate and missed the engineering spaces, or he'd likely have been without power.

"Commander, get me a damage report now! Gunnery, see if we can disable Dixon's ship."

"We can take it out with a single—"

"No, don't take it out, Lieutenant. Just glance it to knock some sense into them."

"Sir, I can't promise that we won't destroy it."

"Just do it, Lieutenant," Jaxton barked, his throat commanding, but his eyes begging. "Sensors, how long until we engage the other Karathian ships?"

"Sir, they're just outside of maximum cannon range. I expect them to fire any second." The officer's voice held a trace of panic.

Jaxton realized he sounded frantic and took a breath. He saw that Dixon's ship had turned away and was fleeing towards the other Hrum formations away from the planet. He did take a second to notice that whoever was plotting the routes was clearly no expert, as they weren't utilizing their build-up velocity well.

"Whoever's in charge of that ship is clearly not fully in control. Either that or he's a beginner to starship navigation."

"Aye, sir," Bradley replied. "What do you want us to do?"

"We continue the attack the Karathian fleet as planned. Task our fighter complement with trying to catch Dixon's ship and try and disable the engines, avoiding human casualties where possible. Have Major Stevens attempt to board it."

The crew, sensing that Jaxton was once more in control of his emotions, got to work. The distance closed until Jaxton's ship could fire his new weapons. Checking his status board one more time, he saw that even with the damage from Dixon's ship, his ship was still fully mission capable. The damaged shields were not facing the enemy, so nothing had to be done in that regard, but he was down half a dozen missile tubes.

"Gunnery, fire our remaining missiles from the undamaged launchers. Fire the Evo cannons, maximum power."

"Aye, sir," replied Lieutenant Lewis. "But sir if we charge them all the way, they'll—"

"I am willing to risk overheating if it'll save a few more of our ships. We don't have the advantage of surprise this time."

Lewis didn't reply, but he immediately began firing.

The lights dimmed as a massive amount of power was pulled from the powerplants. The cannon shots traveled the distance in the blink of an eye, and he began to see flashes as the bolts struck the shields. A few moments later, both the Karathian ships and Jaxton's own supporting ships began to fire. He saw how effective his ships' shots were, and after only a few seconds of continuous fire upon one ship, the bolts began to break through the shields and impact the Karathian hull. Unfortunately, as he'd predicted, the Hrum ships weren't firing blindly like usual, but instead were focusing fire on individual ships and launching fighters. He flinched as one of his destroyers was blown apart from Hrum fire.

"Have the destroyers fall in behind us. Their shields can't withstand the Hrum cannons."

The two fleets exchanged blows. The fighters Jaxton launched earlier were one of the few advantages he still had. The enemy fighters, thinking they were going to be able to charge in unmolested were taken by surprise when Brewster's fighters that he'd tasked to stay with Jaxton made their appearance. Too many Hrum fighters formed up due to Brewster having to split his forces into so many groups to entirely stop them from charging in, but they had clearly not expected the near-invisible fighters to be tailing them. With a nearly five-to-one kill ratio, it wasn't long before not a single Hrum fighter remained. They had launched a few missiles that had targeted Jaxton's own battleship and another battlecruiser. The battlecruiser took a hit near its engineering spaces and had a large section of it now open to space, but it was still in the fight. The missiles did little more than scratch the paint on Jaxton's own ship. The Hrum cannons so rightfully feared were also making their mark, but Jaxton's Evos and the firepower from the rest of his ships gave as good as they got. In the end, what felt like hours, but in reality was only about twenty minutes, left nothing but a smoldering debris cloud of what had been the Karathian ships. Jaxton's fleet had fared considerably better due to the overwhelming effectiveness of his fighter support as well as the better than advertised power of the Evo cannon. His ship had cut through the enemy ships like butter, barely pausing before striking another. He had heard his gunnery officer arguing with his engineering officer at the tail end of the conflict, so now that it was over, he tuned in. Apparently the repeated full-power shots had done exactly what Jaxton had been warned about. The Evo overheated and was now inoperable. The engineering team said that the physical barrel of the gun had begun to warp due to the intense heat and was no longer safe to fire.

"I told 'em. *They'd overheat* I said. I told 'em all..." Jaxton heard one geeky junior engineer saying.

"Those are the risks we had to take," the young gunnery officer replied.

"But now, they'll swell up, um high heat causes expansion, helloooo!"

"Noted, ensign, just see if you can cool them down, okay."

"Aye, sir," the excited engineer acquiesced with one last rolling of his eyes. "I'll try...."

The Arcon sustained very little damage other than that however. The rest of Jaxton's ships weren't quite so lucky. Two more of his ships were heavily damaged, one badly enough that it was little more than a floating hulk and they were evacuating it. In addition, with the loss of Dixon's battlecruiser, he was down to three mostly operational and one barely operational ship and a floating hulk. He stood no chance against the rest of the Karathian ships who were headed in his direction. He wasn't even sure if they'd have time to reload the fighters before they arrived. On the other side of the system, Pierce's ships were locked in battle with the Karathian who had chased them from WOT, and there was nothing Jaxton could do to help.

Dixon's ship was still burning away from the planet, but it was being pursued by a dozen fighters including Brewster, along with four shuttles loaded with marines. It was Jaxton's hope that they'd catch up and that not everyone on the ship was subverted. The fact his sister, and his friend Commander Taylor were both aboard made him sick. He muttered a quick prayer to whatever deity there was. "Please be alive," before refocusing on what he could control.

"Sir, Captain Pierce arrived and is taking up station around the Albion point. He said the Karathian ships should be right behind him," Lieutenant Johnson said. "He also asked if he should dispatch some of his fleet to assist."

Jaxton nodded thoughtfully, looking at the distances involved. The Karathians who were converging on him from the outer edges of the system had a significant velocity advantage. A quick check of the speeds and distances told him that Pierce's ships wouldn't be able to reach him in time to support.

"Tell him to keep his force intact. No point in him weakening his forces when he won't get here to help in time anyways. Helm, let's take up stations around the planet. Gunnery, any chance they can fix the Evo cannon?, and Comms, tell them to get our fighters reloaded as quickly as possible. Have all unessential crewmembers evacuate to the planet. Use the escape pods, we don't have enough shuttles for everyone. They'll be better off down there, where they can hopefully make a difference on the ground. We'll hold them off as long as we can up here."

"Aye, sir," they all replied.

Major Greg *Cold Brew* Brewster felt a sense of dread in his chest. He wasn't entirely sure what had happened, but Captain Dixon's ship, the ship holding Nat, had gone off the rails. Jaxton had ordered him to chase down that ship, disable it, and then board it. He was sure he hadn't wanted Greg to go himself, but he knew he was one of the best pilots in the fleet, and he had the best chance of disabling and not destroying the ship. His fighter and the eleven others who were with him would have stood no chance, but whoever was piloting the ship apparently was no expert and was showing them the most vulnerable part of the battlecruiser while completely ignoring the threat his fighters posed.

"Make sure your missiles are set to proximity detonation and configured for their lowest yield," Brewster growled over comms "The ship's shields are still front-biased, so the rears basically unprotected. I don't want to vaporize the whole damn thing by accident."

His pilots simply clicked their acknowledgments.

A few moments later, as one, the fighters launched their missiles, set to their lowest possible yield. There was still a relatively high chance that they could get unlucky and hit the powerplants and the ship would blow up as they went critical. Even with all the safety features NIS put into their ships, sometimes they failed and the ship would become nothing more than a blob of rapidly expanding gas. It was their hope was that they'd do enough damage to force them into an emergency shutdown without going critical.

Greg watched anxiously on his screen as the missile tracks closed with the much larger ship. Unable to watch, he closed his eyes shortly before they were due to go off. The cockpit fell silent outside of the hum from his engines and his own masked breathing for a long moment.

Then the excited voice of his wingman came over the headset. "We got him! The ship's powerless!"

Greg reopened his eyes as he took in the scene. True to what his wingman had said, their missiles had blown a massive hole in the engineering spaces which had in turn forced the powerplants into emergency shutdown rather than explode. Sadly, they very likely just killed god knows how many crewmembers who were likely unaware they were even doing something wrong. He sent a silent prayer up before replying.

"Major, the ships without power. You can.... Oh no."

Whoever had been piloting the battlecruiser had not accounted for the pull of gravity from the nearby gas giant. If he hadn't lost his engines, it would not have been that big of a deal, but with the loss of power, the ship was almost certainly going to be sucked into the gravity well of the massive planet.

"Oh my god, I killed her," Cold Brew murmured.

"Major, what's the status? Are we clear to proceed?"

Greg heard Stevens' voice as if it was from coming from the end of a long tunnel. His ears were ringing and he thought he might be sick. He watched helplessly as the ship barreled towards the planet, praying that escape pods would begin launching. His prayers went unanswered and he watched as the badly wounded battlecruiser slowly got sucked into the gravity well of the gas giant.

"Major, we have to bug out..."

No reply.

"The enemy ships are approaching, Major."

Silence.

"Major Brewster, if we don't pull back now, we'll—"

"Roger that, Captain," Greg finally acknowledged, shaking his head with a hard bank of his fighter and a quick burn of his engines to blast back toward the NIS fleet. "All birds head back home."

He had no idea what he was going to tell Jaxton.

Jaxton watched as the Karathian ships closed on his position. His engineers said that their Evo cannon was going to be inoperable and would need a yard to repair. He ordered the rest of his ships to use him as a bullet shield, but it felt hollow and pointless. There was little they could do, and nowhere they could run. He tried to find the words to inspire his crew, but none came to mind. At least Pierce seemed to be holding his own. The Karathian ships had shown up shortly after Pierce had formed up around the Albion point and they were now engaged in a fierce battle that Pierce's ships currently appeared to be getting the better end of. He hoped the faith he had put into the young man wasn't misplaced, as he'd likely be in command of the only NIS ships alive in the system in a few minutes. As he looked around, Jaxton couldn't help but think he'd failed them all. Commander Bradley, his long time XO and friend unstrapped from his console, and walked over to him. Jaxton looked up at him with an inquiring eye.

"Sir, it's been an honor. I could not have asked for a better commanding officer." Bradley stood at attention and saluted.

Around the bridge, the others did the same, unstrapping, standing tall with a crisp salute, wanting to show their leader that they had his back. Jaxton found himself overcome by emotion. He'd never been prouder of his crew than he was at that exact moment. He was at a loss for words, but he did unbuckle, stand up and return the salute.

"Thank you all, it's been an honor," he finally managed to get out.

A sudden beeping from the communications console made everyone turn. Lt. Johnson quickly settled back at her station and looked to see what was happening.

"Sir! reinforcements have arrived! I'm receiving a message from Senior Admiral Wellington. He has arrived with a dreadnought, four battleships, and another thirty smaller ships."

The elation from hearing this was slightly muted by the fact that they would not get there in time to save them.

"Sir…" Lt. Chen started to report.

"Lieutenant Chen, they won't arrive in time."

"No, that's not it. The Karathians, sir, they're… they're turning away!" yelled a suddenly very excited Lieutenant Chen.

"They're *what*, Lieutenant?" replied Jaxton.

"They appear to be fleeing, sir. Heading towards the Albion point in the direction of WOT."

Jaxton didn't quite believe what his officer was telling him. He believed the Karathian ships could have engaged him and still managed to retreat before the fresh NIS forces arrived to help. He double-checked the sensor screens and saw what his officer was telling him was true. He shook his head in disbelief.

"Johnson, tell Captain Pierce to disengage and get the hell out of their way. He can't take them on alone, and I think they just want to get out of here."

"Aye, sir."

A suddenly very relieved Jaxton sat heavily in his chair. He'd survived another impossible encounter. Eventually he thought his luck would run out, but he'd take whatever the universe gave him today. He did not yet know the status of Dixon's battlecruiser, but the fact that he had not led his entire fleet to their deaths filled him with so much relief that he could barely focus on the screen in front of him.

"Start rescue operations. I'll be in my office."

"Aye, sir." replied Commander Bradley.

Jaxton stumbled to the couch and was asleep within seconds.

Chapter XXI

On St. George in The Wreathsburg Broadcast Center
Year 3326

Ryan talked briefly with Commander Nord who gave Ryan a brief rundown of what the situation was around the planet. In a very un-Hrum manner, the invaders had mostly left the people alone. After securing government centers, and some of the infrastructure around the planet, the only thing they had really done was attempt to capture as many of the nobility and other important figures as they could. Ryan explained to Nord what they had found in the broadcast center and the hospital. He thought it was likely the Hrum were attempting to do the same thing to the nobility they did get their hands on. Nord, who was a little bit skeptical at first, sat back as he realized the implications of what Ryan was saying.

"They're trying to infiltrate the population by subverting the planet's leadership."

"Aye, sir," Ryan replied

"You can*not* let Izabella fall into their hands, Ryan."

"I don't plan to, sir. Any chance you can send some support our way?"

"Unfortunately not. They destroyed what little airpower we had on the day they arrived. We are too far away to help in time."

Ryan looked away and shook his head.

"Look, try to contact the ships that just arrived. They might be able to support. Hold on as long as you can."

"Will do, sir," he said, just about to close the channel.

Nord spoke up again. "And Ryan…"

"Sir?"

"They can*not* capture the Grand Monarch."

"I understood, sir."

"I hope so. No matter what else happens, she cannot be allowed to fall into their hands."

Ryan paused as what the commander was saying sank in. If it came down to it and they were about to be captured, Nord wanted him to make sure that would not be possible.

"Sir, she will not fall into their hands."

"Good! Good luck, Ryan."

"Thank you, sir. You too."

He closed the channel. He was not sure he would be able to do what the commander asked. He was doing mental gymnastics in his head. His CO all but ordered him to kill the woman he loved rather than let her fall into the hands of those alien murderers. They couldn't take her alive. That was definitely true, but he was still not sure he'd be able to pull the trigger if it came down to it. He shook his head to clear it before returning to the situation at hand.

Assuming the Hrum shuttles carried a similar amount of men as their own, he had to expect there'd be close to three hundred Hrum coming their direction. He was badly outnumbered and most of his troops were greener than a freshly mowed lawn. They'd gotten in touch with Marvin, who indicated he'd successfully taken the hospital, but had suffered horrendous casualties. They wouldn't be able to assist in the defense of the broadcast center as they were too busy freeing the prisoners and treating their wounds. The locals who'd ambushed the Hrum on the road had also made contact and would be arriving shortly before he expected the Hrum to. That would add another thirty or so men to assist in the defense, but almost none of them were trained.

This building was not a military structure, so it wasn't laid out in a fashion easily defensible, but the heavy construction due to the weather in the region did help. Also, most of the men there were familiar with the layout. He didn't need to waste time showing the people where to go. If he ordered them to a spot, they knew where to go. He thought again about trying to flee, but ruled it out. Even the shuttles that the locals had in their motor pool were just easy targets to the Hrum coming down from orbit. He was working with the assumption that the Hrum were going to try and take Izabella alive, and as such, he felt the Hrum wouldn't try and level the building, or strike it with anything except small arms. He hoped he was right because just one of those shuttles could likely level the building with a missile. As with most buildings in this region, there were several subterranean floors. In this building, as with most, they were storage rooms as well as emergency weather bunkers. It was not military grade, nor was it perfect for being on the defense, but it was better than standing with his ass flapping in the wind in a windowed skyscraper.

He had scattered some squads of men throughout the upper floors. They also did have some anti-air equipment that was old, but probably would still work. If the shuttles decided to lay waste to the building, those men were as good as dead. Looking over at Corporal V, he gave the young man a reassuring nod.

"We just have to hold until our reinforcements get here."

"When will that be, sir?"

"Your guess is as good as mine, Corporal, but Grand Monarch Izabella is counting on us. We cannot let her down." Ryan saw the young man's spine straighten a little at the mention of his leader.

"Yes, sir. We will not let her down!"

"Now, can you do one last run-through of the defenses. When our stragglers get here, I want you to get them ramped and ready as quickly as possible."

"Yessir!"

Corporal V jumped to his feet and hustled out of the room. Corporal Kim, who was watching, gave a light chuckle. "Kid's got enthusiasm, that's for sure."

Ryan side-eyed the mysterious man, seeing an opportunity to poke a bit. "Sure does, but you aren't a whole lot more experienced than him. Isn't that right?"

"That's right, sir," Kim said, looking around and squinting up at the bright sky. "War changes a man. I feel more than twice my age."

Ryan gave him a look that said he didn't entirely believe him, but he said nothing. Since leading a team to victory during training ops with the newly formed militia units, Kim couldn't conceal his experience and proficiency, his tactical and leadership skills clearly atypical for a non-com soldier. Digging into Kim's past would have to wait, however. A commotion above indicated the arrival of their remaining men. Kim and Ryan hustled up the stairs to greet them. When they arrived, they saw Dale and Corporal V barking orders. They only paused for a moment to acknowledge Ryan's presence before hustling off to their assignments.

Corporal V turned and said, "Sir, our scouts report they can see the inbound Hrum shuttles. They are landing in the woods. We should expect company soon."

"Very good, Corporal. You know what to do. We got to hold the line for as long as possible."

"Yessir."

The building rumbled slightly as the Hrum shuttles came screaming down from orbit. His guess that they wouldn't just blow the building away was accurate. They initially attempted to land close, but after one of them was blown away by an AA missile from one of the men in the center, they backed off and landed out of range.

"Here we go," Ryan muttered to himself.

Izabella, who refused to hide in the basement, was running around the facility with Ryan encouraging the troops. It was oddly quiet for almost fifteen minutes. He assumed the Hrum were gathering their strength and preparing for the assault. They'd all landed on one side of the facility, but Ryan didn't want to risk being surprised in the same way he'd assaulted the building just a few hours ago, so he didn't move all his men to that side.

"Here they come!" reported Corporal Kim.

Kim's announcement was followed by a spattering of gunfire, as the first Hrum made their appearance along the fence line of the facility. Ryan jogged over and looked out the window, hoping that the Hrum were advancing like they normally did. In a disorganized mob. His hopes were quickly dashed when he saw the telltale signs of an energy shield of some sort. It appeared not only were the Hurm advancing in formation, they also were carrying with them a mobile shield of some sort.

"I hate it when the enemy learns new things," Ryan said. "Hold your fire. Hold your fire. We don't have anything that will breach that shield. Pick your shots if you see an opening, but don't waste ammunition. Kim, is our little surprise ready to go?"

"Aye, sir. Waiting with the engines warm."

"Perfect, call them in."

"Roger that, sir."

Ryan watched as Kim spoke into the radio. A few minutes later, the rumbling of a heavy gunship began to shake the building, and Chomper's repurposed gunship came screaming into the warzone. The portable shield the Hrum were using was sufficient to block small arms fire, but the massive cannons on the gunship shredded it and kept going, ripping apart the Hrum sheltering behind it. They returned fire on the gunship, but it was heavily armored and the rounds bounced off. The commander of the Hrum, realizing that he had to change tactics, ordered all his men to charge, sacrificing shelter for speed. This gave Ryan's men the opportunity to open fire, which they gleefully accepted. The razorback continued to buzz saw through the Hrum for several minutes until five or six of the shuttles lifted off and engaged the gunship. The pilots of the razorback were forced to break off as they fired their own much heavier cannons at them. Ryan hoped that his pilots would survive. One on one, that gunship was more than enough to take on a shuttle or two, but five was asking a lot.

The gunfire picked up as the Hrum began to shoot back, having got into range with their own weapons. Their fire was blind, and not as accurate, but there was still the occasional lucky shot that took down one of Ryan's fighters. Ryan fired his own rifle at the incoming swarm, cooly dropping Hrum soldiers with well-placed bursts of fire. There were too many Hrum to stop, so the mob came closer and closer and it wasn't long before they reached the building and started breaking into the lower levels. Ryan and the locals had done their best to barricade access points, but there just hadn't been enough time to fully block off areas, especially if a heavily armored alien wanted to get into them.

"Corporal, have all our men evacuated off the first floor?"

"Aye, sir."

"Good, blow it."

"Yessir!" The young corporal quickly detached a detonator from one of the loops on his armor, flipped the safety, and pressed the button. A solid *whump* bubbled into the air as the charges they'd placed simultaneously ignited and a fireball blew out every window and doorway to the ground level of the center.

"That'll slow 'em down for a minute," Ryan muttered. "Corporal, get Izabella into the broadcast center room. We'll hole up there."

"Aye, sir."

Izabella didn't argue, but she did run over to Ryan and give him a quick peck on the cheek.

"Stay safe, Commander Drake."

"I will."

She jogged away with the young corporal.

"Kim, I think we can move the men on the other side to help us now. It doesn't matter if they come from the other direction, let's do our best to hold the stairways."

"Agreed, sir, I'll move them." Kim said, sprinting off.

Ryan had ordered the men on the first floor to retreat up to the second once the Hrum had gotten close. This was all a part of his plan to slowly condense his forces into a tight defensive knot in the hopes they'd receive reinforcements soon. He hoped the Hrum hadn't learned any more new things when it came to assaulting a fortified position. He watched as the last of his men pulled back from their original positions to where Kim was sending them. There were far fewer of them than he liked, but there was nothing he could do at this point. There was a brief lull as the Hrum carefully returned to the burnt-out ground level and took their time in clearing it. They also presumably were checking the basement. He thought that his assumption that they were looking for Izabella was proven by observing this behavior.

The calm didn't last, and soon the first Hrum soldiers started making their way up the stairs. Ryan calmly fired a burst, nailing the lead soldier in the visor before ducking behind cover as the follow-up soldiers returned fire. He backed away, letting his men hold the position while he hurried around, checking the other defenses. If the Hrum soldiers kept doing what they were doing, he'd be able to hold on for as long as their ammunition lasted. The staircases were narrow and couldn't fit more than one or two Hrum soldiers at a time. He was beginning to feel hopeful that they'd make it, when gunfire suddenly ripped through the area. He was in a large room, filled with cubicles. On his left, he saw Corporal Kim take a Hrum laser to the shoulder and he was writhing on the ground in pain. Peeking up over the desks, Ryan saw that the Hrum had apparently learned how to rappel. They'd climbed up the outside of the building, and were now firing in from the windows. Ryan fired two more bursts at the enemy soldier who'd shot Kim, nailing him center chest. The Hrum dove into the room, wounded, but still in the fight. The other militia in the room figured out what was happening, and they too began firing at the Hrum who were now pouring in from the exterior as well as the staircase.

Ryan turned to Kim. He was on the ground, flat on his back, badly hurt but still alive. The Hrum laser had burned through his armor, and Ryan saw blackened and blistered skin where it struck.

"Leave me, sir. I'm not going anywhere."

"That's bullshit, corporal. You haven't told me your story yet."

"Not much to tell, sir."

"You know that's not true, but that's not important."

Ryan slung his rifle on his back, and reached down to pick up his wounded corporal. Kim yelled as Ryan lifted him, the wound obviously hurting.

"Quit your whining," Ryan said as he stuck a sidearm into Kim's free hand. "Take this."

Kim took the weapon, but didn't seem all there, so Ryan wasn't sure if he'd be of any help. He took another quick look around. The Hrum assault hadn't let up, but his teams were still valiantly fighting. He dragged Kim into one of the nearby offices and propped him up against the heavy desk.

Over his headset, Corporal V suddenly yelled, "Sir, they're coming in from the outside." V paused, Ryan hearing laser fire in the background, then… "Shit, they're bypassing this floor, and going straight for the broadcast room. They must know Izabella is there."

"Leave me, Commander," Kim demanded. "Give me a rifle! I'll hold on as long as I can."

Ryan looked out through the doors then back down at Kim.

"Go help your woman."

Ryan slid his rifle over his head and handed it to Kim. He clasped his hand and replied, "Give 'em hell, soldier. It's been an honor."

"You too, sir."

With that, Ryan hurried from the room, drawing his sidearm. The fighting on this floor was still fierce, but Ryan ignored it and made his way up to the third floor where there was more fighting. The upper floors of the building were circular in design. He assumed it was to help support the massive antenna that protruded from the top of it. The broadcasting room occupied the center of this floor, and Ryan had come up the stairs near the outside. He burst through the doorway, quickly picking out a target and firing his gun. The Hrum had established a foothold on the floor, and Ryan found himself behind them. He managed to drop two before the others noticed his presence, and returned fire. He ducked down behind a cubicle desk, thanking whoever the builders were for their heavy construction. An explosion rocked the room after one of his men tossed a grenade which exploded and took out a couple more Hrum soldiers. Ryan peeked back over the desk he'd taken cover behind and saw all the Hrum in that room were down. He quickly made his way into the broadcast room, making sure the men saw him before entering so they didn't accidentally shoot him. They quickly barricaded the door behind him as he sprinted in. Izabella and Corporal V were both there, unharmed. He jogged over to them.

"Anything from the commander, Corporal?"

"No, sir. I know the fleet is engaged in orbit, but not much else. I don't know how much longer we can hold." As if to emphasize the point, the gunfire picked back up, and the door began to shake as the Hrum soldiers re-organized and began attempting to break their way in. Ryan was positive now that they knew who was inside, as they didn't use any sort of explosives that could potentially harm the rooms occupants. It was beginning to look desperate.

Ryan looked down at the floor then at Izabella. Her emerald green eyes caught his, and he could only hope that she couldn't see the desperation that he was feeling. Thinking to what the commander had told him, his hand absently wandered over to settle on the grip of his pistol. Could he really shoot the woman he loved, even if it was to protect her from the enemy? What kind of monster would that make him? What if he did it too soon, or worse waited too long and let her fall into the enemy's clutches? He lowered his head and sat there out of ideas for a moment that seemed forever trying to come to grips with what he knew in his heart was right. Then static! Radio squelch! Over his communicator, Ryan heard some crackling before the voice of one of his razorback pilots spoke.

"Anyone left alive in there? We're circling back for another attack run. We managed to shake the shuttles chasing us."

Ryan smiled. That was one tough gunship.

Turning back to Corporal V, Ryan said, "We've gotta get out of here. If we can get on the gunship, we can retreat to the mine." Ryan straightened up and looked out the shattered windows, then crouched back down. "Maybe we can get a vehicle and sneak away or hide out in the mountains until help arrives."

"Sir, there's a landing pad on the roof. We just have to get there."

"I like it, corporal," Ryan replied. He switched back to the channel with the razorback pilots. "We're coming to the roof. Be ready for a hot exfil."

"Aye, sir," the pilot replied. "We'll be there, Commander."

Turning to the men, Ryan continued, "Soldiers, we have to get to the roof. When I say, we're going to charge the Hrum. Toss the rest of your grenades, and we'll burst out the room. We have to make it to the roof."

"Yes, sir," the remaining soldiers in the room shouted.

Ryan was pleased to see that Corporal V was on the ball and knew exactly what he was thinking. He fixed Ryan with a quick smile before pulling out an entire bandolier of grenades and prepared to arm them.

"Sir, just give the order. We'll push them back to allow you time to get to the roof."

"Thank you, Corporal."

Ryan took a quick look around the room. Izabella was quiet, but appeared ready to go. Taking a breath, he picked up a rifle whose owner no longer needed it, checked it and nodded. "Go!"

Virgadamomo quickly armed his entire collection, and tossed them casually out the door. There was a brief pause before the entire building shook as each of his grenades exploded.

"There may have been some plastic explosive in that too, sir," The young corporal said, with a slightly manic smile on his face.

Ryan chuckled, but didn't reply. He made a mental note to never put him and Corporal O'Leary together. They both seemed to have an affinity for over-the-top deployment of explosives. "Let's go. Go go go!!!"

With Corporal V in front and Ryan in the back, they ran out of the room and beelined for the stairs to the roof. Ryan took a few shots at the few remaining Hrum soldiers who had been knocked down, but not killed in the blast. Izabella had just made it through the doorway, when Ryan stumbled. He managed to keep his feet, and slammed the door closed behind him.

He heard Corporal V yelling into the comms, "We're coming in hot. Got Hrum on our heels."

Ryan didn't hear the reply, but he did hear the door behind him blow open. He turned and fired a few parting shots at the pursers before turning and following Izabella. When they reached the landing pad, they saw the razorback pointed in their direction. The ship looked worse for wear, with only three of its four engines running, and one of them smoking. The ship was also peppered with what he assumed were Hrum cannon shots. They waved at the ship, and it shakily flared in for landing. Before it could land, the Hrum pursuing them had reached the roof and were pouring out the door, guns blazing towards Ryan and his men. They returned fire, knocking down the first two. The ship managed to land, and Ryan watched as Corporal V, sheltering the monarch with his body, escorted her up the ramp. He stumbled as a parting shot from the Hrum struck him, but kept going until she was safe inside the bay. Ryan and the two other militia with him continued to fire at the unrelenting tide of Hrum now pouring up the stairs. They slowly backed up to the ramp. Once his heels touched it, he turned and sprinted up. One of the two militia following. The other laid unmoving on the tarmac.

"Go, go, go…" Ryan yelled, as he continued to fire.

The engines on the ship whined and surged as the pilot commanded them to full power. A few Hrum rifle shots peppering the rear as they flew. They'd escaped! The ramp squeaked closed and Ryan took stock of who was left. Corporal V looked like he was in a little bit of pain, but his armor had apparently held, while the other militia member with them appeared unharmed. He walked towards the front of the ship, when he heard Izabella gasp.

"Oh my god!"

Turning, Ryan replied, "What?"

Apparently when he'd stumbled, it hadn't been because he'd tripped. He'd been struck directly in the back by a Hrum laser, and it had burned through his armor. As if his body finally realized it, he began to feel a burning pain from his back. Izabella, who had been strapped down to a seat, began to unstrap and stand.

"Ryan, sit down. Let me look at you."

"I'm fine. When we get to safety, we can look at it. Please stay seated, your majesty."

She looked like she wanted to argue, but relented. Ryan, doing his best to tune out the pain, and moved forward to talk to the pilots. Before he could get there, another explosion rocked the shuttle. The pitch of the engines changed from a deep howl, to a grinding, pained groan.

"We're under attack, more Hrum shuttles," the pilot said, his voice stressed. "They took out one of our last two good engines. I'm not going to be able to keep us in the air. I'm going to try and put us down gently." The pilot didn't sound convinced he'd be able to do that, but Ryan didn't tell him how to do his job. "Buckle up, we're going to crash." The pilot banked and turned and pushed the controls. "Shit, we're going in. We're gonna to crash."

Ryan tried to make it to a seat, but the shuttle dove suddenly, tossing him into the ceiling. He felt his wounded back strike the hard metal roof and he almost blacked out from the pain. Corporal V, who was safely strapped in managed to grab ahold of Ryan's arm and pull him down into the seat. He peeked forward, as he was trying to get the harness on and saw they were moments from hitting the ground.

"Fu..."

With a grinding crunch, everything went black.

When Ryan woke, it was dark. He was being dragged through the woods. As his mind cleared slightly, he realized it wasn't dark, but that he could only see out of one of his eyes. He tried to turn his head and look around, but found he didn't have the energy to do so. Ryan knew his body was broken, but he didn't know the extent of it. He also realized couldn't feel his legs, and as he reached up to touch his blind eye, he felt torn skin and blisters and blood. Lots of blood. To his left, he heard gunfire. Finally, he painfully turned his head towards it. He spotted Izabella, firing a rifle in the direction of where they were coming from. She was screaming and yelling as she shot while someone he could not see continued to drag him backwards through the woods. Ryan wanted to help, but even the small action of turning his head had exhausted him. He coughed wetly, something in his chest was also broken. Using his remaining eye, he forced himself to focus on the beauty of the woman he loved. He only wished that he'd have more time with her. In his badly wounded and delirious state he could almost imagine what their kids would have been like. Headstrong like their mother, athletic like their father, and brave like both of them. He tried to call out, but no words escaped his ragged throat. He could do nothing as his vision slowly faded to nothing, the last thing he heard being the rattle of automatic rifle fire.

To Ryan's surprise, he opened his singular eye once more. The first thing he saw was a very tired and tear-stained face of Izabella hovering over him, holding his hand. He tried to speak, but it came out only a croak. He managed to look around momentarily panicking before realizing once more that only one eye was working. He was in a shuttle, several medical personnel working on him as they flew to where he assumed a hospital was waiting. Izabella said something he could not understand, but he locked his good eye on her and nodded. He managed to mouth, "I love you," before he lost consciousness.

When he awoke again for the third time, he smelled the sterile environment of a hospital. He had no idea how long he'd been out, but judging by the growth of his beard as he scratched his chin, at least a week has passed. He laid there for a moment, eyes closed, his mind trying to process all that had happened, before he finally opened his eyes and looked around the room. In the chair next to him sat a man, the face blurred. He blinked and squinted to bring into focus none other than his big brother, Jaxton.

"Hey bro," Ryan managed to groan out.

Jaxton, who'd been reading a book, jumped slightly at the sound of his voice, but quickly turned and a broad smile creased his face. "I told them you'd wake up early. The doctors said it'd take you at least a day for you to wake once they took you off the meds keeping you asleep and in a coma."

"How long?"

"You've been asleep nine days. Once the medics managed to stabilize you when they picked you up, they transferred you to the Capitol City Hospital where you are now. We almost lost ya buddy."

"Where's…" Ryan strained to sit up.

"Huh?"

"Where's… Izabella?"

"She's fine. She's been by your side since the day you were brought in here. She wouldn't leave you until I agreed to sit here and keep an eye on you. She should be back soon."

"Oh…. well that's good," Ryan said tiredly, his brain still not fully awake after being asleep for so long.

"That's quite the woman you've got there. Although I can't imagine what she sees in you. Especially now. You look like the turd I just left in your toilet."

"Kiss. My. Ass." Ryan groaned, chuckling softly. He tried to sit up, but Jaxton forced him back down.

"Rest. You're recovering, but you took some pretty serious wounds back there. In fact, you're about a foot short!" Jaxton said, clearly amused at what thought was a witty pun.

Ryan looked down as Jaxton pulled back the blankets and saw that his left leg had been amputated just below the knee. "Could be worse, I suppose."

"Yeah?"

"I'm a righty."

"Oh don't you worry brother, that's not all. Along with that, you had a collapsed lung, four broken ribs. Severe laser burns on your back, a massive concussion—though I told the docs you'd always been a little brain damaged."

"Ha. Ha."

"What else… Oh! We also have matching scars now, and if you can't tell, your right eye still isn't working."

Ryan had forgotten that, but after closing his left several times and realizing he still couldn't see out the right one, he discovered his brother wasn't lying. Jaxton, ever the thoughtful big brother, held a mirror up for him to see. His face was covered in scabs. He'd been peppered with shrapnel when the shuttle crashed, and the right side of his face had taken the vast majority of it. In addition, he had a nasty scar running from his jawline, through the center of his eye, and all the way up to his forehead. Whatever had struck him, had cracked his jaw, and destroyed his eye and had knocked him silly.

"You can hardly call that a little love tap I gave you over your eyebrow a matching scar," Ryan said, chuckling painfully."

"Pfft, a scar's a scar! Frankly, I am surprised you're even here," Jaxton said with a smirk. "I told the doctors to just throw you out. I don't know why they wanted to save you so badly. Maybe they don't know ground pounders are a dime a dozen."

"Or as they say on Sapporo: a septum a doozle."

They both laughed, as much from stress relief as humor.

Taking a more serious tone and laying his hand on his brother's shoulder as a sign of brotherly affection, Jaxton continued, "I am glad you're alright though, brother. Life would have been significantly less fun without my drinking buddy."

"That would have been a travesty," Ryan replied dryly. "What happened? How am I alive?"

"What's the last thing you remember?"

"I... remember the shuttle crash..."

"Nothing else?"

Ryan shook his head slowly.

"After the shuttle crashed, you, the Grand Monarch and the two others who survived the crash attempted to flee. You were in pretty rough shape at that point as you were tossed around pretty badly when the shuttle crashed, but you led the way anyways. Apparently, you refused to let anyone look at your wounds."

"I—I don't rem—"

"Anyways..." Jaxton said, interrupting him. "You managed to hike several kilometers towards the mine, fending off attacks from the Hrum or Karathian soldiers the entire way, but before you could make it, you collapsed. Izabella took your rifle while your corporal dragged you the rest of the way. Luckily before they could get overwhelmed, Major Brewster's fighters and some of my marines arrived to rescue you. After that, you were medevac'd here."

Ryan nodded to himself. He did now vaguely remember waking up while being dragged through the forest.

"How's Nat?" Ryan saw Jaxton's face fall as he said their sister's name, making him fear the worst.

"Later, little bro," Jaxton replied, nodding his head towards the door. "For now, I think there's someone here to see you."

Ryan carefully turned and saw a blur, then squinting, realized who it was. Izabella stood in the doorway, tears flowing freely down her beautiful face. As soon as they locked eyes, she ran forward, jumped onto the bed and enveloped Ryan in a hug. After seeing red for a brief moment as Izabella crushed his battered body, he returned the hug with all of his very limited strength. They said nothing, and just held each other as Jaxton and Izabella's bodyguards quietly left the room.

"I thought I'd lost you," she said

"Never, never in a million years, my love." Ryan replied.

She laughed, her tear-stained face looking more beautiful than anyone Ryan had ever seen. She continued to laugh as she climbed off of him, taking far more care than she had when she first arrived. Ryan was grateful as her weight on his chest had been quite painful in his current pitiful state. She didn't go far, just settling next to the bed in a chair and taking his hand. They said nothing for a long time, she just sat there stroking his arm as she held his hand.

"So what should the colors be?" she suddenly asked.

"The *colors*?"

"For our wedding of course."

Ryan turned his good eye on her to get a sense if she was joking. She wasn't.

"Umm, maybe you had best pick that out."

"I think you'd look very handsome in white and sapphire blue. It would match your eyes. All of you Drakes would look so fiercely handsome with your pretty blue eyes."

"Um, sure, whatever you say, that's fine dear."

A voice from the doorway cut in. "He has no idea what you're talking about does he?"

Ryan turned to see a group of broadly smiling people including Jaxton, Marvin, and a subdued-looking Greg Brewster. His brother, the one who spoke, was smiling the widest.

"I will give you all till the end of the week to pay me. You all have my information. I believe congratulations are in order, brother."

Ryan was completely lost at this point, "Izzy, what are they talking about?"

"Do you remember the shuttle ride here?"

"Um.....Yes..." he said slowly, wracking his brain, trying to figure out what had happened.

"Well, when you woke up, I said if we survive this, will you marry me?"

There was a long pause before he slowly replied, "I nodded and said I love you."

"Yep! So you *do* remember! I am so excited! Jaxton, he *does* remember! You owe me a hundred nobles!" She crushed

Ryan into another painful hug before jumping up and chasing after Jaxton as he strutted down the hall. "He remembers!" she yelled once again as she left. The others cleared out after wishing him a quick congratulations.

Ryan's mother always made him promise to not keep secrets from his future wife, whoever she may be, but he figured this one little secret wouldn't hurt. He hadn't heard a word that Izabella had said to him in his delirious state. He couldn't keep from smiling at the turn of events.

"Oh boy, mom and dad are gonna love this…"

Chapter XXII

On St. George in a Small Chapel
Year 3326

The wedding was a small, private affair, or at least that's what Ryan told himself. He tried to ignore the fact that the entire thing was captured on camera for the entire planet to see. Outside of his family, the only people in attendance were a few select friends and a handful of nobles that Izabella had invited. Izabella had been right, as he stood in the front of the church with his brother as his best man, he admitted that the sapphire blue suit did look good on him.

It had been close to two months since he'd woken up from the coma and he was about to marry the love of his life. He had mostly recovered from the horrific injuries he'd suffered in the shuttle crash. The pilot had managed to put the mortally wounded razorback gunship down softly enough that most of the occupants had survived. Ryan, who hadn't fully managed to get strapped down, had been thrown around the bay where he'd lost his eye when he impacted a bulkhead. He had no recollection of it, but apparently he'd gotten up and fought the Hrum who followed them down in their own shuttles while they were attempting to capture Izabella. His leg had been blown off in the process, and he'd taken several other shots from the Hrum rifles. Corporal V, the surviving pilot, and Izabella had dragged him away from the battleground after he'd fallen. They managed to get to the mine entrance, where the militia who had remained there to guard it had held off the remaining Hrum until the fighters from Jaxton's carrier arrived and eliminated the remainder of the Hrum in the area.

After he had woken up, he'd been fitted with an advanced prosthetic that he insisted be made out of the hardest metal possible. He barely noticed it anymore, as he was able to do everything he had been able to with a normal leg. The only thing that was annoying was that he got random ghost itches occasionally that took forever to go away. His eye socket had been crushed when he impacted the bulkhead, and it was not savable. The doctors had done the best they could to fix the damage, but they weren't able to save his vision. He wore an embroidered eyepatch that his brother told him made him look like a pirate until they could fit him for a cybernetic if he chose, but it would take several months before it was ready.

In the crowd, his mother and father sat together, his mother not bothering to hide her joy in the form of tears, while his usually subdued and serious looking father had a look of contentment and happiness on his face. Next to them was a beautiful blonde woman who Jaxton had introduced to Ryan as Dr. Casey, who had apparently agreed to come as his date.

Next to them, an empty space. The space that should have been filled by his younger sister. Words couldn't describe how badly he wanted to see Nat, sitting there excitedly next to their mother. The unfairness of losing someone so young and innocent weighed heavily on his heart. He weaved his head to look through the modest crowd. For a moment he saw her, snickering, bringing a glass of punch to Jaxton, pushing his arm to stop teasing her, and coming up to put a flower in his bride's hair, giving him a congratulatory hug. Ryan blinked and Nat was gone, the hug-feeling fading away. He blinked again and squinted and shook his head. Maybe it was his lost eye's memory, an optical itch of sorts that would last for a long while.

On Dr. Casey's left was a haunted-looking Greg Brewster, who still blamed himself for Nat and Gemma's deaths. Ryan had just found out that Greg and Nat had been seeing each other, and nobody was taking her death harder. No matter how much they tried, neither Jaxton nor Ryan had been able to convince him otherwise.

There was a slight commotion near the back of the room. As Ryan looked up, his heart nearly stopped. His wife-to-be, Izabella, the most beautiful woman he'd ever seen had entered the room and was now walking towards him, her belly not yet showing the secret they planned to share with the family soon. There was a lot of work to do. Much of the planet was in disarray, and the Karathians were still attacking all over NIS space. The Hrum were still a mystery, but nothing mattered at that moment. All he could think about was how excited he was at that moment. Tomorrow they'd worry about the future, but today he'd focus on the here and now. The Karathians had done their best to try and wipe them all out, but they'd failed. Ryan vowed to make them regret their failure.

Austin Davis is an award-winning author of *HRUM*, a thrilling science fiction adventure that marked the beginning of his storytelling journey. Born and raised in Chicago, Austin now calls Utah home. A mechanical engineer by day and a storyteller at night, he crafts immersive science fiction and fantasy tales that captivate readers and transport them to new worlds.

When he's not writing or working, Austin enjoys dirt biking, camping, and exploring Utah's rugged wilderness. He's also an avid reader who loves getting lost in a great book.

Austin lives with his beautiful wife and their two spoiled dogs, who happily rule the household.

You can get **free King's Hounds prelude short stories** when you join my newsletter at: https://thedavisverse.com/

Want to keep up with new releases, behind-the-scenes content, and everything happening across the Davisverse? Find me on my socials here: https://linktr.ee/thedavisverse

THE DRAKE CHRONICLES

Military Science Fiction

Check out all of Austin Davis's books at https://thedavisverse.com

THE KING'S HOUNDS
EPIC FANTASY
WOLFHOUND
THE KING'S HOUNDS BOOK I
FANG & FEALTY
THE KING'S HOUNDS BOOK II
AUSTIN DAVIS
Join the Davisverse newsletter for free short stories and updates.

Good reviews are crucial for indie authors. They play an essential role in helping new readers discover and take a chance on an indie author's work.

If you enjoyed this book, would you take a moment to leave a positive review? It would mean the world to me and help get this story in front of more readers.

Thank you so much for your support!

For the best places to leave a review and help share this book with others who love great stories like you and me, check out my website!

https://thedavisverse.com/

Made in the USA
Coppell, TX
22 May 2026

77663020R10152